CW01630736

DEAD IN THE WATER

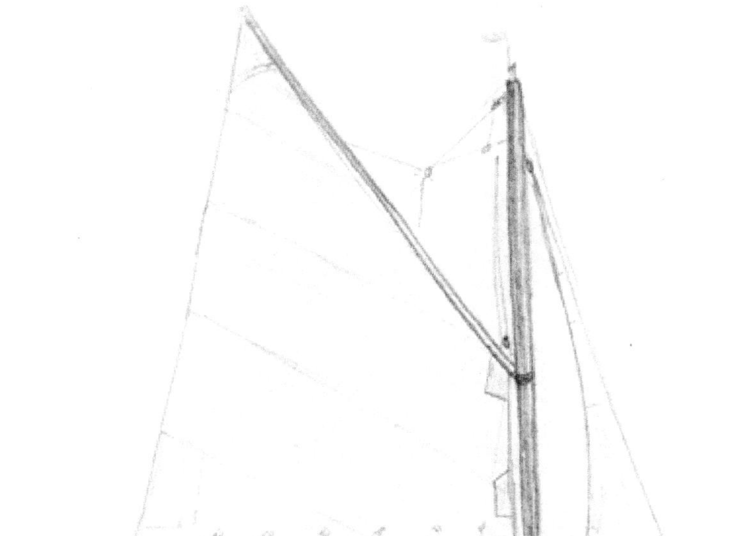

Chris Crowther

Dead in the Water copyright © Chris Crowther

The moral rights of the author have been asserted.

All rights reserved. No part of this publication may be reproduced, distributed, or transmitted in any form or by any means, including photocopying, recording, or other electronic or mechanical methods, without the prior written permission of the publisher, except in the case of brief quotations embodied in critical reviews and certain other non-commercial uses permitted by copyright law. For permission requests, write to the publisher, addressed "Attention: Permissions Coordinator," at the email address below.

This edition published 2024
Taleweaver
Hoveton – Norfolk – England – NR12 8UJ

ISBN: 978-0-9030943-4-4

www.chriscrowther.co.uk

First published this edition in 2016 by Hamilton Publications, Ventulus, Cross Lane, Brancaster, Norfolk PE31 8AE

Cover photo by Lord Paul Sergent www.photographs-r-us.co.uk
Sketches by Sarah Rogers

Other books by Chris Crowther

"Jack Fellows" murder-mysteries

Waterproof

Still Waters

The Water Frolic

Water Under the Bridge

Dead in the Water

Watershed

Children's fantasy adventure

Timecruiser

Flying thrillers

Bladestrike

Pursuit

Chapter One

'Are you sure it's right for us to be attending this meeting, Jack?' queried Audrey Fellows, as she followed her husband towards the church hall. 'Surely the locals would rather sort out their own disputes without outsiders like us getting involved.'

'Loss of countryside is everyone's concern, Aud,' Jack replied as they entered the rapidly-filling hall, 'and, anyway, this is where I'll be operating from this summer, so I need to be in the know.'

'Well, here's someone who'll be able to tell you.' A tall upright figure with a mop of pure white hair and an equally white beard, had spotted their entry and strode towards them with an outstretched hand.

'Jack ... Audrey ... good to see you ... we need all the support we can get to scupper this damned proposal.' Admiral Sir Claude Ashfordby, long-retired as a flag officer, but now an extremely active warden for the village church of St Mark's, was always outspoken when it came to the welfare of his parish. Knowing Jack had been working as a Broads ranger since retiring from the Metropolitan Police, his eyebrows rose questioningly. 'You're a long way from home, Fellows. Are you attending in an official capacity?'

'Not at all, Admiral, but I'll be here on duty very soon, so I need to know what's going on, especially when it involves such a controversial environmental matter. It certainly seems to have stirred up no end of ill-feeling in your community.'

'And so it should.' Sir Claude nodded in the general direction of the village outskirts. 'For goodness' sake, who wants a bloody solar farm blighting the landscape and replacing forty acres of fertile farmland. I can't stand by and see that happen to our countryside.'

'Well, you're not alone by the sound of it.' From the full hall, raised voices and angry words promised an evening of heated discussion, and not all of it well intentioned, thought Jack. He glanced towards two menacing-looking youths in low-slung trousers, standing chewing gum just inside the main door. 'I'm all for protests, Admiral, as long as they stay peaceful. What you don't want are things getting nasty.'

'Ah, that's the ex-policeman in you,' said Sir Claude, smiling, as he led them to a couple of spare seats next to his own. 'Always the voice of reason.'

'And this is the old sea-warrior in you,' returned Jack, sitting down amidst the clearly angry parishioners. 'Always spoiling for a fight.'

'Only if it's a just one, but it'll be good to have you on our side, Jack. Must be a while since I last saw you?'

'A year actually, when I was patrolling the Southern Rivers for a week,' recalled Jack, remembering that the Broads Authority launch for this sector of the Yare had been based on the parish moorings, very close to the admiral's own boat. 'You were doing some work on that beautiful sailing cruiser of yours ... *Curlew*, wasn't it?'

'That's right. Haven't had her out yet this year, but soon will.' He turned to Audrey. 'And you, dear lady ... are you still churchwarden of old Saint Cuthbert's?'

'Yes indeed, Admiral, and the work it involves seems endless, so heaven knows how you find the time to take on this protest as well as your duties at St Mark's.'

'It's not just me though. The whole parish is up in arms.'

'So I can see,' said Audrey, noticing there was standing-room only left in the hall. 'Do you really think you have a chance of stopping it?'

'We'll have a jolly good try. Meet the enemy head on, is my motto ...' Sir Claude indicated the large bear of a man sporting a greying bushy beard, already seated with others on the hall's raised stage, sipping a glass of water while eyeing the audience with undisguised contempt '... and there he is.'

'Bertie Borrett no less,' said Jack, repeating a name he'd heard many times in the last few months, but one never spoken of with warmth. 'Not the most popular resident this village has ever had, I understand.'

'Damned right he's not,' fumed the admiral. 'A bad day for us, Jack, when he bought Providence Farm ten months ago.'

'Just after I did my temporary stint here,' recalled Jack. 'Poor old Providence Farm. Hardly the most appropriate of names anymore. Where was he before that?'

'London, where he should have stayed. Apparently made his fortune in scrap-metal.'

'Well, I guess we're about to hear how he's going to make even more,' said Jack as, up on the stage, the chairman of the parish council got to his feet and called for quiet.

'Thank you, all of you, for coming here tonight for what promises to be a most informative, but highly charged meeting. There'll be a chance for you all to have your say later, but first I'm going to ask the landowner concerned to state his case.'

'Thank you, Mr Chairman.' Borrett's loud, cockney voice filled the hall. Standing there, huge frame all the more intimidating in wide-checked tweeds, he wasted no time in coming to the point. 'The fact is, power demand in this country is growin' daily and I intend to do my bit to supply some of it.'

'... and make yourself a lot of money in the process,' came a voice from the floor, accompanied by much cynical laughter.

'Yeah, well that's the sort of reaction I'd expect from you lot,' retaliated the landowner, 'but you'll change your minds when you 'ear what benefits solar energy will bring to the community.' He held out an ordering hand to the rather nondescript younger man seated to his right, who immediately delved nervously into the briefcase at his feet. Perhaps the fellow should have had the required data to hand, but his momentary fumbling obviously irritated Borrett, who snatched the requested papers with an audible grunt.

'Who's that poor devil?' whispered Jack.

'Borrett's so-called Personal Assistant ... a failed city solicitor by the name of Cecil Watling.'

'Not the happiest of jobs I would imagine.'

'Especially if you only keep it because the boss fancies your wife,' said the admiral in a hushed voice from behind his hand, while nodding towards the petite dark-haired lady seated two rows from the front. 'From what we see, it's Lucy Watling who does the "personal" while her husband does the "assisting".'

'And does poor Mrs Borrett know what's going on?' whispered Audrey, who was finding this exchange altogether more interesting than the man's now endless vociferation of figures.

'I'm sure she does,' answered the admiral. 'Elsie Borrett may be a fine woman, but I imagine it's a case of knowing on which side her bread's buttered. Mind you, she does seem a lady well able to hold her own.'

'She probably needs to.' Jack's gaze had followed the admiral's eyes towards a large woman with strawberry blonde hair, seated on the front row and wearing a rather inappropriate tight fitting dress. She had doubtless once been very good looking, but years of excess and marriage to a difficult husband had certainly taken their toll. Obviously attending the meeting under sufferance, she was showing little interest until a particularly biting remark from three rows back, caused her to turn around so sharply that her large gold earrings audibly jangled. It took only a fleeting withering glare from the lady's heavily shadowed eyes to freeze the offender into silence and bring a smile of approval from Jack. 'Not a lady I'd like to get on the wrong side of though.'

'Shush,' cautioned Audrey, giving her husband a gentle dig in the ribs. But she needn't have worried because the general hubbub was now drowning out most of Borrett's oratory, let alone their own whispered tattle. Finally, despite attempts by the chairman to restore order, even the big man himself had had enough.

'Right, if you ain't goin' to have the decency to listen to what I 'ave to say, I'll let someone else try and drum some sense into yer.' He nodded towards a slim man in striped shirt and lightweight suit, seated to the left of the chairman. 'This 'ere is Mr Edward Asthall, project engineer with Solartech, the company spear'eadin' this development.'

Now it was Asthall's turn to get to his feet and extol the benefits of solar energy. Generally, he was allowed an easier run than Borrett, but when he called for "any questions" there was a forest of hands from the audience.

'Why here? Why not some disused industrial area instead of unspoilt countryside?' asked the first questioner from the floor.

'A matter of availability,' answered Asthall. 'Mr Borrett is prepared to lease his land for this vital, far-sighted project and we're glad to take up his offer.'

'... and pay him bundles of money,' shouted another voice from the floor.

'Yes, well ... that's the way of the world.'

'Not our world, it isn't,' shouted another angry voice.

'I think now would be a good time to have a break,' appeased the chairman, glad of an excuse to give frayed tempers time to calm down. 'After that, we'll throw the proposal open to the floor and then we can judge the consensus of opinion.'

'You do that,' snarled Borrett, screwing his data sheets into a tight roll, 'but don't expect me to stay and listen to it. The one thing you do need to discuss is how deep yer pockets are, because fightin' me is goin' to cost you lot a load of money. I've already taken on a top London barrister to fight my corner, so ...' he pointed the rolled sheets towards the audience as though they were a loaded weapon, '... get hirin' your own and find out how much that costs.' Throwing the papers back into his PA's lap, he then stomped off the stage and pushed his way towards the door.

Several villagers attempted to confront him as he made his passage out of the hall, but the two heavy lads by the door came to his side and cleared a path with much shoving and the odd hard-knuckled push. Finally, they were out and gone with Lucy Watling hard on their heels. Further thoughts on that scenario, however, were interrupted by the tinkling of the refreshment bell as a hatch at the other end of the hall opened and local ladies stood ready to serve. 'Ah good, I could do with a cuppa after that business,' confessed Sir Claude with some relief.

'Let me get them, Admiral,' offered Audrey. 'I can see some of your fellow-parishioners want a word with you and Jack needs to go and check Spike in the car.'

Glad of the excuse of some fresh air, Jack took his cue and left the hall.

* * *

Outside, dusk was just falling, one of those lovely early summer evenings with just the slightest nip in the air, but all the promise of long warm days to come. Thankfully, most villagers had chosen to stay inside for more exchanges over tea, leaving the car park relatively peaceful except for a car just stopped by the main exit with its engine running. It was Borrett's Mercedes and the reason for its temporary halt was Lucy Watling, standing by the open rear passenger window, obviously very upset and gesticulating angrily to the owner seated inside. Jack, approaching his own car parked quite close by, could clearly hear Lucy's agitated voice.

'But you said that after the meeting you'd meet me at the boat.'

'Yeah, well I'm not in the mood anymore, so some other time.'

'This is the second time you've stood me up, Bertie. You've met someone else haven't you? Who is she?'

'You're bonkers, woman. Just buzz off,' ordered Borrett, closing his window and nodding to the churl at the wheel to drive on.

But Lucy Watling was not to be brushed off that easily. Taking a firm grip of the door handle of the moving car, she shouted through the glass, 'You don't get rid of me that easily, Bertie Borrett. I'll find out who she is and tell her a few home truths.'

Once more the car jerked to a stop, and Jack saw Borrett give a quick instruction to the figure in the front passenger seat. That window now silently opened, a tattooed arm came out and Lucy's face was pulled down and into the car. Then came the sound of a vicious slap followed by Lucy being sent reeling back into the bushes behind her. 'Bastard!' was all she managed to shout as the Mercedes purred off and disappeared down the road.

Jack left his own car and dashed to her side. 'Mrs Watling ... are you all right?' he asked anxiously, helping the PA's wife to her feet.

‘Do I look as though I’m all right?’ Lucy pulled a twig from her hair and shrugged off Jack’s helping hand. ‘Bloody men ... why do I bother with them?’ Gulping back a sob, she quickly straightened her skirt before pulling a tissue from her sleeve to wipe away both tears and grime. The fast reddening area on her cheek wouldn’t be gone quite so easily, thought Jack, as she turned on her high heels and, with no attempt at thanks, pouted her way back into the hall.

‘Well, at least *you’re* glad to see me, Spike,’ greeted Jack as he opened his car tailgate to reveal the border collie standing there, tail wagging excitedly at the prospect of imminent exercise. A quick stroke, collar and lead on, and then it was to the grass area behind the hall for a quick scamper. But, with a good chunk of the break already used up, it was a very brief one for poor Spike who soon found himself being ushered back into the car and his master returning swiftly to the hall.

* * *

Back inside, Jack found Audrey just taking her leave of a tall pleasant-looking lady of middle age with a ready smile. ‘Bye for now, Margie ... we’ll be in touch.’ She turned back to her husband. ‘You were a long time, Jack. Spike only needed a short run.’

‘That’s all he got, but there were distractions. I’ll explain on the way home, love.’ He nodded after Audrey’s friend, now returning to a seat beside her husband, further down the hall. ‘Who was that?’

‘Margery Granston. I don’t think you’ve met her, but she ran the flower arranging class I went to last year.’

‘Ah, yes. I seem to remember you got on well with her.’

‘Yes, lovely lady and I’ve offered to help her out in a week or so.’

‘Good ... you’ll enjoy that.’ Jack glanced again at Mr Granston, tall like his wife, but very thin and far more sullen-looking. ‘Doesn’t her husband run his own marine fabricating business?’

‘George? Yes, he has a workshop just on the outskirts of the village.’

‘He doesn’t exactly look a bundle of laughs.’

‘No, but the poor chap has had some money worries which they’re only just getting over.’ Audrey didn’t feel now was the time to go into greater detail. ‘I’ll explain later.’

Jack was content with that, because he was now more interested in peering over his wife’s shoulder at Lucy Watling. The lady seemed to have quickly recomposed herself and was back with her own husband, who had a comforting arm around her shoulders and was obviously whispering words of misplaced concern. At this point the Fellows were rejoined by Admiral Ashfordby, cup in hand, and all set for the second half.

'So, how are you finding this whole business, Fellows?'

'Certainly interesting. Who would have thought such a small Broadland village harboured so many deep emotions and strange characters. Like those two louts we saw with Borrett. His minders, I presume. Are they local?'

'Yes, worse luck.' The admiral pulled a face. 'The Hinnerley brothers, Horace and Alfie. Village delinquents who are frequently up in front of the magistrates. They actually work for Borrett, which must be the first paid job they've ever had.'

'Doing what?'

'Driving him around since he lost his licence for being caught at the wheel with twice the legal limit in his blood. Most of the time, though, they just laze around the boatyard pretending to be busy.'

'Which boatyard?'

'The old Cookcraft yard, here in the village. Borrett bought it the end of last season.'

'Really. That's a shame.' Jack remembered the small family hire-boat business at the end of the dyke, Fred Cook, its cheerful owner, and the helpful yard-hands who always found time to chat to their regular customers.

'More than a shame, Jack,' muttered the admiral with a heartfelt sigh. 'Lovely traditional old yard it used to be. We all knew Fred had been struggling to make ends meet for years and that the hire fleet was running at a loss, but once Borrett got wind of the yard's financial predicament, he jumped in and offered a derisory sum to buy it. Old man Cook swore he'd never sell.'

'So, why did he?'

'Rumour has it, a visit from the Hinnerley brothers.'

'Hmm, that's what we're dealing with is it? So, having got his hands on the yard, what does Borrett do with it?'

'Not much,' explained the admiral with a shrug. 'He straight away got rid of all the old Cookcraft employees, sold off the hire fleet, and now the only boats moored there are his own motor cruiser and the old yard workboat.'

'But there are still parish moorings along the dyke leading to the river, surely?'

'Oh yes, I still keep *Curlew* there, but most of the others have left after a string of so-called incidents.'

'Such as?'

'Oh, boats that were securely moored by their owners being found adrift on the river, fuel contaminated, sails ripped, woodwork gouged, petty thieving ... that sort of thing.'

'The Hinnerley brothers?'

'That's what everyone suspected, but nothing could be proved. In the end, owners simply took their boats away to other moorings. Apart from *Curlew*, there's a canal narrowboat with some live-aboards and that's about it. It'll be good to see the ranger's launch back there Jack, I can tell you.'

The Broads Authority had one launch based at the village staithe, but it was sometimes relocated to replace other launches when they came up for refit. This last winter it had been completing its own at the Authority dockyard and Jack's first job would be the trip back. 'It'll be good to be here again, Admiral ... I think ... though it remains to be seen how relations will be with this new yard-owner.' Jack frowned. 'Seems a funny way do business, if you ask me. The old Cookcraft yard used to make a useful income from work on private boats moored in the dyke, so why drive valuable custom away?'

'You're right, but it was obvious from the start that Borrett had no interest in running it as a working boatyard. He just keeps his own boats in the wetshed and uses the rest of the space for running a small import business.'

'Importing what, exactly?'

'Traditional deck fittings ... cleats, fairleads ... that sort of thing. Buys them in Holland and brings them back in his boat. Top notch stuff actually and pretty cheap too. Wouldn't mind buying some for *Curlew*, but ...' Sir Claude gave a snort, '... damned if I'd ever buy anything from that blighter.'

'Obviously some people do though, if he can make enough profit to cover fuel costs going backwards and forwards across the North Sea. What sort of boat's he got?'

'Big Dutch twin-screw job called *Merlin Magic*, of all weird names, and far too nice for the likes of him.'

'You could say the same of Mrs Borrett,' said Jack, noticing the lady making a determined effort to avoid any contact with Lucy Watling, as she crossed the hall to join their group. Much to Jack's surprise, she greeted Admiral Ashfordby like an old friend, with a peck on the cheek.

'Nice to see you, Claude.' She put an affectionate arm around the admiral's waist and nodded towards the Fellows. 'Ain't you goin' to introduce me to yer friends?'

'Ah, yes,' replied the admiral, blushing slightly, 'this is Jack and Audrey Fellows. Jack's going to be one of the rangers here this summer, so watch yourself in that boat of yours.'

'Just part-time now,' said Jack, taking the lady's hand, 'but I'll be glad to help if you ever have any problems afloat.'

'Not me, you won't,' said Elsie Borrett, with a down-turned mouth. 'Boats has never been my thing. Too much water and far too wet for my likin'.'

'But I understand you own the old Cookcraft yard now, so I'll probably see you there.'

'Not likely, with that ghost hauntin' the place.' Elsie gave an affected shudder. 'You'll not find me hangin' about there for longer than I need to, thanks very much.'

'Ghost ...?'

But before Jack could pursue this line, Admiral Ashfordby broke in. 'You're not leaving now are you, Elsie?'

''fraid so, Claude.' She nodded towards the assembly starting to make their way back to their seats at the end of the break. 'I'm sure you'll all 'ave a few words to say about that bleedin' husband of mine, and me being out of the way will let them flow a bit freer. Done me bit and shown me face, so I'm off.'

'Dear lady,' said the admiral taking her hand. 'I hope you don't think that any of our animosity is directed towards yourself.'

'Course not, love. In fact, anyone who gives old Bertie an 'ard time is an 'ero in my book. So, good luck, sailor, and don't pull your punches.' A wave to the audience, and then she was gone.

'Quite a girl,' said Jack, as this personable lady exited the hall.

'Too good to be married to Borrett,' agreed Sir Claude, nodding. 'Can't blame the dear girl for fighting her husband's corner, but I hope she knows what she's doing.'

'Oh, I think she knows exactly what she's doing,' replied Jack without further explanation, but with a smile on his face. At that time, the chairman was once again calling for silence and he and Audrey were retaking their seats beside the admiral for what promised to be a lively second half.

* * *

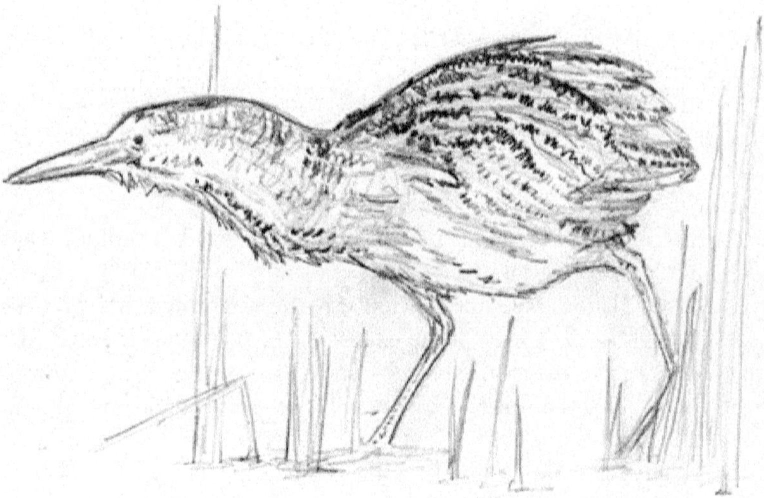

Chapter Two

'So, whatever was going on between Borrett and Lucy Watling, is definitely over now.' Audrey had been listening to Jack's account of the happenings in the village hall car park and formed her own conclusions. They were heading homeward with Spike asleep in the back for most of this long drive that took them along the south bank of the Yare, around Norwich and on to the Northern Rivers.

'Certainly appears that way. She seemed pretty sure it was because Bertie had fallen for someone else.' Jack turned towards his wife and grinned. 'Perhaps we should go to public meetings more often, Aud. Better than any theatre.'

'I'm not so sure, Jack.' Audrey turned back from giving Spike a gentle stroke. 'I don't like seeing people hurt, even if it is just their feelings. There were so many different emotions raging in there tonight. I knew people would be angry about the solar farm, but I wasn't expecting there to be such open hostility towards Bertie Borrett. Not that I blame people for disliking the man after seeing the way he treated his poor PA.'

'... in front of everyone too,' agreed Jack, 'and, if that wasn't embarrassing enough for Watling, it seems as if the whole village knows what's been going on between his wife and boss. And how must Elsie Borrett feel about her husband's blatant affair being aired so publicly?'

'No doubt she's used to it.' Audrey closed her eyes briefly and shook her head. 'Goodness knows why some wives put up with the husbands they do.'

'In her case, I expect for the money,' said Jack. 'It'll suit her to stay married to Bertie, and I should think she's long-since ignored his roving eye. I can't believe there's much love lost between those two anyway, so she's probably only too pleased if he finds his pleasures away from the matrimonial bed. He must be a good ten years older than her, so I bet she's banking on outliving him long enough to spend at least a few happy years working her way through his unspent millions.'

'I don't think you have to be quite that cynical, Jack,' reproved Audrey. 'If Elsie's got any sense, she'd be better off cutting her losses and going for a big divorce settlement now. She certainly has grounds for one.'

'I can't see the likes of Bertie Borrett paying out a fortune when he doesn't have to.' They were well clear of Norwich now, back in darkened countryside and Jack looking forward to getting home for a stiff nightcap. In the meantime, this discussion was helping speed the journey on its way. 'And besides, I'm damned sure he wouldn't want any dodgy dealings coming to light if his finances were scrutinised in court ...'

'... which would surely give Elsie some bargaining power for an out-of-court settlement.'

'You don't threaten the likes of Borrett,' pointed out Jack. 'Elsie has probably seen what happens to those who stick their neck out, and the treatment his minders can dish out.'

'Those tough Hinnerley brothers, you mean. Just the look of those two is enough to intimidate anyone.'

'Which is probably their sole purpose, Aud. Tough as he appears, Borrett probably needs a bit of muscle to watch his back and those two can certainly supply it. Thugs such as them have no scruples. You should've seen the smack one of them gave Lucy Watling.'

'That was despicable, but Lucy must have known she was playing with fire, carrying on with a man like Borrett. She was just asking for trouble.'

'Well, she got it tonight,' said Jack with a chuckle, 'but whether it's over or not, I'm not so sure Elsie will care, because I got the impression she might be having a little fling of her own.'

'Really? Who with?'

'Well, didn't you notice how touchy-feely she was with Admiral Ashfordby? Used his first name too, as if they were quite close.'

'Probably just her way.' Audrey smiled and wrinkled her nose. 'You say the admiral's been a widower for several years, so I suppose he's a bit chuffed to be receiving the attentions of an attractive woman like Elsie.'

'Especially one a good thirty years his junior.'

'Perhaps she just regards him as a father figure. Married to an oaf like Bertie, she must find the admiral's charm and good manners a wonderful contrast.'

'You're probably right,' agreed Jack, 'but I just hope the old sea-dog doesn't go and fall for her. Bertie Borrett isn't the sort of man you'd want to get on the wrong side of.'

'I shouldn't worry, love, it's probably all something about nothing, but I'll try and find out more from Margie Granston when I see her.'

'The flower-arranging lady? You said you were going to tell me more about her husband.'

'Yes, well, a year ago, George's fabrication business wasn't doing too well. He'd tried manufacturing his own boat fittings, but they'd proved too expensive, weren't selling and it looked like he'd go bust completely. He even had to sell his beloved boat to pay off debts at around the time Bertie Borrett moved into the village.'

'And ...'

'... to crown it all, Borrett started importing better quality and cheaper fittings from Europe.'

'That can't have helped.'

'No. According to Margie, George thought that might be the final kiss of death to his own business, but then, unexpectedly, things started looking up.'

'Really? How?'

'She didn't say exactly, but I gather the two men arrived at some sort of working agreement where Borrett does the importing and George the selling.'

'That's good, but George must be the only man for miles around who's actually benefitted from Borrett moving here.'

'Well, they seem to have sorted something out. Actually, things looked up for the Granstons in more ways than one because, while money was tight, Margie decided to earn a few pennies from flower arranging commercially. She's doing the flowers at St Mark's on Friday week, so I'm going over there to help, which will be good practise for me ...'

'... and, as you'll be working together in the church where the admiral's warden, she might be able to bring you up to speed on all the village gossip.'

Audrey gave an exasperated sigh. 'Don't ask me to do your nosing, Jack Fellows. If you want to know what's going on there, you should talk to Sir Claude yourself. Borrett's probably making life difficult for him just now, so I'm sure he'll appreciate some man-to-man support and a friendly chat.'

'Yeah, you're right,' conceded Jack, 'and, anyway, there's something else I want to pick his brain about.'

'Oh no, don't tell me,' groaned Audrey, knowing full well what was coming next. 'I bet it's to do with the ghost that Elsie mentioned, isn't it?'

'I am a bit intrigued, and it was interesting that she wasn't more forthcoming, which makes me all the more determined to find out more about it.' He gave his wife a playful nudge. 'Just a mystery to investigate, Aud. Admit it, you like a bit of intrigue yourself.'

'I would, Jack, except in your case it always unearths something far deeper and sinister.'

'Yes, well, this is probably just another of those Broadland ghost stories with a smidgen of truth that's been embroidered into something weird and romantic.' They were in their own narrow lane now and another minute had Jack backing into the cottage driveway and switching off the engine. 'Home again, Aud. Not as grand as some, but perhaps one filled with a little more marital harmony.'

'It will be as long as you don't go looking for trouble, Jack,' warned Audrey. 'You start patrolling again in a week, so just concentrate on looking after all those boating holidaymakers, and leave the villagers to sort out their own problems. Go and have a drink with the admiral by all means, but don't get too deeply involved in anything else.'

'I think the solar farm business will take care of itself anyway after tonight,' chuckled Jack. 'The meeting showed Bertie Borrett that the locals won't be quite the pushover he thought they'd be. After being given such a hard time in the hall followed by that unpleasant altercation with Lucy in the car park, he's probably glad to be back at Providence Farm enjoying a bit of peace and quiet.'

* * *

'You bastard!'

In the large kitchen of his farmhouse, Bertie Borrett ducked as the cut-glass tumbler of vodka narrowly missed his head and shattered against the dark walnut of the built-in freezer.

'You really are the pits, ain't you?' Elsie blinked back an alcoholic haze, picked up the bottle and prepared to follow up the tumbler with a better aim, but her husband grabbed her arm just in time.

'You stupid cow ... you could've killed me.'

'Yeah, well 'bout time someone did.' The fight had started almost the minute Elsie had walked in after making her own way back from the hall. She'd derided him for his womanising and he'd called her "a burned out lush". It was an accusation hard to refute with a fair amount of vodka already inside her so now, slumping into one of the chairs around the big farmhouse table, she lowered the bottle, grabbed a second tumbler and poured another good three fingers-worth. 'One day you'll bleedin' well get what you deserve, sleepin' around with anythin' in a skirt, and then just dumpin' them when somethin' better comes along.'

'You don't know what yer talking about.'

'Yes I do. People like Lucy Watlin' who you obviously gone and ditched tonight. Don't you deny you ain't been messing with that trollop ever since she came 'ere.'

'Yeah, well, she's out of my life now, so why worry?'

'Because I know you and your rovin' eye, Bertie. You've got another lined up, aint yer? Probably the one you've been dishing all that cash out on.'

'What cash?'

'The thousand odd you've been gettin' out of our account every month, that's what. Spending it on the woman you keep scuttlin' down the river in the workboat to see, no doubt. An' don't think I don't know. I been to the yard a few times and found it and you both gone.'

'That's just for a few bits an' bobs at Reedham. You know I can't drive any more. I've got to get around somehow.'

'I thought that was why you employed those two Hinnerley morons from the village. They've got to be good for somethin', surely.'

'Yeah, lookin' after the yard an' runnin' my import business.'

'What, the few bits of fancy metal you scuttle back an' forth across the North Sea for every month?' Elsie gave a derisive sniff. 'I don't call that a business. More like an excuse to visit the 'ot spots of Amsterdam if you ask me.'

'Yeah, well I'm not.' Bertie sat down in exasperation and poured himself a shot of vodka. 'Those are quality boat fittin's that I get from Holland an' you should be pleased I'm finally doin' somethin' straight.'

'You? Straight? Do me a favour. You've never done an honest thing in your life, Bertie Borrett, and I know, sure as 'ell, you 'aven't started now.'

'What about the solar project then? That's straight enough.'

'Oh yeah, perfect that is. I thought movin' 'ere might mean a new start, but no, you immediately get into some scheme that has the whole population turned against us.' Elsie took another swig of her drink. 'And one that could probably bankrupt us before you're finished. Like what you said tonight about 'iring some top London lawyer ... what's that all about?'

'It's about gettin' the better of all these daft protesters. I can 'andle them well enough at a local level, but when they get their 'eads together and start lodgin' appeals, I'm goin' to need someone who knows the law to push things through.'

'You've got Cecil. I thought the idea of takin' on a solicitor as your PA was to cut down on all those legal bills. And, God knows, we've 'ad enough of those over the years, with all them scrapes you got yourself into.'

'Watlin' couldn't argue 'is way out of a paper bag,' muttered Bertie, giving a dismissive snort and choosing to ignore Elsie's other observation. 'Why d'yer think 'e got booted out of 'is last job and couldn't get another as a solicitor? Watlin' was useful enough settin' up the office, but now that's done 'e can clear off.'

'Because you've lost interest in 'is missus more like, poor beggar.' Elsie looked as if she was about to be sick, but managed to recover enough to ask, 'So, who'll look after all that sort of stuff with 'im gone? Not me, I can tell yer.'

'Damned right,' agreed her husband for the first time this evening. 'The way you put away the booze, I wouldn't trust you to pay the milk bill, let alone run my business. You ain't even fit to do the cleanin' these days. Now I 'ave to pay someone just to keep the place lookin' 'alf decent.'

'And why should I after all these years?' Elsie glanced at her reflection in the kitchen window and tried to wipe away the crow's feet at the corner of her eyes. 'If you want me to look the part round 'ere, it won't be by being on me 'ands an' knees as a scivvy. I need a bit of time these days to keep my looks goin'.'

'Tarting yourself up for your own bit on the side more like.'

'What d'you mean by that?'

'I mean all these supposed shoppin' trips you keep doing with nothin' to show for it. Do me a favour. You've got some bloke on the side.' Borrett paused to point a warning finger straight into his wife's face. 'Well, no-one double times me, so get yourself ready for a divorce, and before I get rid of Watlin', I'll have 'im close our joint account an' cut you out of my will an' all.'

Elsie put down her glass of vodka. 'You mean you're goin' to leave me penniless?'

'You got it in one.' And then he was gone, slamming the kitchen door behind him and noisily stomping up the stairs to his lonesome bedroom.

It left Elsie somewhat stunned as she contemplated a future very different from what she'd ever envisaged. Life with Bertie Borrett had been no picnic, but at least it provided the material niceties in life. She looked at the bottle beside her, its level dropping as surely as her apparent fortunes. Her husband never made idle threats and a future without access to his money was a very bleak prospect indeed.

In an attempt to find some consolation, she thought of dear old Claude, his charm and unceasing chivalry. What was that he always said? "Meet the enemy head on." Perhaps it was time for her to do just that, and very soon too if she were to salvage any reward at all from all those wretched years of marriage.

* * *

Several miles away, other mischief was being planned. With the midnight hour long past, the brothers Hinnerley sat in their battered pickup truck, staring beyond an ancient wooden lych-gate to where ethereal moonlight bathed the roof and tower of the church it served. It was Alfie, the younger one at the wheel who spoke first. 'You sure this is the one, Horace?'

The older brother put away the folded map. 'Course it is and no alarm system neither. Just a load of lead up there all set for the taking.'

Only two hours before, they'd dropped their employer off at Providence Farm, locked the Mercedes in its barn and collected their own vehicle from the open out-building. Then back to the boatyard where a trailer had been hitched up and tools and ladders loaded into the back before another hour's drive through the darkened countryside to this remote parish, well to the west.

'You reckon it's safe to get started then?' Alfie was always glad to defer to his older brother's judgement.

'Yep. The village is a good half-mile away and we're long past closing time. They'll all be tucked up in their little beds, snoozing away while we do a mod on their precious church. You get them there gates open and I'll get the truck right up to it.'

Soon the pickup and trailer had been backed up the shingle track to the church and positioned close to the porch. Climbing out, Horace allowed himself a callous laugh. 'These religious types are always spouting on about helping those less fortunate, so let's do ourselves a bit of self-service.' He nodded into the open back. 'Grab the ladder and I'll bring them tools.'

Ten minutes and the brothers were twenty-five feet up on the fifteenth century roof, prising off the pliable sheets of protective lead before rolling them up and dropping them into the churchyard below. Carelessly slinging one roll too wide, Alfie managed to hit a gravestone below, breaking off its upper half.

Horace gave his brother a half-hearted punch. 'Watch it, Alfie. You're making enough noise to wake the dead.' It was a sick joke, but one they enjoyed as they resumed their destruction.

Dawn was still a good hour away when they were finished, both truck and trailer loaded with their haul of valuable metal. As they sped back through the lightening countryside, the first drops of rain started to spatter the windshield. Alfie switched on the wipers. 'Seems like we're in for a right downpour.'

Horace nodded. 'Yeah. What a mess they're going to find when they next turn up for their communion. P'raps we ought to hire ourselves out as a clean-up team. Sort of make the dosh at both ends.'

Once again the cab rang with laughter as the pickup and trailer, low on springs with a full load of lead, sped ever eastwards.

*   *   *

Chapter Three

'Agghh! It makes my blood boil.' At the Fellows' breakfast table, Jack slammed his cup back into its saucer and turned the newspaper so that Audrey could see the offending article. 'Would you believe it. Another local church having the lead taken from its roof. That's the third this month.'

In the week since the public meeting, Jack had been busy getting back into the swing of his ranger duties. At the Broads Authority dockyard in Trowse, he'd joined regular rangers on their patrols, some of which extended down to the lower half of the Yare, where he'd half-expected to see Sir Claude Ashfordby already afloat in *Curlew*. But there had been no sign of the admiral, possibly because the old seadog was still too involved in his fight against the proposed solar farm.

Jack wished him luck, but was content to let local politics take a back seat for now, as this morning he would be taking his own launch, refit complete, out of the dockyard and down river to the village, where it would be based for the rest of the season. With his ranger uniform back on and this enjoyable trip in prospect, he'd started the day feeling good with the world. That was until he'd read about the lead thefts.

'Now Jack, don't go getting upset about things you've got no control over,' soothed Audrey, popping on her specs and leaning a little closer to see the photo of an anguished vicar and warden looking up at their ravaged church roof. 'Oh dear, how distressing for them. Wasn't the last theft like this only a week ago?'

'That's right, the same night as the solar farm meeting. The inside of that church was badly water-damaged when heavy rain seeped through onto pews and flooring and ruined the chancel.' Jack tried to calm himself down by pouring another cup of tea. 'The cost of repairs for these churches runs into hundreds of thousands.'

'The insurance companies will pay for that, surely,' said Audrey, trying to find a crumb of comfort in this whole sad business. 'I know our own St Cuthbert's is well covered for that sort of eventuality.'

'That's only because we invested in CCTV.' Jack could well remember the year of fund-raising needed to purchase the four surveillance cameras for their parish church. He tapped the relevant passage in the article. 'It says here that the insurance only covers the first seven and a half thousand if the church doesn't have CCTV. Our thieves have obviously sussed their targets well, by only going for churches in remote locations and without surveillance cameras.'

'I just hope Admiral Ashfordby's church will be spared then,' said Audrey, starting to clear the breakfast things. 'I remember him telling me at a diocesan meeting how much St Mark's wanted to get cameras installed, but that they just didn't have the five thousand pounds it would cost.'

'Most churches struggle to pay their normal bills without having that burden thrust upon them. Perhaps the admiral should convince Borrett that he'd get the parishioners on his side if he offered to donate the money to install cameras.'

'Can you really see the admiral going to that bully, cap in hand for favours, Jack?'

'No, not really, and it probably wouldn't do him any good if he tried, because Borrett isn't the type who'd even know the meaning of good will.' Jack picked up the paper once more and mulled over the details. 'It can't be easy getting rid of stolen lead these days. Apparently, since 2012, it's been illegal for scrap yards to pay cash for it, and, with the police keeping firm tabs on any untraceable valuable metal turning up, fencing the stuff must be a problem.'

'Wasn't Borrett once in the scrap metal business, Jack?'

'Yes, that's right. In London apparently. Hmmm, that's a good point, Aud. Perhaps a closer nose around the Cookcraft Yard might be even more appropriate than I thought.'

'Jack, please don't go jumping to conclusions. Bertie Borrett might not be the nicest or most honest of people, but surely he wouldn't jeopardise his whole future here by getting involved in something like that?'

'He would if it was worth it financially.'

'So how much do they get for this stolen lead?'

Jack tapped the paper. 'Says here that its market value is a thousand pounds a tonne and you get about seven from a typical church roof.'

'Peanuts for the likes of Borrett.' Audrey, leant over her husband's shoulder and scanned the rest of the article. 'And anyway, it says here that the police are launching an intensive investigation, so you just stick to patrolling the river, love, and leave crime- busting to those whose job it is. As regards Borrett, I'm sure the admiral is keeping a wary eye on him and his dealings.'

'I'll find out when we meet up,' said Jack, swigging back the remains of his tea and getting up from the table, 'I was hoping to see him out on *Curlew*, but he doesn't seem to be sailing yet.'

'Well, why don't you give him a ring today when you've got a minute ...' Audrey glanced at the clock and stood up, '... but you'd better get a move on now or you'll be late.' She handed her husband his jacket and lunch bag before ushering him to the door, where he paused just long enough to give her a goodbye kiss.

'Right, I'm off but, yes, I will give Sir Claude a quick ring. See you this evening, love.' And then Jack was stepping out into the early morning sunshine to spend his first day this year doing the job he loved.

* * *

That was certainly not a situation enjoyed by Cecil Watling that fine morning. Sitting at his desk in the small Providence Farm outbuilding that served as his office, Bertie Borrett's PA couldn't help but mull over the chain of events that had brought him here. Money was the root of all evil, ran the saying, and, in his case, he'd proved it dead right.

Not that he'd ever had much of it, growing up in a working class family on a council estate. But one thing he had been blessed with was academic ability, a gift that had taken him to university and the study of law. He'd chosen that subject, not for humanitarian reasons or because it particularly interested him, but purely as a means of becoming very rich.

The reality though, after graduation and as a trainee solicitor, was somewhat different, with a miserly salary mostly spent on bare sustenance and repaying his student loan. After qualification, he'd managed to get into a practice specialising in litigation, but seeing his clients getting huge amounts of damages from often dubious accidental injury claims only frustrated him further. And then he'd met Lucy.

She worked as a senior medical secretary in a nearby doctors' practice, which Cecil's law firm regularly used for professional advice regarding accidental injury claims. They frequently spoke on the phone and Lucy's manner and sensual voice attracted the young solicitor enough for him to make up an excuse to visit the surgery to collect a medical report. Faced with this stunningly attractive, petite brunette, Cecil had been instantly smitten, asked her out for a drink and been flattered beyond words when she'd actually accepted. He knew he was no great catch for someone as beautiful as Lucy, but despite his shortcomings, their relationship grew.

Deep down, Cecil always suspected it was more his job that had attracted her, but as long as she continued dating him, he kept his thoughts to himself and accepted that the one undeniable thing they did have in common, was an unrelenting desire for money.

Unfortunately, that was something Cecil still had little of when he and Lucy married, and even less by the time they'd over-stretched their finances on a flat and furnishings. Added to that was the realisation that, although she continued to work at the surgery, his new wife was a shopaholic who squandered all her salary, and some of his, on clothes, make-up and hair appointments. It wasn't long before Cecil found himself engulfed in debt, but it was then that Lucy came up with the solution.

On her insistence, they'd kept their romance and marriage a secret, even to their respective employers. Lucy had argued it might raise conflicts of interest and, in his naivety, he'd accepted that reasoning. Only later did he suspect it was all part of her plan and by then it was too late.

It had been a very simple scheme that had immediately eased their financial problems, so much so that they decided to repeat it again ... and again. Eventually, they were living the high life they'd both always dreamed of, and one that could seemingly continue indefinitely. And so it would have if fate hadn't intervened.

But it had and they'd both lost their jobs and only avoided criminal proceedings and Cecil being struck off, by cashing in their worldly possessions and repaying every penny embezzled.

And so, homeless and penniless, salvation had come in the form of this job with Borrett, secured only by Lucy's undeniable charms.

'So, what are you doing other than just feeling sorry for yourself?'

Cecil looked up with a start, so engrossed in his musings that he'd failed to even notice Lucy come through the door. Their home wasn't far away, a workers' cottage on the edge of the farm, close enough for them both to be at Borrett's beck and call when he needed, Cecil in the office or Lucy in his bed. 'No, just thinking of all that might have been.'

'Yes, well you might instead be thinking of what it *will be*.' She was dressed in just denim jeans, check shirt and flat sandals, so much more attractive to Cecil than the phoney glamour his wife normally portrayed.

'What brings you here, Lucy? Not something you do very often these days.'

She perched on the edge of his desk and absent-mindedly played with a paperknife. 'Oh, just interested in what thoughts you might have about what you'd do if you didn't have this job.'

'Why, don't you think I'll have it much longer?'

Lucy's laugh held little humour. 'Come off it, Cecil. We both know I'm the only reason Borrett employed you in the first place and why you've kept your job this long. If it wasn't for me, you'd still be stacking shelves at the supermarket.'

'If it wasn't for you, I'd still be practising as a solicitor.'

'Don't you dare try and blame me for that!' Cecil jumped back in fright as Lucy brought the paperknife down to impale a document on his desk. 'That deal I set up would still be raking in the money if you hadn't gone and blown it.'

'I wasn't me. It was just bad luck.'

'You make your own luck, Cecil.' She let go of the knife, folded her arms and fixed her husband through narrowed eyes. 'You really are pathetic, aren't you? The way you let Borrett humiliate you like he does.'

Cecil removed the knife from his desk and pointed it at his wife. 'It's you that does the humiliating, Lucy ... by going to bed with the man.'

'Yes, well ...' she touched the red mark on her cheek, '... that's all over now and so will your job be just as soon as Borrett has worked out how he can fire you, without giving you any compensation.' Her tone mellowed just slightly. 'Believe me, Cecil, I was only doing what I did for us. It was our financial security I was thinking of and now, once again ...' she glanced outside and across the field towards their cottage, '... we're going to lose our home, our livelihood and everything we've worked for.'

'Perhaps not.' Cecil, sat back and turned the knife over in his hands. 'How do you know I haven't been working on securing our own compensation?'

Lucy blinked twice and leaned forward. 'Go on.'

'I haven't spent the last six months playing dogsbody to that arrogant bully without learning a little bit about his business.' Cecil knew he had his wife's attention and his manner was appropriately patronising. 'If legal training teaches you one thing, Lucy, it's how to extract information from the most obscure data.'

Her eyes were wide open now. 'So, tell me, what did you find?'

'That our dear Bertie Borrett has more money than even you would imagine, and it's all involved with that crazy business in Holland.'

'What, you mean importing those boat fittings? He can't make much from selling them ... just pocket money.'

'If you call well over a million euros, "pocket money".'

'A million ...' Lucy shuffled just a little closer along the desk. 'Are you sure?'

Cecil nodded sagely. 'Couldn't be surer. Of course, if you look at his books and UK bank accounts, it shows a business barely holding its own. But sorting out his office, I came across a number pencilled into the cover of a file. That number looked suspiciously like a foreign account number to me. It didn't take much finger work on the computer to come up with the details of an account at a Dutch bank. A bit more delving in the files and I had a PIN number and got access to it.'

'... to find ...?'

'... it held a six figure sum.'

'My goodness.' Lucy sat back in amazement and ran fingers through her hair. 'Where on earth did that come from?'

'Goodness knows.' Cecil threw the paperknife back onto the desk. 'Some devious business, I have no doubt, but the important thing, Lucy ...' he lowered his voice conspiratorially, '... is where it's *going*.'

'Going? Going where?'

'Into an offshore bank of our own. In fact, some of it's already gone.'

She sat up abruptly. 'You're kidding! How much?'

'Not much. Just a little taster by way of an experiment.' Cecil leaned back in his chair, concealing the satisfaction he felt at, for once, having his wife's full attention. 'First I set up a bank account in Spain under Borrett's name, but with me as principal signatory. And then I made a day trip to London a few weeks ago.'

'Yes, I remember you were pretty cagey about the reason. So, you were actually ...?'

'... paying a visit to Canary Wharf and the London branch of Borrett's Dutch bank. I'd printed out a request on his letterhead for a thousand euros to be transferred to what, ostensibly, seemed another account of his in Spain. I made this first transaction personally just to identify myself as his PA. Forging the pathetic scribble he uses for a signature was no problem and with such a modest amount and my obvious legal credentials, they didn't hesitate to accept the transfer to the Spanish account.'

'... which, in reality is our own foreign account. Well done, Cecil,' complimented Lucy. She gave her husband a big kiss on the cheek before frowning slightly. 'But won't Bertie see what's happened when he gets his next Dutch bank statement?'

'Of course he will, but the last thing he wants is any paper trail leading back to England, so he has all his statements sent to a box number in Amsterdam. For the same reason, they're not forwarded from there and instead he only collects them on his regular trips to Holland. He's not off again for another two weeks and by then we'll have cleaned him out.'

'You mean ...?'

'Yep, the lot. Equivalent to about a million pounds.'

'Phew, Cecil, what a coup.' Lucy could hide neither her admiration nor vindictiveness. 'Serve the bastard right, I say, and I'd love to see his face when he discovers just how much he's been shafted.'

Cecil shook his head. 'That's one pleasure you won't have, because by then we'll be long gone. And, if Elsie knows about that Dutch account, which I'm sure she doesn't, she wouldn't have been seeing any of it anyway, so it'll be no loss to her.'

'How do you mean?'

'Because the day after that public meeting, Bertie asked me to draw up a new will that effectively cuts his wife out of everything.'

'Well what do you know.' Lucy's chuckle was spiked with more than its fair share of malice. 'So, even our smug Mrs Borrett is finally getting her come-uppance.' She threw her arms around his neck. 'Oh, Cecil, I knew you had it in you really, but tell me exactly just how you're going to pull off this wonder-heist?'

'Later.' Cecil unwound his wife's arms. 'And don't go stupidly giving the game away. No gloating or even a hint that you're anything but the dumped mistress. In fact, it'd be better if you didn't make contact at all with the Borretts for the next week or so. Stay in the cottage pretending you're licking your wounds and work out how you're going to spend all those euros.'

Normally, Lucy didn't take kindly to being told what to do by her husband, but now she just grinned and said, 'That shouldn't be a problem for me.' She gave him a passionate kiss and softened her voice. 'But I think we can allow ourselves a little celebration tonight, Cecil. I'm going home to sort out a special meal ...' she purred, giving a saucy wink, '... and don't be late, because that's not the only treat that'll be waiting for you.'

After she'd left, Cecil sat back in his chair and allowed himself a smile of satisfaction before he returned to his computer and keyed in the now-familiar password. He had some very important transactions to negotiate in the next few days.

* * *

Chapter Four

Out on the river, Jack's own priorities were rather more modest and certainly less sinister.

After his eight o'clock start from the dockyard, it had been a pleasant, leisurely passage downriver to his patrol area in morning air sufficiently chilly to produce pockets of mist that only added to the almost ethereal charm of the low-lying land of the Yare valley. Still early in the day, it was a charm that had been shared by just one solitary heron, motionless as a statue as it scanned the limpid waters for a first glimpse of fish breakfast, and giving Jack a slight sense of guilt as his widening wake lapped against the mud banks.

Now, however, two hours into his passage, the easterly wind was freshening slightly, bringing with it just the faintest tang of the North Sea and a slightly chillier reminder that this was still early summer. Not sufficient though to deter several boats already on the go. Being past Easter, but well before the main school holidays, most out this morning were craft either owned or hired by an older generation fulfilling the dreams that had sustained them as they worked their way towards retirement. In general, these boaters were a pretty experienced lot who required little help or guidance from the rangers, allowing Jack to relax as he cruised eastwards, admiring the new paint and varnish of winter-restored classic yachts and the smartness of hire boats just re-launched from their boatyards. Scanning ahead, he again hoped to see Admiral Ashfordby's *Curlew*, out on such a lovely day and peeling off the first miles of the thousand-odd the old salt sailed every year. But, though several other sailboat masts marked the river's winding course, there was no sign of the familiar tan sail with its namesake depiction stitched into the fabric. Perhaps he was already moored at one of his favourite spots where he liked to mix with other boaters and regale them with nautical anecdotes, non-the-less entertaining for being oft repeated. However, even further on, there was no sign of boat or admiral and finally Jack pulled out his mobile and keyed the number.

It rang several times before '... Ashfordby.' The gravelly voice still carried its old authority, though this morning it was tinged with just a suggestion of tiredness.

'Admiral ... Jack Fellows here ... surprised you're not out on the river making the most of wind and sun.'

'Oh, hello Fellows. No, not today. Catching up with some sleep, actually.'

'Oh, I'm sorry. Did I wake you?'

'Yes, you did, but what can I do for you?' The tone wasn't unfriendly, but reproving enough to make Jack feel slightly guilty.

'Just wondering if we could meet up for a drink and a chat sometime.'

'Oh ... well ... it won't be for a while yet. My evenings are pretty tied up these days. Give me a call in a week or so and we'll take it from there.'

'I see. Okay, Admiral, I'll do that. Sorry to have disturbed you.'

'That's okay, Fellows. Goodbye.' And the phone rang off.

Frowning slightly, but determined not to make any unfounded assumptions, Jack switched off his own phone, shrugged and continued on around the next bend in the river.

He was abeam Langley marshes now, a flight of greylag geese squawking past in echelon formation, the blue skies above seemingly bigger than ever and this beautiful vista marred only by the mighty storage silos of Cantley Sugar Beet Factory, just coming into view. Minutes later he was passing the popular old wherry watering hole of the Red House pub and, after that, the factory itself.

Such industrialisation always came as something of a shock amongst the encircling rural landscape, but Cantley was indeed a vital part of the local economy, producing as it did, an annual two-hundred thousand tonnes of sugar from 1.3 million tonnes of locally grown beet. Years before this beet, and the coal and oil needed to feed the process, had been brought along the Yare by river transport, but in the last quarter century that transportation had all given way to road. Motoring past the empty wharves, Jack recalled his many encounters with the huge sugar-beet lorries that thundered down the country roads between September and February, a period known as "the campaign". Such musings though were soon left astern with Cantley itself as he continued downriver on the fast ebb, following yet another twist of the river's meander. Now, ahead and on the south bank, he spotted a type of boat relatively uncommon on Broadland waters.

She was a canal narrowboat, lying alongside the floating pontoon mooring provided for boats wishing to visit the Hardley Drainage Mill. The mill itself lay just inland, a fine example of restoration of the once numerous turning pumps that had kept the marshes drained for centuries.

Jack's attention, though, was focussed on the boat, its slender forty foot steel hull adorned with tubs of flowers and with a column of wood smoke slowly rising from the tall brassbound chimney for'ard.

Always a popular stopping place for boats in transit, Hardley's floating pontoon negated the need to worry about the Yare's significant tidal range, but this morning, the narrowboat was the only vessel moored there. Jack slowed for a better look. On the side of the after-cabin, skilfully worked amidst traditional roses and castles, was the name - *Faith and Hope* – while standing by the helm at the stern was a young woman. As Jack drew nearer, he could see she was keen to attract his attention.

'Ahoy! Can you help us?'

Swinging around on the ebb tide, Jack brought the launch alongside and handed across a line.

* * *

Only a little further downriver and just beyond the village dyke, was Providence Farm from where, upstairs in the master bedroom, it was possible to see the river and passing boats. That was not a scene being enjoyed at this moment, though, by Bertie Borrett, who instead was downstairs at the big farmhouse kitchen table, scoffing a late breakfast of four rashers and two eggs. It was not a meal lovingly prepared by Elsie any more than he would admit to enjoying it. Rather, this breakfast table was more a no-man's-land between opposing forces than a place for domestic socialising, a scene of morbid silence broken only by the chomp of Bertie's noisy mastication.

Seated opposite, Elsie wondered, not for the first time, how she had ever found anything in the least bit attractive about this man. 'So, when are you scuttlin' across the North Sea again?' she asked in an effort to break the almost monastic silence.

Bertie didn't answer until he'd slowly chewed another mouthful, not through any sudden attack of manners, but purely as a device for showing his wife that everything was going to be on his terms. Finally, he pushed the plate away, wiped his mouth with the back of his hand and answered with another question. 'Why d'you want to know that?'

'Oh, just plannin' my days.'

'Working out when the coast is clear, more like.'

'I wish ... and don't do that,' she scolded as Bertie swept some errant crumbs from the table onto the floor.

'Why not. That's what the cleaner's for ain't it?'

'Not today it's not. It's 'er day off.'

'Off!' Bertie's bloodshot eyes did an intolerant roll. 'I don't pay for days off.'

'No, you don't, and think yourself lucky we've got anyone, because no decent local girl would work 'ere with your reputation.'

'Who'd want 'em anyway?' He gave a loud belch. 'But, in answer to your question, I might be runnin' across to Holland sooner than I thought.'

'You don't say. Missin' you, is she?'

'Give me a break, woman. It's just that my supplier wants to clear out old stock and is offering me a deal.'

'Good for 'im. The sooner you're out of my 'air the better.'

'Yeah, well at least it'll give you time to get it re-coloured,' fired Bertie, as a departing shot as he stomped out of the kitchen for the privacy of his study.

Not that Bertie ever actually studied anything in this small locked room just down the hall, except his magazines from the top shelf of the newsagents or the file he now took from the top drawer of his desk. Squeezed into his big captain's chair, he paused for a few contemplative seconds before opening the buff cover.

In the file were a number of email printouts and letters but, most important of all to him, a seven-by-five inch photo paper-clipped to its inside. It showed a young woman, blonde, pretty and dressed in the regalia of a barrister-at- law. Bertie sat for a long time just gazing at it.

* * *

Newington Causeway, in the London Borough of Southwark, lies between the Elephant and Castle and Borough High Street, a hundred miles south of Broadland geographically and a world away environmentally. It does, however, boast several important buildings, one of which is the Sessions House wherein sits the Inner London Crown Court.

It was in the corridor outside Court Six this fine morning that barrister Lynsey Butterick paused to breathe a sigh of relief, pulled off the itching horsehair wig and shook out her blonde ponytail. But any satisfaction this gesture allowed was immediately neutralised by a voice from behind.

'Shouldn't you at least wait until you're in the robing room before doing that?'

It was a modulation as familiar as it was pompous, but Lynsey still jumped slightly, knowing she was indeed in slight violation of court etiquette.

'Miles ... what are you doing here? Aren't you supposed to be prosecuting that conspiracy-to-steal?'

'I was until old Justice Frobisher deemed there was no case to answer and threw it out.' Miles Rotherby-Jones shrugged sloping shoulders beneath a gown that also effectively covered an expanding waistline. 'Another example of the CPS failing to give me sufficient hard evidence to do the job.'

'I think that's the same excuse you made for the last case you lost, Miles,' said Lynsey, who had never had much respect for her colleague's advocacy skills.

'Yes, well, perhaps when I take silk, I'll be given more winnable ones.'

'Perhaps.' Lynsey made no effort to disguise the scepticism in her voice, knowing that, despite his professional and personal shortcomings, Miles held two main ambitions in life, they being to put "QC" after his own name and "Mrs" and "Rotherby-Jones" either side of hers. She didn't hold out much hope for the former and none at all for the latter.

Rotherby-Jones adjusted his wig, beneath which sprouts of thinning red hair seemed as intent at escape as their predecessors. 'But you seem pretty pleased with yourself. Presumably, the handling-stolen-goods you were defending, came off well?'

'Yes, very well.' Lynsey wasn't by nature a gloater, but for Miles' sake she did give an exaggerated smile of satisfaction. 'A "Not Guilty" from the jury after only thirty minutes deliberation so ...' she threw her wig onto a nearby bench, '... that's why I'm quite literally letting my hair down.'

'You could do that better by letting me take you out for a meal this evening.'

'No thank you, Miles.' She chose to be just a little abrupt in her rejection. 'I've got a lot to sort out here before I leave in a few days.'

'For Norfolk?' Rotherby-Jones gave a dismissive sigh. 'You mean you're actually serious about accepting that ridiculous wind-turbine brief?'

'It's a solar farm actually, Miles, and yes, I really am going to handle it.'

'You must be mad. Here you are, for a girl, building quite a reputation as a criminal lawyer, and you seem determined to throw it all away on some misguided crusade for alternative energy.'

'It's not misguided at all. If you weren't so blinkered, you'd realise there are going to be more and more of these cases as fossil fuels run out.

Harnessing energy from the sun and wind's the only way forward, and I intend to be instrumental in getting these schemes up and running. It's something I can do ... even as a girl.'

The sarcasm, however, was lost on Rotherby-Jones. 'You realise, of course, that you'll be ruffling up a lot of feathers with public opinion as it is. People aren't going to want acres of solar panels or wind turbines in their backyards, so your views aren't going to make you many friends.'

'Oh, so getting criminals off the sentences they probably richly deserve is the way to people's hearts, is it?' Lynsey took off her gown and threw that on top of the wig. 'Quite honestly, Miles, I'm sick to death with crime and this whole charade of justice. There's another world out there, and I aim to find it, starting in Norfolk.'

'You call "Norfolk" the real world? And what do you know of this chap Borrett you're going to represent?'

'Only what his solicitor tells me. That he's got a genuine interest in fostering alternative energy and is determined to push this project through.'

'But have you ever met him?'

'No, of course not. No barrister meets their client much before representing them.'

'That's different, Lynsey. You tell me you're actually going to stay with this man.'

'Not *with*, Miles, but as a guest *of* ... on his boat, actually.'

'You're joking. You know nothing about boats.'

'No, but I'd like to learn. And, anyway, his solicitor tells me *Merlin Magic* is very comfortable, so I won't be exactly roughing it. At least I'll be getting some fresh country air.' Lynsey wrinkled her cute nose. 'That has to be better than the foul prison smell of urine and stale food which seems to be the background to most of my client interviews.'

'I can see you need a break,' conceded Rotherby-Jones, reluctantly, 'but you're surely not intending to stay up there any longer than necessary?'

'Perhaps I am. I always wanted to see the Broads and, from what I know of the area, it might be a good place to settle down.'

'On your own, you mean?' Rotherby-Jones shook his bewigged head. 'But what about us?'

'What do you mean, "us"?'

'Well, I thought we had ... well ... some sort of understanding.'

'Really?' Lynsey folded her arms. 'Believe me, Miles, the only understanding *I* have is that if and when I'm seeking male companionship, the last person I'll choose is a pompous, emotionless, supercilious, self-righteous prig like you.'

'Well ... I say ... that's a bit ...'

But Lynsey wasn't listening. Instead, she was snatching up her wig and gown and giving her loose hair one more defiant shake before turning on her high heels and clicking down the corridor and out of the door without even a backward glance.

Rotherby-Jones watched her go, well aware that in the last hour he'd suffered defeat in both court and love. It was not a situation easily accepted by someone so conceited. That, of course, was not something he would ever recognise, but what he did know was that Lynsey had misjudged him badly on one point at least. For, far from being emotionless, Miles knew he possessed one characteristic that could be as destructive as it was powerful – one that even now was building inside him. Just how dangerous that could be, Lynsey Butterick, would soon find out.

*   *   *

Chapter Five

'Thanks for stopping. I hope you can help.' Back on the Yare, the slim young woman at the stern of the narrowboat leaned down to take the line Jack was handing across, her face lit by the most ready and natural of smiles.

'I hope so too. That's what we're here for. What's the problem?'

As if in answer, a man in his mid-thirties, clad in oil-stained overalls, emerged from the machinery space beneath the girl's feet. 'The engine, it is running too hot ... no cooling water.' The accent was distinctly French and at variance with his tall height and short fair hair. He wiped a smudge of oil from his cheek with one hand while the other held something wrapped in cotton waste. He held it out for Jack to see. 'The problem, it is this water pump wheel.'

'You're right, mate, it's the impeller,' confirmed Jack, examining the small plastic component and seeing that several of the blades were missing and the others badly worn. 'Do you keep a spare onboard?'

'We did, but Marcel used it to help another boat with the same problem,' explained the young woman, tucking a tendril of long dark hair behind her ear. She glanced around at the surrounding marshland, the red brick mill gaunt against the arcing sky and the absence of any other habitation. 'Unfortunately, we don't have a tender, so it's impossible to get to a boatyard and we don't know any number to call for help.'

'First thing is to find you the part,' stated Jack. 'There's a boat chandlery at Brundall several miles upriver from here which will have one.'

'Ah, yes, Brundall. That is where we launched this vessel just a month ago.' The young Frenchman nodded to the pair of bikes lashed atop the narrowboat's roof. 'We would go ourselves, but it is many kilometres to a river crossing.'

'No problem,' reassured Jack, taking out his mobile. 'They deliver to boatyards throughout Broadland every day. If they haven't left yet, I'm sure they'd deliver the part to a local staithe and I could collect it for you.'

'Oh, that would be wonderful,' said the relieved young woman. 'Our moorings are in the next dyke downriver. Perhaps they could deliver it there.'

'You mean near the old Cookcraft yard?'

'Yes that's right, on the parish moorings.'

'Which is where this launch is normally based.' Jack explained how it was just returning from a refit. 'So, I'll ask them if they can deliver there. What sort is your engine?'

With the relevant data, Jack was soon through to the chandlers and another minute found him switching off and smiling. 'Just caught them before they left, but they've got the part and will drop it off at the yard in about an hour. It'll be no problem for me to call in there, collect your impeller, bring it back to you here and still complete my patrolling schedule for the day. I'll be a couple of hours, but at least it will get you out of a fix.'

'Our time's pretty much our own,' smiled the young woman, 'so that'll be perfect.'

'Yes, I am obliged to you so much,' added her companion. He nodded down into the cabin. 'Will you let us please say *merci* by sharing with you at least a *café*.'

Jack glanced at his watch. He didn't want to arrive at the yard too early and, besides, he was keen to find out more about this appealing boat and its intriguing owners. 'Thanks, that would be lovely.'

More lines were secured to the narrowboat's cleats and then the ranger was climbing aboard to join the couple on the open afterdeck. The young woman held out her hand. 'Welcome aboard *Faith and Hope*. My name's Charity Howden and this is my boyfriend, Marcel Carbonne.'

'Good to meet you both.' Jack duly introduced himself while noting the boat's gleaming paintwork, shining brass tiller extension and neatly coiled ropes. 'A smart craft you've got here and well-named, now I know yours.'

'Just a little play on words, but, yes, she is a lovely cosy boat.' Charity Howden indicated towards the open cabin door. 'Come below and let me show you more of her.'

In spite of *Faith and Hope*'s narrow beam, she was indeed a haven of comfort, though practical as well, with even a small workshop set up at the aft end of the cabin. Further for'ard, the couple's loving care became apparent with handmade curtains framing each rectangular window and most woodwork adorned with cleverly worked carvings. This homeliness was most pronounced right up in the bows where a wood-burning stove crackled away, filling the cabin with the evocative aroma of burning timber and a comforting glow. While Charity placed a shining brass kettle on the hob, Jack was content to shed his jacket and settle down into one of the couches along the cabin side. Marcel, sat opposite, still wiping the oil off his hands with a paper towel. He had the rugged looks of a man well-used to the open-air life, but with keen perceptive eyes that mirrored a smile as ready as his girlfriend's. 'It is our luck that you came by this morning.'

'In a way,' said Jack, 'but my colleague or I will be doing daylight patrols of the river every day now the season's started.' He glanced around once more at this couple's ordered way of life, clearly something established over a long period. 'So, where were you before coming onto the Broads?'

'On the UK canal system,' called Charity from the galley.

Marcel pulled a map from an adjacent bookcase. 'We have travelled this whole country by canal,' he proclaimed proudly, waving a now-clean hand across the spider's web of lines that marked the inland waterways of England. 'Finally we arrived at your Norfolk port of King's Lynn.'

'The canal authorities are becoming increasingly intolerant of any liveaboards without a permanent mooring,' explained Charity, 'and, as it was so close to the Broads, we thought it would be good to move *Faith and Hope* here.' She placed a mug of steaming coffee at Jack's side. 'We checked first with the Broads Authority and found that our length wouldn't be a problem.'

'You're okay with forty feet,' confirmed Jack. 'We've a few narrowboats on the Broads, but the longer ones have limitations put on their cruising. I see you're tolled and registered, so obviously you intend to stay a while?'

'Yes, for a year at least. It cost most of our money having it craned out, transported to Brundall and then craned in again, so we want to make it worthwhile.'

'Well, it's great to see you here,' said Jack, taking an appreciative sip of his coffee. 'You're obviously someone who loves boats and the water?'

'She's always has,' chimed in Marcel, 'ever since she was a little girl.'

Charity nodded. 'That's right. I don't know what it is, but somehow I only feel at peace with myself when I'm close to the water.'

Jack smiled, knowing something of how this adventurous young woman felt. 'Living afloat must be your ideal way of life then. Have you been doing it for long?'

'Yes, for several years now, since my first marriage broke up.' She reached across to the sideboard for a biscuit barrel and opened it in front of Jack. 'After that upset I felt the need for a complete change of lifestyle and so, with my divorce settlement, I bought this boat in a very neglected state, gave her a complete makeover, a new name and me a home to live on the canals. Two years ago I even took her across the channel to cruise the French canals and, down by Lyon, called in at a yard and met Marcel who worked there. We hit it off and have been together ever since.'

'Why back here?' queried Jack. 'I would have thought the southern French canals would have been a warmer option, if nothing else?'

'Yes, very much so,' agreed the Frenchman with a nod, 'but England, it was Charity's real home and I too wanted a change in my life anyway, so coming here, it was no problem for me. I am good with my hands and boats and can work wherever I find myself.'

'Is this woodcarving yours?' asked Jack, stroking the carved end of the bookcase.

'*Oui*, just a *hobby*.'

'But a very accomplished one, as is your English,' complimented Jack.

'Ah, but there I have the advantage of living many years of my childhood here,' explained the Frenchman. 'You see, my father's job brought us to London, where we lived until I was eight. Then my parents' marriage, it dissolved and *ma mere* took me back to her native Provence.'

'And now you're back and very welcome,' smiled Jack before asking, 'So, do you have a job here?'

'Not a job,' admitted Marcel, 'but if any *mariniers* need work on their boats, then I am happy to help. We have a small workshop on board and so I and *Faith and Hope* both earn a few cents.' He smiled across to Charity. 'After all, it is not fair that my girlfriend, she has to be the . . . how do you say? . . . breadwinner.'

Charity shrugged. 'I'd rather be doing something than nothing, and who earns the pennies is irrelevant to me.'

'So, *you* have a job?' probed Jack, while trying not to sound too nosey. 'Doing what, exactly?'

'Oh, just some local cleaning. It doesn't pay much, but it does get us free moorings.'

'That must be handy,' acknowledged Jack, 'but how?'

'Well, it almost seemed as though it was meant to be, the way it worked out,' she explained. 'We were looking for somewhere reasonably permanent, but were finding it almost impossible for a forty-foot boat. Then we came across that dyke, which seemed to have a lot of free slots, so we went to the boatyard at the end to see if it would be possible to stay.'

'Hmm. So what sort of reception did you get?'

'Not very friendly at first,' admitted Charity. 'There were just a couple of very surly youths who went out of their way to be as unhelpful as possible. We were at the point of walking off when the owner's wife turned up.'

'Elsie Borrett?'

'That's right. Do you know her?'

'I've met her . . . go on.'

'Well, when we explained our situation, she was very sweet and asked if I'd like a job. She said she needed a cleaner, but found it impossible to get anyone from the village and that, in return, she'd try and get us a mooring.'

'The Borretts own the yard, but not the moorings, which belong to the parish,' explained Jack, 'so how did Elsie manage that for you?'

'By pulling a few strings with someone she knows on the parish council.'

'Not an Admiral Ashfordby, by any chance?'

'Yes, that's right. Lovely old man. He owns a small sailboat moored close to us.'

'*Curlew*.'

'That's the one. Anyway, Elsie brought him down to meet us, and he said that as there were so many empty berths, we could stay there if I cleaned for Elsie. I'm not sure how the finances work regarding the moorings, but they seemed to be able to work something out between them.'

'Did they now,' pondered Jack, almost to himself. 'So, how do you find *Mr* Borrett?'

'Very different to his wife. Not at all friendly and he doesn't seem to approve of her employing a cleaner. I just stay out of his way as much as possible.'

'Very wise,' agreed Jack. 'So, how long do you intend to keep working there?'

'Oh, just long enough to get a bit of money behind us again, especially as Marcel has started to earn a few pounds locally as well.'

'Working on boats?'

'*Oui*,' answered the Frenchman for himself. 'I think it was the admiral who put the word about that I can do work on boats and suddenly, *voila*, I have much work. And so, while Charity is *domestique* at Providence Farm, I take this boat to whoever needs me and do the little jobs and everyone is happy.'

'Sounds like a good deal all round.' Jack, raised his coffee mug in salute. 'Well done.'

'Yes, and the pennies do come in handy,' confessed Charity. 'I think most of Marcel's customers are owners who used to moor in the dyke and had their work done by Cookcraft's. Apparently, when Mr Borrett bought the yard, that all stopped, which was a problem for them, but good for us. They keep Marcel so busy that we hardly have time to cruise *Faith and Hope* for our own enjoyment. Today's my day off from cleaning, so we decided to snatch just a bit of time on the river together ...'

'... only to find the engine, it runs hot,' completed Marcel with a Gaelic grimace.

'Well, you'll soon have it running again once I get back with your part.' Jack helped himself to a biscuit. 'And, who knows, perhaps the boat maintenance business will expand to the point where you don't have to clean anymore, Charity.'

She nodded enthusiastically. 'Yes, that would be great wouldn't it? At least then I'd have more time to spend on my real interest.'

'Which is ...?'

'Ghost hunting.'

Jack almost choked on a crumb. 'Did I hear right. You mean looking for ghosts?'

'Yep, ghosts, UFO phenomena, crop circles and anything else that falls outside what we consider normality. Paranormal investigations cover all these aspects, but the supernatural is what I'm particularly interested in.'

'Well, you're in the right area for that,' assured Jack. 'Broadland has more than its fair share of ghostly legends, so you won't be lacking in ones to study.'

'Quite, and an important part of investigating the paranormal is all about deciding what's fact and what's fiction. And I don't have to go far to find material,' she added, 'because the old Cookcraft yard has an intriguing reputation of its own.'

'So I've heard.' Jack put down his coffee. 'Could you tell me about it?'

'It's a long story. Have you got time?'

Jack glanced at his watch. 'Afraid not. I need to get going if I'm to be there when the part arrives, but I very much want to hear it. I'm off duty tomorrow. How about then?'

* * *

'She'll be 'ere tomorrow. I've just got an email.'

It was afternoon now and Bertie Borrett's news, as he sat down at the kitchen table for tea, initially puzzled wife Elsie. 'Who will?'

'My London barrister.' Bertie thumped the table. 'That'll sort out Admiral bloody Ashfordby and the rest of these country bumpkins.'

Still barely on speaking terms with her husband and quite certain that he'd already taken steps to divorce and disinherit her, Elsie no longer cared about the solar project or any other of her husband's interests ... bar one.

'You said, "she'll be 'ere". You mean this expensive lawyer you've 'ired is a woman?'

'Why not? She's interested in green issues and she's got 'erself a reputation for winning cases.'

'And you've got a reputation for winning women.' Elsie sat down at the table opposite and shook her head sadly. 'I should've known there was some other angle to this stupid business.' She fixed her husband with a withering eye. 'You fancy this lawyer bird, don't yer?'

'Don't be daft.'

'I'm not ... anymore. I knew you must have some other poor female on the 'orizon when you gave Madam Watlin' 'er marchin' orders.'

'You're crazy, woman.' Bertie swigged back his tea and stood up. 'I've never even met the girl.'

'Oh, "girl" is she,' countered Elsie. 'And what difference does it make that you 'aven't seen her in the flesh? A bloody photo'd be enough to give you the 'ots and I bet you've looked 'er up on the internet and fancy yer chances. Sure as 'ell she hasn't seen yours or she'd be runnin' the other way.' Even as she said it, Bertie's fist came up and Elsie knew she'd gone too far. In that milli-second she played her last line of defence. 'Go on, Bertie Borrett, 'it me, and give me all the dirt I need to take you to the cleaners.'

The fist paused in mid-strike, wavered and then lowered. 'Not this time, bitch, but I'll make bloody sure that one day soon you'll wish you never said that.'

'Not as much as I wish I'd never said "I do" all those years ago,' shouted Elsie to her husband's disappearing back as he slammed his way out.

Before collapsing into a chair sobbing, she heard his study door unlock, open, close and then lock again.

* * *

Once more Bertie pulled open the drawer, took out the file and sat staring at Lynsey Butterick's photo. Already, he was excited beyond words at the thought that the next day he would be meeting her for the first time. It was an indulgence he only allowed himself a few minutes to enjoy, though, because he had much to do. Lynsey had given him the arrival time of her evening train into Norwich Station and he'd get the Hinnerley brothers to meet her. That way he could be ready on *Merlin Magic* for when she got there.

A quick phone call would get that sorted, but first there was something even more important to organise, something he needed to do that would take more money than he wanted Elsie to see leaving their joint account.

Bertie switched on his computer and emailed his Dutch bank.

* * *

A mere half mile away, Jack Fellows was just nearing Bertie Borrett's yard. After leaving the narrowboat, it had been a twenty minute run downriver to the village dyke, and another ten to slip past the little-used parish moorings. Only Admiral Ashfordby's *Curlew* was moored there, but its owner was nowhere to be seen. Doubtless he'd been glad to have the narrowboat and her pleasant crew as neighbours and, at the same time, score a few brownie points with Elsie Borrett for swinging the moorings-for-cleaning deal. Jack continued on to the collection of old wooden and slightly dilapidated buildings that comprised the yard.

Even on this sunny day, they had a forlorn run-down look, as though mourning the passing of happier times. Now the hire craft were all gone and with them, the holidaymakers whose jollity and excitement Jack remembered, as the background to so much of the yard's everyday work. Sad at seeing such change, he brought the launch alongside the rotting quay-heading and hopped ashore.

There were two main buildings – a largish enclosed workshop with an office, and a wetshed. Parked between them were two pickup trucks, one a battered mud-streaked black and the other, a better cared-for dark blue. As yet, no person had emerged to question his presence, but these vehicles meant that someone was probably around somewhere, which was a pity because he'd hoped for an uninhibited snoop about. For what, he wasn't sure; only an inherent instinct that everything here was not as it should be. Regardless, he secured the launch and went into the wetshed.

There were just two boats filling this open-sided building. One was *Tugger*, the old wooden workboat. Twenty-foot and mainly-open, she had a small cuddy for'ard and a large sturdy samson post midships for towing broken-down cruisers back to base. In her Cookcraft days, she had been well-tended and kept smart in white, red and blue enamel. Now she was as neglected as the buildings in which she lay, with gashes scouring her paint-peeling sides and assorted rubbish and filth filling the open well.

Astern of, and towering above her, was a large steel motor-cruiser with

Merlin Magic painted on sleek white bows. The admiral had been right about her being a handsome vessel, with all the classic lines of a 1960s Dutch-built sea-going motor yacht. Flush-decked with a midships wheel-house and her stub mast lowered in its tabernacle, she just about squeezed into this covered berth. Jack wandered around the shed's narrow creaking walkways, examining the boat in greater detail and frowning at the lack of care and maintenance. Atop the guard-rails, the mahogany capping was worn to bare wood while various ropes lay about the deck, frayed and uncoiled. The boat had been blessed with classic brass portholes and ventilators, but these were stained with green verdigris, unlike the other handling gear such as fairleads, cleats and even the large samson post on the foredeck, that were also of brass, but seemingly brand new. Doubtless, these bright shining fittings were examples of Borrett's imports from Holland. They certainly stood out on *Merlin Magic* against teak decks crying out for a good scrub and a hull scarred and streaked with rust, doubtless a result of heavy handling and poor seamanship. Even the bolts holding the new fittings to the deck were obviously the old originals, unpolished and badly worn from clumsy spanner work. Jack was just feeling the ragged edge of one of these bolts when ...

'What d'you want?'

He spun around, aware his absorption with *Merlin Magic* had prevented him hearing others enter the wet-shed. Now he stood facing the Hinnerley brothers, the older Horace with his shaved head, tattoos and air of latent menace, and behind him, both literally and metaphorically in his brother's shadow, Alfie, trying to look equally tough and managing only what passed for a sinister grin. In his long police career, Jack had more than once encountered similar hostility as he poked his nose into places he wasn't wanted. In some ways he liked this sort of reaction, because it invariably confirmed his suspicions that here was something to hide. He dealt with this now as he always had in the past – by ignoring the other's question and firing one of his own. 'Who's in charge here?'

Horace Hinnerley's stained teeshirt stretched slightly as he puffed out his chest.

'Who wants to know?'

'Jack Fellows ... Broads Ranger.'

'So, we got your boat back here now.'

'Is that a problem?'

'Not as long as you stay out of our hair.'

'I will if you comply with the by-laws.' Jack went to *Merlin Magic*'s bow and tapped the fading toll disc. 'Has Mr Borrett paid this year's yet?'

'Probably.'

'I'll check that. Is the boat going out soon?'

'Next week.'

'Another trip to Holland?'

'Why would I know that?'

'Because this boat is too big for single-handing, and so you probably go with him, Hinnerley.'

'How d'you know my name?'

'You'd be surprised what I know, but answer the question.'

Horace decided this was not a man to prevaricate with. 'Yeah, just me and Alfie go as deckhands.'

'Hmm.' Further discussion was interrupted by the crunch of tyres on gravel. Jack glanced outside to see the chandler's van with replacement impeller just arriving. Ignoring the Hinnerleys, he went out, thanked the driver for good service and, within a few minutes, was heading back down the dyke towards the open river, thoughtful about his altercation with the yardhands, and slightly sad that the old Cookcraft yard should now be such an unfriendly place.

* * *

'You thieving bastard.' Bertie Borrett brought his bearded face right up to Cecil Watling's and thrust a warning finger almost up his PA's nose. 'You chose the wrong man to try and swindle this time, Watlin', but you'll pay for it in more ways than one.'

In the PA's office at Providence Farm, the atmosphere was hostile, bordering on violent.

'Wh ... what are you talking about?' stammered Cecil, physically drawing back, almost falling over his chair and ending up with his back to the office wall. 'I d ... d ... don't know what you mean.'

'Like 'ell you don't. I mean you've been dipping those sticky fingers of yours into a certain bank account of mine.' Knowing he was certainly master of this conversation, Borrett drew back. 'You see, I'm going to need quite a bit of dosh very soon and so I did something I don't do normally and that's contact that bank to check the balance. That's when I found out there'd been a recent transfer to another account I'd never 'eard of in a bank I'd nothin' to do with. But a bit more dabblin' told me the transaction had been done by my PA.' Borrett suddenly thrust forward once more. 'You!'

Not for the first time in his life, Cecil knew he'd been rumbled. Once again it was time for damage limitation. 'So, what are you going to do about it?'

Borrett sank back into the chair opposite his PA's desk, smiled sickeningly and said quietly, 'Nothin'.'

'Nothing?' Cecil knew this was too good to be true, but he pushed his luck. 'You mean you're going to forget it?'

'Yes, that's exactly what I'll do as long as certain conditions are met.'

'Which are?'

'That you sling your 'ook as far as the job's concerned, that you put back every penny you've nicked plus a bit of interest, that you never ever breathe a word of my overseas 'oldings to a livin' soul and finally ...'

'... finally?'

'That you and that bitch of a wife of yours are out of the cottage by noon tomorrow.'

'Those aren't conditions,' gasped Cecil, 'they're ... they're a recipe for breaking me.'

'But what are the options?' asked Bertie with outstretched palms. 'Me informin' the police, your arrest, trial and bein' banged up for a very long time.'

Literally with his back to the wall, Cecil tried one last desperate stand. 'You wouldn't dare, Borrett. I know too much don't I?'

'You certainly do,' agreed his boss, 'but remember I know some very nasty characters who'd soon do you over if you so much as thought about draggin' me down.'

Cecil gulped and blinked. 'All right. I agree ... except for one thing.'

'Which is?'

'That I haven't a clue where Lucy and I can go. I'll need at least another day in the cottage to sort something out.'

'I've got my barrister, comin' up from London tomorrow evenin', Watlin'. She was goin' to stay on my boat, but now she can 'ave your place instead.'

'Lynsey Butterick? It was me that talked her into acting for you. For that alone, I deserve a bit of slack,' pleaded Cecil. 'Just give me time and then we'll be out and she can have it.'

'You don't deserve no slack,' spat Borrett, 'but I must be gettin' soft or somethin'. All right, she can stay on *Merlin Magic* tomorrow night an' you've got twenty-four hours to put that money back and then skedaddle.'

And with that, he stomped out of the office leaving his ex-PA contemplating the prospect of breaking the worst news possible to his own demanding wife.

* * *

*   *   *

Chapter Six

'And so you collected the engine part for the narrowboat and dropped it off to them?' At the kitchen sink, Audrey continued pan scrubbing as she listened to her husband's account of his day's activities.

It was evening in the Fellows' household, Spike walked, supper eaten and just the washing up to complete before settling in. After such a fine day, a frontal system had moved in, bringing wind and rain to lash against the kitchen windows.

Jack wiped another plate and put it in its rack, pleased with his day's work and content now with a bit of domesticity. 'Yep. Charity sent me a text to say "thanks" and that Marcel soon had it fixed and running.'

'All part of the job for you, Jack, but as you're going to be close neighbours for the summer, helping them out certainly got your friendship off to a good start.'

'Yes, I couldn't wish for better. They're a lovely couple which is more than can be said for the lads at the boatyard.'

'The Hinnerley brothers,' guessed Audrey with a frown. 'Apart from seeing *them*, did you manage to find out any more about what's going on there?'

'Enough to harden my suspicions that all is not what it should be.'

'And what exactly makes you think that, Jack? Your "bobby's instinct", no doubt.' Audrey wrung out her dishcloth with just a little more vigour than usual. 'We know Borrett is a wealthy man, so perhaps he simply bought the yard because it's got a large wetshed for his boat.'

'If that's the case, Aud, why's he paying those yobbos to work there, because however those two occupy their time at the yard, it certainly isn't maintaining *Merlin Magic*.' Jack dried another plate. 'It's a crying shame to see what was once such a fine vessel, so woefully neglected. The only decent thing about it now is its deck fittings.'

'... which will be samples of the ones Borrett imports,' presumed Audrey.

'I guess so, but that whole business is a bit of a mystery. Running a big boat backwards and forwards across the North Sea won't be cheap, let alone having two hands to pay.'

'And then, presumably, he has to share some of the profit with George Granston.'

'If there is a profit, Aud, because I can't see there being a lot.'

'Well, let's hope Borrett quickly goes broke and then we'll all be shot of him,' said Audrey a little caustically, having heard quite enough of the man over the last few days and keen now to change the subject. 'In the meantime, I hope he doesn't make life uncomfortable for the couple on the narrowboat.'

'So do I. I know a lot of people, including the Authority, tend to regard live-aboards with some suspicion, but they seem a decent pair just living the dream.' Jack grabbed a glass and polished away thoughtfully. 'Personally, I think gypsying around in a boat like that must be pretty idyllic, and I wish I'd had the courage to do it myself when I was younger.'

'Yes, well don't get any ideas now you're older, Jack. I think we'll spend our remaining years here with a permanent roof over our heads, thank you very much,' said a determined Audrey, ' but I wish them well.'

'Amen,' agreed Jack, holding up the glass in a mock toast. 'But let's hope Marcel can build up his boat repair work, because Charity's too intelligent a girl to be scrubbing floors for the likes of the Borretts.'

'Probably more worthwhile than her other activity though.' Audrey's religious leanings meant she hadn't been particulary receptive to this other aspect of Charity's life. 'Ghost-hunting, for goodness' sake!'

'Paranormal Investigator, is how she describes it,' corrected Jack, who was slightly more open-minded on the subject. 'How successful a one, I'll find out when I meet her tomorrow afternoon.'

'... which is when I'm going to St Mark's to help Margie Granston arrange the flowers,' reminded Audrey, taking the glass from her husband before it got polished to destruction, 'so we can go together.'

'I can certainly drop you off en route,' agreed Jack,' but I'm actually going to meet Charity in Loddon now. That was the other reason she texted me. They'd had a call from a boat-owner with steering problems, so Marcel needs *Faith and Hope* to do the job. Charity's cleaning for Elsie Borrett in the morning and after that, biking into Loddon to do a bit of shopping, so I suggested we could meet there.'

'As long as I get to the church in time to meet Margie ...' Audrey tipped out the bowl and wiped around the sink with perhaps a little more energy than was necessary, '... and you get to find out what this boatyard ghost is all about, we'll both be happy.'

... or until I find out what's really going on at that yard, thought Jack, but didn't say. Instead, he hung his tea-towel on the oven handle and followed his wife and Spike into the lounge for an evening's relaxation.

* * *

... which was a far cry from the scene of domestic disharmony being enacted at Providence Farm on this stormy night.

'I can't believe it.' Elsie Borrett had reached the end of her long and painful tether. 'So now you're bootin' Cecil and Lucy out of their cottage so you can use it for this fancy lawyer you're bringin' up from London. You've got it all planned, ain't you?'

'I didn't plan any of it. I only found out this mornin', that Watlin' was rippin' me off, the thievin' bastard.'

'Takes one to know one.'

'Yeah, well, whatever, Watlin's on his way out ...' Bertie shot his wife a meaningful look, '... like anyone else who gets the wrong side of me.'

'Don't I know it.' Elsie poured herself a third vodka. 'So, when's she arrivin' anyway?'

'Late tomorrow evenin' by train into Norwich. I'm sendin' the Hinnerleys to collect 'er.'

'I thought you'd be rushin' to do that yourself?'

'I don't have a licence no more, remember? And anyway, I'll be busy makin' sure the boat's okay. Being a softy, I've given the Watlin's twenty-four hours to get out, so Lynsey'll be spendin' the first night on *Merlin Magic*.'

'Oh, "Lynsey" now is it? And, more to the point, where will you be spending *your* night?' Elsie gave a half-humoured laugh. 'Poor cow. I'm not sure which is worse – 'aving to sleep on that damp old barge or with you.'

'She's not that sort of girl.'

'Oh really? How d'you know that? I thought you'd never met before.'

'I ain't, but I can imagine,' blustered Bertie. 'And anyway, she's comin' because she genuinely believes in things like our solar farm and wants to see it 'appen.'

'Pull the other one,' sneered Elsie, 'but don't count on me to get the cottage ready for 'er.'

'I wouldn't count on you for anythin' no more,' declared Bertie, snatching the bottle away before Elsie could have a top up. 'And don't worry your 'ead anyway, because I've already asked your domestic to clean the place up, once the Watlin's have cleared out.'

'What, Charity? You've no right. She works for me.'

'And I pay 'er ... like everythin' else around this place, includin' that flashy car of yours which you need to make the most of 'cos, like you, that'll be goin' in the next few days an' all.'

'Right, I will then,' declared Elsie, grabbing her car keys and jacket from their hooks and striding to the outside kitchen door. So, I'm off for a night out and don't wait up.'

'Don't worry, I won't.' With the rattle of wheel-spun shingle and the diminishing roar of his wife's sports car down Providence Farm's long drive, Bertie found himself smiling for the first time in days. Things were working out even better than he'd hoped. Slugging back the remains of Elsie's vodka, he took out his mobile phone and keyed the favourite number.

* * *

'Gosh, what a filthy night.' Lucy Watling let the lounge curtain of their cottage drop back into place and rejoined her husband on the sofa, one hand warmly caressing his neck. 'I shan't be sorry to leave this stinking climate, darling. I'm sure they have plenty of rain in Spain, but I bet it's warmer than here.' She allowed her fingers to continue into his hair. 'Is the money thing actually done yet?'

'Err ... not quite ... tomorrow though ... it has to be done by then.'

Lucy's hand paused momentarily. 'Really, why's that?'

Cecil's lawyer's brain meant he could still think quickly when he had to. 'Because Borrett is off to Holland ahead of schedule ... something to do with a special deal he's been offered.' He gave her a reassuring smile. 'So, we don't want him finding his account empty before we've done our bolt.'

'No, of course not, but ...' Lucy glanced around their cottage lounge with its ancient brickwork, beamed ceiling and inglenook fireplace, '... I did come to quite like this place.' She snuggled closer to her husband. 'In some ways, I'll be sorry to leave it.'

That'll be sooner than you think, thought Cecil as he loosened his tie and prepared for what was undoubtedly the last night of passion he'd ever enjoy with Lucy.

* * *

Chapter Seven

St Mark's Church, like so many in Norfolk, nestled on the periphery of the parish it served. This was a reminder of the Black Death when many a village was burned to stop the spread of that deadly infectious disease. Only the churches were spared and, when eventually the villages were rebuilt, they were often well away from what was still considered contaminated ground. Such dark history though was far away from Audrey's thoughts as Jack drew up outside the tree-shaded 14th Century building, with its even older Norman round tower and ancient thatched lych-gate. One thing that was missing though was any sign of Margery Granston.

'Looks like I'm here first,' said Audrey, gathering her things, 'but don't you hang around, Jack. I'm sure she won't be long.'

'Okay, love. Text me when you're ready for pickup.'

With Jack on his way to his rendezvous with Charity, Audrey strolled around the ancient churchyard, enjoying the early sunshine. She was just reading yet another gravestone inscription when the sound of a heavy vehicle arriving at the church gates announced Margery's arrival. Minutes later, the lady herself was bustling up the church path, sweating slightly in Barbour jacket and sensible shoes, arms brimming with flowers and full of apologies. 'Sorry I'm late, Audrey, but I had to get a spare set of keys from the vicar.'

'That's all right, Margie, but I was half-expecting Admiral Ashfordby being here to let us in. After all, he is churchwarden.'

'Quite, but he's been a bit unreliable of late, so the vicar told me to hang on to the keys until Sunday's evensong.' In the porch, Margery selected a large key from the ancient bunch and then she was turning the lock and the heavy oak door was swinging open. 'We used to leave St Mark's unlocked all the time,' she explained as they entered the cool interior, 'but we suffered some vandalism and two thefts before the PCC decided we couldn't afford to any longer.'

'What a shame,' sympathised Audrey. 'Did they ever catch the thieves?'

'No, though we did have our suspicions.'

Audrey could well imagine who, but decided not to press Margery on the point and instead used her comment about Admiral Ashfordby as an excuse to pursue that line. 'I always took the admiral to be the most conscientious of men.'

'He was.' Margery paused to lay the large bundle of flowers she was carrying down on a pew. 'It's only in the last week or so that he's become a bit odd.'

'In what way?'

'Well, no-one's seen him out and about in the village – at least not in daylight – which is so out of character. I was driving home late the other night though, and saw him scuttling up the road. I stopped to ask him if I could give him a lift and, although he was as charming as ever, he made it quite clear he wanted to be left alone. I did ask him if everything was all right and he just said he was very tired.'

'Yes, that's the same response my Jack got from him when he tried to arrange a drink and chat.' Time, Audrey thought, to carry this conversation just that little bit further. 'You don't suppose, do you Margie, that he's found himself a lady- friend?'

Margery paused to politely consider the suggestion, though Audrey was sure it had doubtlessly crossed her mind well before now. 'Possible, I suppose. It's been a few years now since his wife passed away and he deserves a nice companion, lovely man that he is. Who do you think the lucky lady might be?'

'Elsie Borrett.'

'Good heavens!' Margery's hand went to her mouth in surprise. 'Surely not?'

'I know they don't seem the most compatible of lovers,' agreed Audrey, 'but they do seem very chummy when you see them together, and he's certainly very charming – a characteristic you'd never attribute to her dreadful husband.'

'I think Elsie would be glad of *any* man, quite honestly,' said Margery a little uncharitably, 'what with her brassy manner and flirty ways.' She clasped her hands together, the way many women did when disclosing confidential knowledge. 'I do know for a fact that Bertie suspects her of having an affair.'

'Who told you that, Margie?' Indulging in gossip within the confines of a church seemed less than proper to Audrey, but she knew Jack would be glad of any information she could wrangle.

'Bertie himself, to my George. I told you how they'd formed a working relationship. Well, he told George, in a confidential moment, that he was sure Elsie was having a fling with someone.'

'But didn't say who?'

'No, I don't think he knew himself but, from what you say, Aud, it could well be the admiral.'

'Sadly, yes.' Audrey wanted to see Admiral Ashfordby happy again, but not at the cost of locking horns with Bertie Borrett. 'Let's just hope it's a passing fancy.'

'Yes, if only for the sake of this church,' agreed Margery, slightly downcast. It was time to change the subject and Audrey picked up some of the flowers from the pew. 'Anyway, Margie, we can at least get St Mark's looking nice. You just tell me what you want me to do.'

'Right, we'll start with the altar pedestal,' said Margery, shaking away other thoughts and leading the way up the stone-paved nave, sunlight filtering through the lancet windows either side and illuminating the ancient carved wall plaques that served as memorials to many a long-dead worshipper. In the chancel, St Mark's magnificent stained glass window threw its own multi-coloured beams onto the hanging banners, empty choir stalls and polished altar rail. Here Margery and Audrey paused to make their devotions, though the sacred symbol itself was missing from the table. 'We have a beautiful brass cross,' pointed out Margery, 'but thank goodness it's kept locked in the vestry cupboard between services, or that might have been stolen too.' Mention of the cupboard though served to remind her of something else. 'Oh gosh, we need the vases and they're kept locked in there as well. I meant to get them out before we came up here.'

'I can go and get them if you like.'

'No, that's okay.' Margery once more brought out the large bunch of St Mark's keys. 'I'm not sure which of these is which so it's better that I do it.' She glanced at the flowers, now spread out on one of the choir stalls. 'But we'll need some greenery, Audrey. It's lying in the back of George's pickup truck. If you could go and fetch a selection while I sort the vases, it would be a great help and then we can get started.'

Leaving Margery searching for the vestry cupboard key, Audrey made her way back out into the sunshine to the small parking area on the other side of the lych-gate where George Granston's pickup truck stood. It was only a moment's job to gather some of the best greenery before returning to the church.

Inside, Margery had left the vestry and was standing once more before the main door holding two large plain vases. What Audrey immediately noticed though was the sudden change that had come over the flower arranger in just the few minutes she'd been left alone. Now this normally self-assured lady looked visibly shaken, as though she'd just seen something particularly disturbing.

'Margie ... are you all right? You look as though you've seen a ghost.'

'What? Oh yes ... I mean no ...' Margery blinked twice as though to shake herself back to reality. 'I'm fine, Audrey. Just a few things on my mind, that's all.' And then she was off up the aisle again with just a brusque, 'Let's get on with this arranging, shall we?'

Audrey could only shrug and follow.

* * *

Just a few miles down the road in Loddon, Jack parked his car in the town's market square and found Charity Howden's very traditional shopping bike already outside the café where they'd arranged to meet. The girl herself was sitting at the corner table, her hands cradling a mug of tea.

'I hope I'm not late,' he apologised after getting himself a coffee and joining her.

'No, I think I'm a little bit early,' she smiled back. 'And sorry you had to drive so far, but I try and fit these shopping expeditions in with Marcel's boat jobs. That's the snag of living our entire lives out of one forty foot narrowboat.'

'No problem,' assured Jack, 'and, anyway, I had to bring Audrey to St Mark's so she can give the village flower arranger a hand.'

'Margery Granston?'

'Yes, that's right. Do you know her then?'

'Only slightly. More her husband George, actually,' explained Charity between sips of tea. 'Admiral Ashfordby asked Marcel to fit some new cleats and other fittings on *Curlew*. Apparently, he'd fancied the ones Borrett imports from Holland, but didn't want to deal directly with the man himself.'

'That's right,' agreed Jack. 'The admiral assured me in no uncertain terms, that he'd never do business with Borrett.'

'Mmm, I believe there *are* issues there,' said Charity, pursing her lips before adding, 'but anyway, Marcel solved that problem when he heard that George Granston was actually handling the retailing.'

'Ah, I heard that Granston had gone into business with Borrett,' said Jack, adding a spoonful of sugar to his coffee. 'So George sells these imported deck fittings rather than manufacturing ones of his own?'

'Exactly. Apparently Borrett soon realised his unpopularity was keeping prospective buyers away and that George Granston, with a workshop in the village and valued customers from miles around, would provide the perfect outlet.'

Jack shrugged. 'I'm always glad to hear of amicable solutions, but it still puzzles me how the two of them can make any money out of it.'

'True, but they seem to be making a go of it. I went with Marcel to collect the admiral's fittings from George's workshop, last week, and he said things were looking up. We were impressed with his setup and could see he was well equipped with good tools, the latest in welding gear and even his own forge for the bigger jobs.'

'I can't say I know Granston that well. What's he like?'

'Oh, he's okay at a strictly business level, though perhaps a bit grumpy, and I wouldn't want to get on the wrong side of him.' Charity fiddled with her spoon while she thought this over. 'I suppose he's not the sort you'd imagine being married to Margery. She arrived while we were there and told us all about her flower arranging, but George showed absolutely no interest. In fact, he seemed quite offhand with her.' Charity brightened with a smile. 'But you say your Audrey's with Margery this afternoon?'

'That's right. At St Mark's Church.'

'Hmm. There's a place I'd like to investigate further.'

'Really?' Jack put down his cup. 'Tell me more.'

'Not much to tell really, other than what I've observed in the dead of night.'

'You mean you've been up there on some sort of ghost watch?'

'No, at least not with any success. The thing is, you can see St Mark's from our narrowboat when we're on the mooring. I'm a light sleeper at the best of times and often get up in the early hours for a cup of tea. If it's a nice dry night, I'll sometimes go out on deck to enjoy the moon and stars. And that's when I've seen them.'

'Seen what?'

'Lights… in the church… dim ones, but moving around. The second time I saw them I got dressed and went up there to see what was going on.'

'... and discovered ...?'

'... nothing.'

'Nothing?'

'No, not a thing. All inside was completely dark and the church door was locked securely enough to keep out an army.'

'Did you report this to Admiral Ashfordby? He's the churchwarden.'

'Yes, I know, and I did talk to him about it, but he didn't seem particularly interested and tried to assure me it was just a trick of moonlight shining through the stained glass window.'

'But you don't believe that?'

'No. The moon that night was in the wrong quarter of the sky to shine through that window and anyway, others in the village have seen the lights as well. At least one went up to the church to check it out and, like me, found the place dark and bolted.'

'Hmmm, interesting.' Jack felt just the slightest concern that Audrey was there now with only Margery Granston for company. Deciding he wouldn't delay in collecting her, he pressed on with the prime aim of this meeting. 'But, I believe the staithe and boatyard have an eerie history of their own, don't they? Or at least they do according to the villagers.'

'And with good reason,' confirmed Charity. She pushed forward her cup. 'Do you mind getting me a refill, Jack, and I'll tell you all about it?'

* * *

At that very boatyard, it was more earthly matters that were bothering the brothers Hinnerley.

'Just our bleeding luck,' grumbled Horace, 'that tonight of all nights, we have to go to Norwich Station and do a pickup for the guv'ner.'

'S'pose we could put off this church job 'til another night,' suggested Alfie.

'No we couldn't.' Horace usually dismissed any of his brother's ideas, and brushed this one off more acridly than most. 'From what I gather, this bird's a lawyer, so the sooner we do this job, the better. With her hanging around the place I can't see us being able to do much more anyways.'

'You sure it's safe, Horace?'

'Yeah, course it is. The thing is, old Borrett has said to use his Merc while he waits here and gets his boat ready. Well, I'm guessing he'll be too tied up tonight to notice our comings and goings ...' Horace gave a dirty laugh, '... so, what we'll do is collect her ladyship like he wants, but in our pickup. Then we can just drop her here and scootle straight off to that there church. We'll have the job done and the truck loaded and back here before he even sees the light of day.'

'Sound's right good, Horace,' enthused an eager Alfie, who was constantly in awe of his brother's devious mind. 'Mind you, I can't think what the boss is a thinking of, having some legal type around poking her nose where it's not wanted. It's bad enough having that there ranger's launch back here again.'

'She's something to do with the solar farm business, so the boss told me.' Horace paused to spit into the dyke. 'But you know the guv'nor, he'll be so busy fancying his chances with her, he won't care what we're up to tonight.' He nodded outside the boatshed. 'Come on kid, we need to get loaded before we head for Norwich Station.'

They'd just started piling their tools and gear into the truck when Horace's mobile rang.

* * *

'Sorry you missed your tea, Aud, but I hope this makes up for it.' Jack slid the tray of drinks and snacks onto the wooden table, took his pint of lager and sat down opposite. 'You sure you don't mind driving the rest of the way?'

'No, of course not. You're on duty tomorrow, so sit back and enjoy your drink.' Audrey raised her glass of tomato juice. 'Cheers, Jack.'

'Cheers and thanks, Aud. It's good to be able to enjoy a pint again.' They were at the Woods End pub, Bramerton, sitting at an outside table with the late afternoon sun still warm and the Yare flowing gently past, just feet away. It had been Jack's idea to make this slight detour on the way home and now, with the first deliciously cold mouthful of lager already slipping down, he sat back and relaxed.

'Yes, and in such a peaceful setting.' Audrey watched a women's racing eight go slicing past, oars pulling through the water in unison with barely a splash. 'Now, that's what I call an energetic pastime ... at least compared to my afternoon's flower arranging.'

'Yes, how did that go, Aud?'

'Oh, very well. Margie's very talented and I learned so much.'

'Good. Nothing strange happen while you were there then?'

Audrey paused in opening her bag of crisps and gave her husband a puzzled look. 'That's a strange question, Jack. What have you in mind, exactly?'

'Well, anything spooky?'

'No, of course not ... well nothing "spooky", but perhaps a bit odd?'

'Really.' Jack raised his brows. 'What happened?'

Audrey shook her head. 'I wish I knew. Whatever it was, happened when I went out to collect some greenery from her husband's pickup truck.'

'Was that a blue pickup truck?'

'Yes. Is that important?'

'Only to confirm it was Granston's I saw parked outside the boatyard the other day, which isn't so surprising, seeing as the two have a business relationship.'

'Quite ... ' Audrey threw a crisp to a rather persistent mallard, '... but, more important Jack, did you satisfy your curiosity as to who or what haunts the old boatyard?'

'Yes indeed, but I'll explain later. First tell me about this odd thing that happened to you.'

Audrey related going back into the church and finding Margery Granston looking unaccountably shocked.

'And she didn't give a clue as to what had upset her?'

'None at all.'

'And you didn't see anything yourself that would explain it?'

'No, nothing.'

'Then we have to assume it was something she saw or heard in the vestry ... something that certainly disturbed her, but which she didn't want you to know about.' He helped himself to one of Audrey's crisps and smiled. 'Probably a mouse eating the communion wafers.'

Audrey grinned and shook her head. 'I don't expect we'll ever find out, Jack, but you did ask me if anything spooky had happened, which tells me you know something.'

'Only some odd night-time happenings that Charity told me about.' Jack explained the mysterious lights in St Mark's.

'And she says others have also seen them?'

'Yep.'

'Well, I'm glad I didn't know this earlier,' said Audrey, twisting her empty crisp packet into a spiral. 'Even in daylight, I think I would have felt a little edgy.'

'I thought you didn't believe in ghosts, Aud,' chided Jack with a chuckle. He looked around to admire their setting – the wooded banks rising behind them, the sprawling pub with its cream plastered walls and red pantiled roofs. 'Do you know, a hundred years ago this used to be a favourite stopping place for pleasure steamers from Norwich. There was a chap who called himself Billy Bluelight who used to run alongside them all the way here along the riverbank. Before racing them back again, he'd chant a little ditty, "My name is Billy Bluelight, my age is forty-five" ...'

'... "I aim to get to get to Carrow Bridge afore the boat arrive",' completed Audrey, a little triumphantly.

'That's right!' exclaimed Jack. 'How did you know that, Aud?'

'You're not the only one who researches Broadland folklore, Jack.'

'So it seems ... except, of course, his real name was William Cullum and he stayed forty-five for many years, according to local legend.'

'Stories build up over time,' said Audrey, 'no doubt like the one Charity's been filling you in on, to do with the parish staithe.'

'You could be right, Aud ...' Jack took a swig of his lager, '... seeing as this one's based on an event that also happened about a hundred years ago.'

'Is this a true story?'

'Very much so, and quite a tragic one for those involved.'

'Go on.'

'Well, some old fishing boat was lying alongside the staithe, skippered by a grizzled rogue of a character well-known locally as something of a lech. Unfortunately, that fact wasn't known by a young woman who happened to stop by, and got into conversation with him. She was in the area looking for work and was heard to ask if he knew where she might find accommodation.'

'Don't tell me,' surmised Audrey. 'He offered to let her stay on board for the night?'

Jack nodded. 'No-one really knows for sure what really happened, but the facts are that in the early hours the boat caught fire, the skipper escaped, but the girl perished. According to him, she'd accidentally knocked over an oil lamp and became trapped, but when her body was finally recovered, a post-mortem revealed she'd actually been strangled and was probably dead before the fire started.'

'Poor girl. How terrible. I hope he was arrested for murder.'

'He was indeed, tried at Norwich assizes, found guilty and hanged.'

'Justice was certainly tougher in those days,' declared Audrey. 'And now, I suppose, we go into the realms of fantasy. It's inevitable, isn't it, with a story like that, there has to be a ghost associated with it. I suppose you're now going to tell me the spirit of this girl has been seen?'

'... walking the staithe at night,' admitted Jack. 'Charity Howden wants to investigate it, but she's keeping an open mind until then.' He finished his drink. 'Looking at it another way, this could all be Bertie Borrett putting it about that the staithe's haunted, just to dissuade casual visitors.'

'Put them off what, Jack? Just what is it you think Borrett has to hide in those old run-down sheds?'

'I'm not sure, Aud. Just an instinct that there's nefarious work afoot at the old Cookcraft yard which I aim to suss out before I'm finished there.'

'You and your instincts, Jack,' scorned Audrey. 'But anyway, your theory's a bit shaky, because if this story of ghosts and ghouls is meant to keep people off the staithe, it certainly hasn't worked with Charity Howden, who's dead keen to see more, or with Admiral Ashfordby either, who still keeps his boat there.'

'... talking of whom,' added Jack, keen now to get on firmer ground, 'did Margie have anything to say about our dear admiral's odd behaviour?'

'She did indeed.' Audrey related all she and Margery had discussed, particularly about her sighting of the admiral scuttling through the village late at night, and Bertie Borrett's suspicion that his wife was having an affair.

'Hmm, well, if it's with the admiral, that would certainly account for the old boy's odd behaviour and tiredness,' acknowledged Jack with a smirk.

'It's your tiredness tomorrow that concerns me,' said Audrey. 'Just how early do you intend to start out?'

'Three o'clock, Aud.'

'*What* time?'

'You heard perfectly well. You sure you wouldn't like another drink?'

'No thanks.'

'Right, let's hit the road again then.' Jack stood up and gave his wife the car keys leaving her to merely shrug and ponder just where all this was leading.

* * *

Chapter Eight

In the privacy of his village cottage and preparing for an even earlier clandestine undertaking of his own, was Admiral Ashfordby.

For over a week now, he'd been indulging in this nocturnal activity and realised it was beginning to take its toll. Although the first to admit that this change in his lifestyle would have been easier when he was twenty years younger, so far even his octogenarian years had failed to stem a dogged determination to see this through. By spending the daylight hours sleeping and recovering, he'd managed to keep going and only hoped the end result would be worth it. Whatever, no-one would be able to say he'd failed in his duty.

And so, with darkness setting in, the admiral prepared for another strenuous night by showering early, trimming the white beard to perfection and getting out his best kit, at the same time pleasantly aware that embarking on this little adventure had more than put a spring back into his old heels.

He was certainly fully aware of the risks he was taking and knew if he wasn't careful and got found out, there would be hell to pay. But in a lifetime in Her Majesty's navy, from his early service as a raw midshipman to an admiral commanding fleets, he had never shirked risk or been unprepared to take a gamble. Life's a gamble, he used to say to himself and now that dictum was more pertinent than ever.

Another principle he had always lived by was to tell nothing but the truth. Unfortunately, like many small villages, the inhabitants of this one, fine people though they generally were, always wanted to know everything that was going on. This meant they asked a lot of questions and, mindful as he was that most already had their suspicions, he didn't want to give untruthful answers. And so he kept his head well down during the hours of daylight and avoided any contact with the parishioners. Of course, this made everyone, especially his fellow church-goers, even more curious, and he still had to be careful. Only a week ago the flower-arranging Margery Granston had caught him in an unguarded moment, making his way stealthily through the village. He'd tried to fob her off but, even in the darkness, he'd seen the scepticism in her eyes. Ah well, he was too old now to care what others thought, especially tonight when the object of his love could only benefit from his removal of this particular blight on the village.

It was fully dark outside now. At this time of the year, the nights were still quite long and this one might feel even longer before it was through. As though preparing for yet another naval engagement, Admiral Sir Claude Ashfordby KCB, checked himself in the mirror, straightened once more his Royal Navy tie and strode out into the darkness. This was one job that had to be done.

* * *

Equally determined not to be late for her tryst was Elsie Borrett. Tonight she hadn't even needed to make any excuses to her bullying husband for her abandonment of the marital home. For Bertie had left early to get his boat out of the wetshed and alongside the staithe. She knew this was in preparation for the arrival of his lawyer and was under no illusions what Bertie's idea of hospitality would involve. That her husband would also be planning to spend the night on board *Merlin Magic* was something she accepted. But, as far as Elsie was concerned, this was only for the good, for it meant that for the first time she could spend at least part of the night with her lover.

This thought did not engender any feelings of guilt for Elsie, being married as she was to an outrageous philanderer. In a way, she felt she had no axe to grind at this. When she'd married Bertie all those years ago, she'd been well aware of his reputation as a womaniser and his trail of numerous abused and abandoned girlfriends. In her naivety though, she'd thought she might change him by bringing love and domestic stability to his life. But it had been a forlorn hope that lasted only the first year of marriage, after which the extra-marital flings began, as did his abusive behaviour towards herself.

And in the end, she had given up trying to be a faithful wife. Now she was an adulterer too and, knowing the process of being cut out of Bertie's will was already underway, she was bent on revenge. Tonight, her dear husband would find that not all his plans worked out as he intended, as she dealt him a blow of which he had not the slightest inkling.

It wasn't a course that Elsie had undertaken lightly and one only conceived in the deep love she had for her new man. After Bertie, his caring, attentive manner had shown her another world, and his personal determination and bravery, the inspiration she needed to carry through this bold conspiracy.

Elsie glanced again at her watch. A couple of hours now, and the Hinnerley brothers would be picking up the barrister at Norwich Station. That alone caused her to smile. She could imagine the shock awaiting the London high-flyer when she encountered those two morons waiting to drive her to her first night's accommodation in a cold damp boat with the notorious Bertie. Well, good luck, whoever you are, thought Elsie as her own slick wheels sped her ever faster towards her rendezvous.

* * *

Unaware of the arrangements being made for her, was Lynsey Butterick, feeling increasingly excited, if not a little apprehensive, as she set off for a new phase in her life.

It had been a hectic last day at her London flat, clearing a backlog of correspondence, paying bills and generally setting things up for an extended and open-ended time away. Now, as she waited at London's Liverpool Street Station, it was almost a relief to know all that was behind her and she was finally on her way. Once again, she glanced upwards to the departure board to find out from which platform her 20:30 to Norwich would be leaving. And then, just as the board announced "Platform 12", she heard the ring-tone of her mobile. She let go of her suitcase handle, shrugged the straps of her rucksack off her shoulders and pulled the phone from a side pocket. Much to her dismay, the caller was the last person she wanted to talk to right now but, after a moment's hesitation, she begrudgingly answered it.

'Miles ... what do you want?'

'To have this last try at talking some sense into you.' Rotherby-Jones' voice certainly carried an edge of desperation. 'For goodness' sake, Lynsey, forget this mad idea and come home.'

'Which home, Miles?'

'Mine if you want.'

'Well I don't want, Miles. My train's about to leave.' She scuttled towards the platform, dragging her wheeled case behind, phone pressed against her ear with one shoulder, rucksack slung over the other while at the same time pulling the one-way ticket from her purse. 'So, please just go and get yourself another life and leave me to live mine.'

'Perhaps you won't.'

'Won't what?'

'Live it ... much longer.'

Lynsey pulled up, just short of the ticket barrier. 'I'm sorry, Miles. Do I take what you've just said as some sort of threat?'

'Take it how you please.'

'Then I'll give it the contempt it deserves,' she almost shouted into the phone before switching off and stuffing it back into her rucksack.

Minutes later she was in her reserved seat and, not long after that, the train was gliding out of the station and accelerating ever faster northwards for Norwich and the Broads. She should still have been feeling the excitement of this first step into the destiny she felt was hers, but lingering instead was the slightly unnerving intonation of Rotherby-Jones' parting words. Lynsey tried to dismiss them as the desperate last attempt to stop her leaving. She always knew Miles wouldn't give up the chase without a fight and realised her final rejection must have served as a humiliating blow to his inflated ego. Well, tough, she said to herself, before turning her face to the window and watching the last of suburban London slip swiftly into the past.

* * *

By contrast, Bertie Borrett was feeling nothing but excitement as he prepared *Merlin Magic* for his guest. Wife Elsie's departure on her own romantic excursion had added a new dimension of freedom to his plans for this night, and now he felt like a teenager on a first date as he scuttled about the boat making sure it created a good impression. To this end, since coming aboard, he'd been tidying cushions here, cleaning the odd surface there but, more important than anything, checking that the full-size double berth in the stern quarters was made up and inviting. To this end, he'd even arranged some flowers both for saloon and bedroom and sprayed furniture polish over the built-in units in an effort to combat the all-pervasive odour of damp and diesel.

It was the Hinnerleys' job to keep the outside of the boat clean and Borrett would have got them to clean the interior too, but having had them crew *Merlin Magic* on his trips to Holland, their lack of hygiene and squalid living had been all too apparent. So, for this special night, it was better that they didn't even set foot on board and instead, collect Lynsey from

Norwich Station. He had serious misgivings about sending them off on this mission, but had little choice. He just hoped that the comfort in the back of the Merc would offer some consolation for having to share it with the two reprobates in the front, and that the experience wouldn't be too daunting for her. He'd given them strict instructions, after dropping her here at the staithe, to get lost a.s.a.p. in their tatty pickup truck.

Bertie glanced once more at the bulkhead clock. A couple of hours yet before Lynsey arrived. He went to the cocktail cabinet and checked the drinks before selecting some soft music on the stereo. All was ready for his own little romantic interlude.

Perhaps it was just as well that Bertie was blissfully unaware that his Mercedes still stood behind the buildings at the entrance to the staithe and that it was in the battered pickup truck that the Hinnerleys would ultimately collect Lynsey Butterick.

* * *

'But you never normally go to the workshop at this time of night, George.'

Margery Granston looked up from watching television, to see her husband putting on his coat.

'No, but I've a propshaft to finish off. I promised to have it ready for a boat in Brundall by now. I can't let the owner down.' George Granston continued to the door.

'Of course you can't, George, but you wouldn't have got behind with that work if you hadn't become involved with Borrett's import business.'

'Becoming involved, as you put it, is the only thing that's kept our business afloat, Marge. We were all set to go under before he offered to let me retail the fittings. Now that's our bread and butter and the bigger machine jobs, the jam.'

'I'll be glad when we have enough "jam" not to have anything to do with that horrible man,' persisted Margery, 'and anyway, I can't believe you've got so much other work that, after being goodness-knows-where all day, you have to go out again this evening. When will you be home?'

'I don't know. I might be gone all night.'

'All night! Again!' Taken completely aback, Margery switched off and joined her husband by the door. 'What on earth's come over you, George? There can't be anything at the workshop that needs you to be there *all night*.'

'I'll be the judge of that,' responded her husband off-handedly. He opened the door. 'So, don't wait up.'

'Well, I can't see me sleeping,' protested Margery. 'And what about food? Can't I do you some sandwiches and a flask?'

'No, I'll be all right ... and the less you know, the better.'

And with that, George Granston closed the front door behind him, leaving his confused and somewhat disturbed wife to listen only to the growl of his pickup truck disappearing down the road.

* * *

Spared such worries, was Lucy Watling, and only because she was tucked up in bed fast asleep. Asleep so deeply, in fact, that she'd failed to hear Cecil get up, dress, creep downstairs and exit the cottage.

Normally, Lucy was not a sound sleeper, but this evening's slumber owed more to the sedative her husband had slipped into her bedtime nightcap, than any inherent peace of mind. Certainly, peace of mind was not something she would have had if she'd known that, as she slept, husband Cecil was speeding down the road towards the village staithe in their car.

* * *

It was the River Wensum that Lynsey Butterick was crossing as her train trundled over Trowse railway bridge just minutes from the terminal of Norwich Station. In spite of the darkness, it was possible to make out pockets of mist beginning to form above the black ribbon of the river below and the blurred red and green lights of a boat threading its surface, presumably heading for a night berth in the city. It was a cheering sight to Lynsey, a reminder of the promise of mild adventure that had brought her here in the first place. The train slowed further and was soon pulling into the station itself.

As she heaved her rucksack off the overhead rack, she checked the time – ten-thirty, and bang on schedule. At such a late hour, she was glad that someone would be here to meet her. She'd texted Mr Borrett en route to confirm her arrival time and he'd replied to say that two of his staff would be there to drive her to his boat. And so now, emerging through the ticket barrier into the large and rather splendid concourse, she eagerly scanned the expectant group of awaiting picker-uppers for any possibly holding a card bearing her name. There were none and, what was worse, she seemed about to be accosted by an unsavoury-looking specimen. But, even as Lynsey glanced around for the nearest British Transport policeman, the figure glanced at the notesheet he was holding and asked, 'You Butterick?'

'Y ... yes.' Now she saw the paper was in fact a photocopy of her own image, replete in gown and horsehair wig. Disturbing enough, but more so when the fingers holding it each bore tattooed letters spelling H –A –T –E. 'And you are ...?'

'Horace.' The accent was decidedly rural and his insolent attitude made it obvious that late night pickups from Norwich Station were something he could do without. He nodded towards the exit and turned on his heel. 'This way.'

Lynsey followed. In her legal life, she'd defended many such individuals and tried never to be judgemental. Nevertheless, as this one led her out past the taxi rank and into the short-stay parking area, she found it hard not to take an instant dislike to him. The surly manner and fact that he hadn't even offered to take her suitcase were things she could just shrug off to ignorance, but it was the intimidating, arrogant way he strutted his burly body that she found particularly disturbing. Her sense of ill-boding was only intensified when they reached the vehicle sent to collect her – a battered pickup truck, behind the wheel of which sat another almost identical youth of the same ilk.

'Me brother Alfie's driving,' explained Horace, gruffly, as he opened the passenger door for her. Lynsey realised he did this only to ensure she clambered in first and sat between them, a prospect she didn't relish. In an effort to establish some sort of authority, she passed him the handle of her case and gave him her rucksack, only to see them casually thrown into the exposed and filthy open back on top of tools and ladders. He indicated again the waiting bench seat. 'We got things to do, so get in quick.'

Yet Lynsey hesitated, not only to delay the moment, but to also take in her surroundings. Behind her, the station building with its domed clock-tower sat floodlit and enticing. She knew she still had the chance to return inside and buy a ticket straight back to London, but the thought of Rotherby-Jones' gleeful gloating that she'd crumbled at the first hurdle was beyond contemplation. She looked the other way, past the station railings to where some large boats lay at moorings and, beyond them, the lights of a large hotel shining through wisps of soft mist rolling up the river. Even so, through the picture windows and lit by shaded table lamps, she could see people enjoying food, drink and companionship. How tempting to retrieve her luggage, cross the road and book one night's stay to reassess her options and future.

'You going to get in or in't you?' Horace snapped, impatiently.

Lynsey paused for only one more second to reassure herself that, uncouth as these lads appeared, they had not actually been threatening. She would certainly have severe words with Mr Borrett, when she met him, and complain about the totally unacceptable treatment his disreputable employees had subjected her to. Definitely not something she had any intention of tolerating in the future if he expected her to stay working for him. In the interim, it would be quicker and easier just to get on with it. And so Lynsey climbed in, trying not to notice the odour of caked mud, unwashed bodies and the damp seat.

'Okay, Alfie, we wasted enough time already,' moaned Horace as he climbed in beside her and squeezed unnecessarily close. 'Get a move on.'

Scowling, but saying nothing, his brother started the engine and they were off.

* * *

Several miles away, Audrey Fellows had issues of her own to clear up. 'Did I really hear you correctly back at Bramerton, Jack? That you're going to be leaving for work at *three* in the morning?'

'Yep, and for a couple of reasons you'll probably find pretty barmie.'

'I can guess one,' sighed Audrey as she put on some moisturiser before climbing into bed. 'Not St Mark's Church, by any chance?'

Jack gave a slightly embarrassed smile. 'Well, I thought this might be a good opportunity to see if I can spot anything significant.'

'Like ghostly lights, you mean?'

'That or something more earthly. I can't help feeling there are strange goings on there that shouldn't be.'

'I can't think what.'

'Neither can I, but it just might have something to do with Admiral Ashfordby's increasingly uncharacteristic behaviour.'

'You surely don't think he's using St Mark's for some sort of ... secret assignation? For goodness' sake, as churchwarden, he'd never even consider such a ...'

'I know, I know,' interrupted Jack, 'and, anyway, I also want to have a nose around the yard before anyone else is there.'

'Hoping to see what? The ghost of that girl?'

'No, of course not. It's human activity of a very different kind that I suspect is going on there.'

'Such as?'

'I don't know, Aud. That's why I want to make an unexpected visit.'

'I don't know why you have to get so involved in things,' groaned Audrey, 'but just promise you'll take care and not take any risks.'

'Scouts' honour.'

'And what if none of this "nosing about" produces any results and you find yourself hours early for work?'

'I might well end up not being that early, actually,' Jack replied. 'It could be a slow drive there because, with the high pressure we've got at present, the forecast is calling for fog and ...' Jack glanced outside to where their porch light was already surrounded by a halo of white precipitation, '... by the look of it, it's beginning to settle in already.'

'But at least the weather girl forecasted fine weather for later in the day,' recalled Audrey, 'so that fog should soon clear away.'

Perhaps in more ways than one, thought Jack, but didn't say, as he switched off his bedside light, hoping to snatch a few hours' sleep.

* * *

Jack was correct about the fog settling in, and it was the last thing Linsey Butterick needed on her fraught journey eastwards. Gazing out of the pick-up truck windows as it sped along dark winding B-roads, she saw the flat countryside beyond soon become wreathed in an opalescent blanket while the occasional hamlet that flashed past was lost in the ominous reflection of their own headlights.

'Don't you think you should slow down?' Lynsey forced herself to make the warning, praying not only that the journey would soon come to an end, but also that she would be alive when it did.

When this nightmare passage had begun, she'd hoped at least to catch a glimpse of some of Norwich's historic buildings as they passed through the city centre. Instead, they'd quickly traversed the outskirts, past supermarkets and the football stadium, before ending up on a multi-carriage by-pass which quickly filtered them off onto a quiet country road. Much to Linsey's alarm this, and the worsening visibility, prompted no slackening of their speed.

As conditions deteriorated, Lynsey guessed they must have reached lower-lying marshland and hoped this meant their destination was near. Finally, after a particularly vicious swerve to avoid running off the road, they ground to a stop just short of a flint wall, causing Lynsey to let out an involuntary shriek.

'Yeah, well we need to get there, and quick,' grumbled Horace as Alfie reversed back onto the road.

'... and in one piece, which we won't if your brother continues to drive like a maniac,' yelled Lynsey.

With slightly reduced speed, they drove on for another thirty minutes before turning off the road and onto a rough track, at the entrance of which Alfie brought the vehicle to a halt. 'This is it.'

Lynsey looked as far as she could along the twin beams of illuminated fog. Apart from some overhanging trees, there was nothing to see except the track disappearing into a milky void. 'What do you mean "this is it"?' she protested with mounting anger. 'Where's Mr Borrett?'

'Waiting for you on his boat.'

'I can't even see a boatyard, let alone a boat. Where are they?'

'At the end of that there track.' Horace opened his door, got out and hauled Lynsey's luggage from the back.

'You mean you're not taking me all the way?'

'It's not far to walk. Here ...' he shoved her rucksack onto her lap and dumped her case clear of the truck, '... keep following the track an' you'll soon be there.'

'Urrgh!' was all she could utter in exasperation as she clambered out, hitched the bag over her shoulders and grabbed the handle of her case. 'Thanks for nothing.'

'You're welcome.' It was difficult to tell whether Horace's words, as he jumped back into the cab, were insolent sarcasm or just total ignorance at his own lack of courtesy. Whatever, with a roar of power, the pickup immediately reversed out of the track entrance and back onto the main road where it was immediately swallowed up by the all-enveloping clag .

Lynsey watched the disappearing glow of its tail-lights with mixed emotions. She was still furious at such cavalier handling, but also relieved at finally being shot of the churlish Horace and Alfie. Then she looked around her. With the truck gone and no other lights to guide her, she was standing in total darkness in the eerily silent gloom. Suddenly she felt terribly alone and vulnerable, as a little shiver of apprehension iced its way down her spine. It was a time to take control of her emotions. 'Come on, Butterick,' she said out loud to herself, as she had many times before when facing frightening courtroom battles, 'you can hack it.' And so, with an equally firm grip on herself and the handle of her suitcase, she set off along the deserted track.

"Not far", Horace had said, but she placed as much faith in his promises as she had in his brother's driving. If anything, the fog seemed to be thickening and she judged she must be very close to water. Now her fear was of stepping off into an unseen dyke or river, and she wished she'd thought to include a torch in her kit. A light, any light, would have been some source of comfort.

And then she saw one, just a flickering glimmer at first, but an enticing indication that there was something at the end of this fog-bound track. She pressed on with a quicker step, dragging her case behind, its small wheels struggling to cope with the uneven terrain. The light was getting closer and brighter and, eventually, a shape started to emerge around it.

It was a boat, the light a welcoming glow behind a porthole that, to Lynsey's tired eyes, shone now like a beacon of hope. She gave an audible sigh of relief, knowing that soon she'd be in warmth and comfort. And then, just a second later, she stopped in her tracks.

Although she heard no sound, she sensed that she was being watched. Too afraid to breathe, she turned around slowly and caught the slightest glimpse of something lingering there in the swirling fog, just feet away.

And then it was gone. She stood motionless, now breathing heavily and too terrified to move, wondering if her overwrought senses were playing tricks on her or whether she really was being spied on.

She shook away stupid thoughts and once again, pulled herself together. Only yards to go now and this grim final part of her journey would be over. Carrying her case, she picked her way across the intervening grass, taking care not to trip over the mooring lines, stepped cautiously right up to the boat, and peered through a porthole. A bearded dark-coated figure was moving in the flickering light beyond. She knocked on the hull and almost immediately heard booted feet climbing wooden steps. She unhitched her rucksack and prepared to board.

*　*　*

Chapter Nine

That fog was still dense the next morning as Jack drove slowly along in a world reduced to just a few hundred metres in the twin beams of his dipped headlights. Not for the first time since leaving home in the early hours, did he ask himself just what he was doing there.

The answer, he knew, was his lifelong principle of always sticking to any plan he'd made. He liked to think of it as determination, though Audrey always called it stubbornness. It had served him well enough along the road of life and now, as he drove slowly along this actual road, he glanced at the dashboard clock and noted that dawn was still a good hour and a half away.

Even then, it would be another few hours before the fog began to clear, it being a common fallacy that the sun always burned it off. In inversion situations like this, the result could often be the opposite when its convecting rays would first stir up the cold air close to the earth's surface and mix it with the warmer layer above, thickening the hanging precipitation yet further. That was undoubtedly what would happen today and Jack realised that not only was he going to be late for his own investigations, but that the start of his patrol could also be seriously delayed. Nothing he could do about either now though, and so he kept on, straining his eyes for any unexpected traffic.

Thankfully, at this early hour on such a gloomy Saturday morning, the roads were empty. In fact, since leaving the increasingly obscured lights of Norwich and joining the minor road to the village, he'd not seen another vehicle. That didn't mean the way ahead would be clear, and so he crawled onwards, trying to keep alert and focussed, thankful he had his Sat Nav to track his progress, but realising again, his illogical liking for fog.

It was a strange fascination, but one he'd always had. In a way, he felt selfish, knowing of all the disruption and risks this phenomenon caused, but an element that enshrouded all it touched with an air of mystery ... and Jack loved mysteries.

Perhaps this harked back to his boyhood days growing up in the East End of London, when pea-soupers would descend for weeks on end, bringing the city and suburbs almost to a standstill and deadening all but the mournful wail of ships' sirens from the nearby Thames.

Thoughts of that river, now so far away, recalled other memories of his early days in the Metropolitan Police, serving on launches in their Thames Division. Fog then meant ghostly wharves and shrouded warehouses in which the wrongdoer flourished and those on patrol needed to be extra vigilant.

Jack shook himself out of his reminiscence, aware he needed to concentrate and relieved to find the car still on the road and travelling along at a steady fifteen mph.

A quick look at the Sat Nav showed he must be close to the river. He shuffled more upright in his seat and slowed to a walking pace. Even so, he was totally unprepared for what happened next.

Suddenly, as if materialising from out of the ether, the figure of a young woman appeared in the road ahead, arms waving, and obviously wanting him to stop. In spite of his snail-like speed, Jack only just managed to jam on the brakes and come to a skidding halt as she collapsed out of sight beyond his bonnet.

'What the ...' He jumped out and ran forward, unsure whether he'd actually hit her.

In the swirling vapour of the car's dipped headlights, she lay there, unmoving and seemingly lifeless.

* * *

Not for long though. Even as Jack bent down, she raised her head and struggled to sit up. He put a steadying hand on her shaking shoulder. 'Are you all right?'

'Yes ... yes, I think so.' Her tee-shirt and jeans were soaked by condensing fog while strands of blonde hair lay lank across her face. As Jack went to help her up, whether due to cold or shock and probably both, her whole body began to tremble uncontrollably. 'I ... I'm s ... so sorry for jumping out at you like that, but ... but I needed you to stop.'

'Don't worry ... let's get you warm.' He took off his waterproof jacket, wrapped it around her shoulders and helped her into the front seat of the car, before climbing once more behind the wheel and turning the heat to FULL. Then he leaned into the back, pulled the flask from his lunch bag and poured a mug of hot steaming black coffee. 'Here, have this.'

She smiled weakly and took a tentative sip, cradling the warm mug in her shaking hands as if it contained nectar from the Gods, while Jack glanced up and down the road, worried that another vehicle might emerge at any second and not see them in time. He slipped into gear and eased forward. 'Just relax and calm down while I shift us to somewhere safer.' Only a few hundred yards further on, the gateway to a field emerged through the fog. He pulled in and switched off. By now she'd drunk all the coffee. He topped up again from the flask, steam rising into her straggling hair, which she brushed back to reveal eyes heavy with fear and fatigue. 'Feeling better?'

She nodded, her obvious shock giving way to relief. Wiping away a tear, she took another sip of coffee. 'Th ... thank you for stopping.'

'Don't mention it, but just what are you doing wandering around at this time of morning without a coat on?'

She didn't answer immediately, but instead glanced at Jack's uniform white shirt and black trousers. 'Are you a policeman?'

'I was once, but now I'm a river ranger which is a sort of policeman.' He took her cold hand in his. 'Jack Fellows.'

'Lynsey ... Lynsey Butterick ... and I can't tell you how good it is to meet you, Mr Fellows ...' her voice was articulate and full of gratitude, '... you've been a life-saver.'

'That bad was it?'

'Worse than bad.' She sniffled back more tears. 'I ... I'm here from London to take up a new post with a local landowner and ... and ...'

She was still struggling to make herself coherent, but Jack was already ahead of her. 'Not Bertie Borrett, by any chance?'

'Yes, that's right, but ...'

'... and you must be the lawyer he was hiring.'

She nodded again. '... but not if I'd had any idea of what lay in store ... that horrendous ride in a pickup truck ... and then the way Mr Borrett tricked me onto his boat ...' She started to cry again and Jack passed her a tissue.

'Just start from the beginning.'

'Yes ... sorry ...' She took another sip of her coffee. 'Well, as I say, it was arranged I'd stay on his boat this first night ...'

'At his boatyard?'

'Yes. I got picked up at Norwich Station by two of the hands. A dreadful pair by the name of ...'

'... Horace and Alfie Hinnerley.' Jack said their names with distaste. 'Yes, I know them, so go on.'

'Well, they dropped me at the entrance to the staithe and I made my way through the fog to the boat. After I'd knocked on the side, Mr Borrett came up and took me down into the cabin.'

'On a foggy night like this, you must have been glad of a bit of comfort.'

'It wasn't that comfortable, I can assure you ... or clean,' she explained in a tremulous voice, wrapping Jack's coat just a little tighter around her. 'I'd never met the man before and I took an instant dislike to him. He almost immediately started making lewd remarks and disgusting suggestions. Just to gain some time, I made the excuse that I needed to change and asked to see my cabin. He showed me into a little cubbyhole of a room, but it was only as I closed the door that I realised the lock was on the outside. I heard a bolt slide and knew I was a prisoner.'

'This is serious stuff,' said Jack, shocked that even the likes of Borrett could behave in such a crude and reckless manner. 'So, did he let you go or did you escape?'

'I escaped ... by banging on the door and saying that I'd got changed and would he let me out, but when he unbolted it, I just barged past and made a run for it.' She was clearly still traumatised by the experience and tears were once more rolling down her cheeks. 'Unfortunately, he obviously knew his boat better than I did and caught up with me in the main cabin where, in panic, I grabbed the nearest thing to hand, which was the oil lamp on the table, and hit him with it.'

'Good for you.' Jack smiled and gave her shoulder a reassuring squeeze. 'Hard I hope.'

She gave the glimmer of a smile back. 'Not really. I only dazed him slightly. But when I threw the oil lamp down, it started a small fire, which must have distracted him. Not for long enough, though, because by the time I'd got the hatch undone and stumbled up on deck, he'd caught up with me again. But I still managed to get away and leg it down the staithe. I'm a good runner, Mr Fellows and it didn't take me long to lose myself in the fog. All I wanted to do was put as much distance as possible between me and that scene back there. I've spent the rest of the night stumbling around, totally lost, terrified out of my mind and imagining that face looming out of the fog at any time. I was just about all in when I saw your lights.'

'You've had a rotten experience,' said Jack, saddened to the core that any man could behave so badly. 'We need to get you straight to a police station and Borrett arrested.'

'I'm not sure.' She bit her lip. 'It'll be just his word against mine, Mr Fellows. You know as well as I do that if he's charged, he'll just say that I encouraged him. Win or lose, my reputation will be ruined, so it's better if I just head back to London and write the whole thing off as a bad experience.'

'No, you can't do that,' insisted Jack firmly. 'As a barrister, you of all people should know the law must win out. If Borrett gets away with this, it'll only be a matter of time before he tries it again.'

'I suppose you're right but ...' she hesitated, as if reluctant to explain further, '... but there is something else.'

'Go on.'

'Well, I told you I managed to get away when he grabbed me on deck, but I didn't explain how.'

'But now you're going to.'

'Yes.' She paused and bit her lip. 'You see, I pushed him overboard.'

'What, into the dyke?'

'Yes. I was only trying to fend him off, but he stumbled backwards against the deck rail, and the next thing I knew he was over the side and in the water.'

Jack could only laugh. 'Well, I should think a good dunking at least cooled his ardour.'

'Yes, but what if he couldn't swim? What if he drowned and it was my fault?'

'Look, I'm on my way there so, if you're that worried, let's go straight to the staithe and check.' Jack took the coffee mug from her still-trembling hand and screwed it back onto the flask. 'That way we'll at least put your mind at rest.'

'I can't ever go back there.'

'I can understand how you feel, Lynsey, so what I suggest is that I ring the police first and get them to meet us at the boatyard. That way we'll keep things official, you safe and get Borrett arrested on the spot.'

'If you really think that's for the best, Mr Fellows.'

'I do ... and the name's Jack.'

'Okay ... Jack ... I guess now's as good a time as any to face my demons.'

'Good.' Jack took out his mobile phone. Knowing exactly who he was going to contact, he keyed the number and, feeling only slight guilt at disturbing his friend's slumber, let it ring. But it answered surprisingly quickly. 'Bailey, Jack Fellows ... sorry to wake you at this early hour ... oh, you're already up ... right ... we'll join you there.' Jack switched off, frowning.

'You seemed to know him,' Lynsey said, concerned at this brief one-sided conversation and Jack's sudden ominous silence.

He quickly regained his composure. 'Yes, Detective Inspector Bailey. Good man. We've worked together on a number of cases now.'

'But, you didn't explain what had happened.'

'No, I didn't need to.' Jack slowly put his phone away. 'That's because Bailey's already at the boatyard. He's been there an hour now.' He turned to face her. 'Lynsey, I'm sorry, but the news isn't good.'

* * *

Chapter Ten

If ever Jack could have wished fog away, it was this morning. They'd come crawling into the village after just a couple more anxious miles, its outer houses and inner thatched cottages eventually materialising ghostlike through the swirling fog. Set on slightly higher ground further on, the church of St Mark's remained completely hidden in its own enveloping blanket.

Those miles, though, had seemed endless, with the gloom outside more than matched by the cloud of despair that Jack's news had brought to Lynsey Butterick.

'You say they've found his body in the dyke.' She closed her eyes and slowly shook her head. 'I should have stayed to help him, shouldn't I?'

'You were desperate, Lynsey, and no-one would think straight in the kind of situation you found yourself in.'

'That's not how the courts will see it, Jack, as you and I both know.' She ran shaking fingers through her damp, tangled hair. 'I've been responsible for killing someone and I still can't believe it happened.'

'You were defending yourself against a man well known for his licentious ways, and that's what your legal defence will establish ... if it ever comes to that,' consoled Jack, while trying to keep any misgivings from his voice. He nodded ahead to where the boatyard track cut left from the road. 'We're here now, so try not to think too far ahead. We'll just take things one at a time.'

Even as they lurched down the potholed track, the blurry outline of the boatyard became visible with numerous ghostly blue flashing lights reflecting off the fog. To Lynsey it must have seemed like the anteroom to hell itself. 'You will help me, won't you, Jack?' she pleaded, tugging nervously at his sleeve.

'Of course I will.'

Beside the boatyard sheds were Borrett's Mercedes, Elsie's sportscar and another unidentified car. There were also marked and unmarked police cars, an ambulance and two fire engines, one of the latter hard by the mooring where *Merlin Magic* still lay, a sad shadow of the boat Jack had inspected just days before. With her wheelhouse contorted by recent fire, she lay listing thirty degrees to port, her stub mast collapsed and lying tangled across the deck and that sweet hull, buckled and blackened by smoke. Lynsey climbed out of the car, seemingly hypnotised by the scene. 'But ... How? ... Why? ... I can't ...'

Jack put a restraining arm on her shoulder as a familiar figure in dark-blue raincoat detached himself from the grouped police, medics and firemen, and came striding across to join them.

'I know this is your patch now, Jack, but I didn't expect you here this soon.' Detective Inspector Bailey had the look of a man not expecting to spend his Saturday morning by a fog-shrouded dyke.

'Neither I you.' Jack glanced towards the burned-out boat and, more ominously, the sheeted figure lying inert by the water's edge. 'Bertie Borrett no doubt.'

'Yes. His wife's already identified him,' said Bailey, nodding towards the distraught figure of Elsie Borrett, standing nearby in the comforting arms of Admiral Ashfordby, 'but how did you know that, Jack?'

'I'll tell you later. Have you got a cause of death yet?'

'Yep, the doc's already done a preliminary which suggests he died from drowning, but there's also a suspicious head wound, so I guess we're looking at murder.'

'Or involuntary manslaughter,' countered Jack.

Bailey's eyebrows went up at least one notch. 'You already seem to know something I don't, Jack. In fact, would you like to explain just why you're so near to the crime-scene on this cold foggy morning?'

'Gladly, but first ...' the ranger scanned the surrounding personnel, 'have you got a female officer here, Bailey?'

'Yes, my DC.'

'Good, then I'd like her to look after that young lady,' he indicated Lynsey who was staring transfixed at the lifeless form lying just yards away, 'while you and I have a private chat.'

* * *

'That's quite a story, Jack.' The two men were sitting in Bailey's unmarked car where the ranger had given a full account of the morning's drama. 'Do you believe her?'

'Yes, I do. She's an intelligent woman, Bailey, a barrister-at-law. Why on earth would she concoct a hair-brained story like that?'

'Because it shifts the blame onto the victim, doesn't it?' Bailey rubbed lost sleep from his eyes. 'I don't know, Jack, somehow it just doesn't ring true.'

'In what way?'

'That a rich local landowner would entice a barrister, of all people, up here with, according to her evidence, the sole purpose of sexual conquest.'

'Borrett had a reputation for womanising,' argued Jack, 'and, although Lynsey insists they'd never met previously, her name and photo had appeared in the press in connection with a fairly recent case. From that, we can only assume Borrett formed an unhealthy obsession and hatched his plot.'

'But he must have known he'd never get away with it,' persisted Bailey. 'And how did he manage to entice her here anyway? My understanding is that barristers are hired by the solicitor, not by the client direct.'

'Borrett's PA *is* his solicitor, so it wouldn't be difficult for him to engineer things his way.'

'I'll need to have words with this PA,' said Bailey, taking out his notebook and pen. 'What's his name?'

'Cecil Watling and he lives with his wife at Providence Farm.'

'The Borrett's domain,' said Bailey, writing down the details before slapping shut his notebook. 'The thing is, Jack, whatever the true sequence of events here, your young lady ...' he glanced back into his notebook, '... Miss Lynsey Butterick ... admits to hitting Bertie Borrett over the head and shoving him overboard, thereby bringing about his death.'

'But not with malice aforethought,' pointed out Jack, using the old terminology.

'Perhaps not but, for the moment, its going to be treated as murder and I'll have to take her in.' He went to get out, but Jack held him back.

'Okay, but just a couple of questions first, Bailey. For starters, who reported finding the body?'

'The fire service when they arrived, but they'd been called by the old boy over there ...' once again, Bailey consulted his notebook, '... Claude Ashfordby.'

'Admiral, Sir Claude Ashfordby KCB, actually,' clarified Jack.

'Hmm, rank, title *and* decorations,' said Bailey with another rise of the eyebrows. 'He'll make a good witness.'

'And what *did* he witness, actually?'

'Flames coming from the boatyard. He was up and about and saw the blaze. Apparently keeps his own boat here and had a personal reason to be worried. So he dialled 999 and came down himself to investigate.'

'What time was this?'

'Ten past three. He remembered checking his watch as he made his way here and the fire service have confirmed the time of the call.'

'Strange,' said Jack, frowning, before moving on to another aspect that puzzled him. 'And you say it was Mrs Borrett, who identified the body?'

'Officially, yes, though it was your admiral who first told us who it was.'

'You didn't waste any time getting the next-of-kin down here, Bailey.'

'I didn't need to. She was already here.'

'Really? So early, on a dark and foggy morning. Why was that?'

'I don't know, because I haven't taken any formal statements yet.' Bailey climbed out of the car followed by the ranger. 'I reckon the first will be your young barrister with her strange tale of abduction.' He went over to the marked police car where Lynsey sat in the back with Bailey's DC. They both climbed out as the men approached, but it was Bailey who spoke. 'Miss Butterick, Jack Fellows here has related the story you told him. Do you admit assaulting Mr Borrett and pushing him overboard?'

Lynsey lowered her head and said simply, 'Yes, I did it.'

'Right ... Lynsey Butterick, I'm arresting you on suspicion of murdering Bertram Borrett. You don't have to say anything, but it may harm your defence if you do not mention, when questioned, something which you later rely on in Court. Anything you do say may be given in evidence.'

'Murder?' Lynsey gasped and took one step back. 'How can it be murder? I was just defending myself.'

'That's something to be discussed during your interviews,' said Bailey. He nodded to one of the uniformed constables who took Lynsey's arm.

'I can't believe this.' She blinked hard and cast despairing eyes around the grim scene before her. Finally, they seemed to focus on *Merlin Magic*'s blackened hulk. 'That boat ... can I have a closer look?'

Bailey shrugged and nodded approval to the PC, who released the lawyer's arm.

They moved closer to the wreck where firemen had started up a motor-driven pump and begun the process of pumping out. Jack guessed it was water used to extinguish the blaze that had caused the list in the first place and already *Merlin Magic* was starting to right itself. Standing on the quay-heading, Lynsey leaned across and tapped the blackened hull. 'It's steel.'

'That's right,' confirmed Jack. 'Built in Holland of the finest.'

'But the boat I was on was wooden.'

'The boat in there is wooden,' said Bailey, indicating the workboat, *Tugger*, lying in the wetshed.

'No, that boat is way too small. The one I was on was about the same size as this one, but wooden.'

Bailey stepped forward. 'It was dark and foggy, Miss Butterick. You can't be sure.'

'But I am,' insisted the young lawyer with an emphasis she must have used many a time in court. 'This is a completely different boat.'

Further discussion was interrupted by one of the firemen on board, emerging from below holding a partially burned article. He handed it across. 'This yours, Miss? We found it in a cabin down there together with a large suitcase with the same label.'

It was a red canvas rucksack, scorched and ruined but, even worse, it still had Lynsey's name and address label attached to its straps.

* * *

'Right, I think that answers that one,' said Bailey with a nod to the PC, who now firmly led Lynsey back towards the awaiting car. But, the young lawyer still wasn't ready to leave this scene of tragedy. Instead, she stared at the surrounding dilapidated wooden boatyard sheds.

'These buildings ... they weren't here last night.'

Bailey had the look of a man who'd had enough of his time wasted this early morning, but it was Jack who spoke. 'I think you'll find they were, Lynsey. My guess is that they're at least a half a century old.'

'No, I know you'll say it was the fog again, but I walked to here and I ran back and there was never so much as a shed to get in my way.'

'The trouble is, Miss Butterick,' said Bailey with enforced patience, 'you don't appear to have a single witness to confirm any of what you've told us so far.'

'You mean you don't believe me?'

'You know how the system works,' said Bailey bluntly. 'Can you come up with anyone who can substantiate your, frankly implausible, story?'

'I don't think so ... unless ...'

'Unless what?'

'There might have been someone.'

'Really? Who?'

Lynsey shook her head. 'I don't know. I just had the feeling that there was someone else there. Someone watching me in the fog.'

'What sort of someone?'

'It's hard to be definite with such poor visibility and the darkness, but ... I think it was the figure of a young woman.'

Standing there in the early dawn, Jack felt a slight chill run up his spine, and not only due to the clammy near zero temperature. Any further thoughts or discussion were now interrupted again, this time by the approaching beams of another vehicle's headlights lurching up the track towards them. It came to a grinding halt before the main boatshed, a battered black pickup truck from which two equally disreputable looking figures emerged.

'The brothers Hinnerley,' said Jack as if answering Bailey's unspoken question. He glanced across to Lynsey and she nodded.

'Yes, these were the two who collected me from the station.'

'Is that correct?' asked Bailey of the older looking scruff.

'Who wants to know?'

'Police. Answer the question.'

'Yeah, we brought her here.'

'Not all the way, you didn't,' challenged Lynsey. 'All you did was dump me at the end of the track.'

'Yeah, well it were foggy, weren't it?'

'That's not the reason you gave at the time. You said you had work to do.'

'Okay, let's not get bogged down with details at this stage,' interrupted Bailey. He turned back to the brothers. 'So, if it was too foggy before, what are you doing here now?'

'We was driving by and saw all the lights and come to check.' Horace looked around at the collected emergency vehicles and uniformed officers. 'What's going on?'

'There's been a ... an accident, if it's any business of yours.'

'Yeah, well it is 'cos we work here.'

'Is that correct, Mrs Borrett?' asked Bailey, turning to Elsie, who had pulled herself together a little and was now joining them on the arm of Admiral Ashfordby.

'Yes, they're ... they *were* my husband's yardhands.'

'What d'you mean "were"?' asked Horace, as though fearing his employment might have been terminated. Then he remembered Bailey's reference to an accident. 'You don't mean the guv'nor ...?'

'... has been found drowned under suspicious circumstances,' answered

Bailey, 'so I'd like to know what you were doing in the early hours of this morning.'

'Drowned ... suspicious!' Horace Hinnerley seemed genuinely shocked before his natural truculence kicked in. 'Why d'you want to know? You think we had something to do with it?'

'You were at the crime-scene at about the critical time,' answered Bailey. 'According to Miss Butterick here, it was you who collected her from Norwich Station and dropped her at the yard.'

'Yeah, but that's all we done and we di'n't come any further than the end of the track.'

'So, where did you go after that?'

'Nowhere. We just went on home an' watched telly, di'n't we Alf?'

'Yeah, just watched telly,' confirmed the brother, parrot-fashion.

'You told me you had to go off on some job,' insisted Lynsey.

'Yeah, well, it was too foggy weren't it,' replied Horace with a shrug.

'Lack of visibility didn't seem to worry you when you were driving like maniacs earlier.'

'Yes, all right, Miss Butterick,' broke in Bailey, 'I'll do the questioning if you don't mind.' He turned back to the brothers. 'So, you just drove home and watched television. Hardly the most exciting Saturday night for a pair of young lads.' The DI was making no attempt to disguise his cynicism. 'And I suppose, you have no witnesses to substantiate this?'

'Course not.'

Bailey decided now wasn't the time to press for further details of the brother's evening viewing. 'Okay, we'll leave it at that for the time being, but early next week I'll want a full statement from you two. Give my DC your contact details and we'll let you know time and place.' He turned to the admiral. 'I suggest you take Mrs Borrett home. We'll be in touch later regarding written statements from you both.'

With admiral and widow gone, Lynsey turned again to Jack. 'Why won't anyone believe me? These buildings definitely weren't here when I came earlier.'

It was Horace, glad of a diversion, who gave a scathing laugh. 'What you talking about? These sheds have always bin here.'

Without even attempting to respond to this, Lynsey instead turned to Bailey. 'Inspector, can I ask one more favour before I'm taken into custody?'

There was defiance in her voice now, a crisp clarity as though she were already cross-examining an important witness. Even Bailey sensed this was no young lady to mince words with. 'Which is, Miss Butterick?'

'That I view the body.'

Jack intervened. 'Lynsey, is that wise?'

'It's not a nice sight, Miss,' added Bailey. 'Are you quite sure?'

'Yes, of course I am. I've seen many photos of bodies before, Inspector.'

'Yes, but you could distance yourself from those.'

'I assure you, I'll be fine.'

The little procession made its way over to where the body lay covered by a sheet. At a nod from Bailey, a constable lifted back the end covering the head.

Lynsey took a deep breath, bent down and looked. Then she stood up and said firmly, 'This isn't the same man.'

* * *

Chapter Eleven

'Is that really what she said, Jack?' Audrey paused before removing a shepherds' pie from the oven as she listened to her husband's account of the morning's drama.

'Word for word. She reckoned the bloke on her boat was slim and swarthy, the complete opposite of Borrett's thick-set body. The only thing both men had in common was a beard and even that was different, Bertie's being bushy and flecked with grey, while her assailant's was dark and wiry.' Jack bent down to stroke Spike who, as usual, had parked himself under the dining table, waiting for any titbit his master could slip him without his mistress noticing. It was Saturday evening now with the Fellows all set to eat.

Audrey put the pie on the table. 'So, you have two very different descriptions of the victim.'

'Exactly.'

'And was it?'

'Was it what?'

'The body of Bertie Borrett that you saw at the staithe?'

'Oh, it was him all right,' confirmed Jack, unfolding his napkin and taking an appreciative sniff of the dinner about to be served. 'Poor Bertie was pretty ugly in life, but I can tell you he was even uglier in death.'

'Yes, well spare me the details, Jack,' ordered Audrey, keen now to return to less morbid issues. 'So, from what you've said, there can't be any doubt that this ... what's her name?'

'Lynsey Butterick.'

'... this Miss Butterick must be lying.'

'But Aud, she just isn't the type.' Jack spooned himself a generous helping of pie before continuing, 'She's a barrister for goodness' sake ... sworn to uphold the truth ... so why should she?'

'I don't know, Jack,' admitted Audrey rather haughtily, 'but haven't you noticed something very familiar about this story of hers?'

'You mean, that it's very similar to what happened at the yard a century ago?'

'Exactly, virtually a carbon copy.' A bowl of mixed veg crash-landed onto a spare dinner mat.

'You all right, Audrey?'

'Yes, of course I am. Why do you think I'm not?'

'Oh, just that you seem a touch rattled, that's all.'

'I'm quite all right, thank you, Jack,' she insisted with slightly exaggerated politeness while taking her seat opposite, 'but I can't believe you're getting yourself involved yet again in another probable murder case. It's none of your business, so just let Bailey deal with it all.'

'A boat in my patch has burned at its moorings, Aud, so that definitely *is* my business, and I still have to file my report on that.' Jack paused to help himself to some greens. 'And, as regards Lynsey, she's probably never heard the old story and, even if she had and needed to make something up, she'd surely concoct something far more believable than that.'

'Yes, well, as a lawyer, I'm sure "Lynsey",' emphasised Audrey with little fingered speech marks, 'did her homework before coming here and knew full well that Borrett was a lech and couldn't be trusted with women. Being aware of his reputation, did she really think it would be wise to stay on his boat, unchaperoned?' She shook out her napkin as though it were a ship's mains'l catching the breeze. 'My guess is that Borrett completely mistook the vibes, came on too strong and things got out of hand. Knowing she'd possibly killed him, she did a runner, met you and realised she had to come up with a quick sob story.'

'That's a bit unfair, Aud,' complained Jack between mouthfuls. 'No, she's too clever a girl to come up with a tale so implausible. If things had happened like you imagine, she knows enough about court pleas to realise she'd be far better off telling the truth.'

'And if it does come to trial, what charges might she face?' Audrey's tone had softened just a little.

'She's been arrested on suspicion of murder, but that could well get reduced to manslaughter.'

'Where is she now?' asked Audrey, finishing what little helping she'd served herself.

'Great Yarmouth PIC.'

'PIC?'

'P.I.C. Police Investigation Centre.' Jack pushed away his plate. 'The old days when you were just banged up in the nick have long gone, Aud. In the last five years, we've got purpose-built centres in Norfolk, separate to the station, where suspects are taken. The poor lass will have her fingerprints and DNA taken before being assessed by the duty officer, and then be locked up in a cell. Bailey's unlikely to see her in person while she's there and any communication will, most likely, be made through video link. That means I won't get another chance to see her for a quick, off the record, chat.'

'Why would you want to?'

'Because I think she's the victim in all this, Aud, and I promised I'd help her. It was me who assured her she wasn't to blame and convinced her to stay and face up to what happened.'

'You really think she's innocent, Jack?' Audrey poured them both a glass of water. 'From what you've just told me, she's admitted causing the death of Bertie Borrett, so surely she must have done it.'

'... in self-defence, and anyway, she's adamant it wasn't Borrett she pushed overboard, or even the same boat. Added to that, there's the time factor.'

'What time factor?'

'Well, Lynsey reckoned she got into Norwich at ten-thirty. Even in the fog, that journey to the staithe can't have been much more than an hour so by the time she boarded the boat, it must have been before midnight. But Admiral Ashfordby reckons he spotted the fire at around three in the morning.'

'Yes, but she said she was locked up in a cabin, so she could well have lost all track of time. It does raise another question though – whatever was the admiral doing up at that time of the morning anyway?'

'Probably couldn't sleep.'

'... or, was sneaking home after spending half the night with the victim's wife.' Audrey was in no mood to take prisoners on matrimonial fidelity this evening.

'Yes, that thought occurred to me,' admitted Jack, 'but I hope we're wrong.'

'... because that would put him on the list of suspects?'

'Exactly. Motive and opportunity. After all, there he was at the staithe and with Elsie. Now, what on earth was she doing down there in the early hours? That's another one that needs answering.'

'But do any of them need answering, Jack, when you already have a prime suspect?'

'Yes, because it's just too much of a coincidence that others were there at around the same time. No-one would have been out at that time in the morning in such atrocious conditions, without having a very good reason.'

'Like the Hinnerley brothers?'

'Just so. I wouldn't trust those two further than I could throw their case files. What were *they* doing out in their truck in the early hours?'

'I dread to think, Jack.'

'I know what you mean,' said Jack, grimacing. 'But, having said that, they did at least give us a bit of useful information.'

'Really? What?'

'They told us who owned the other car.'

'What other car?'

'The one parked at the yard between Borrett's Mercedes and Elsie's sports car.'

'And ...?'

'... it was the Watlings'.'

'What, Cecil and Lucy's?' Audrey was recalling her brief encounter with the pair at the public meeting.

'Yep. Bailey got the number from the Hinnerleys and Lucy answered. Apparently, she sounded pretty groggy and when Bailey said he needed to speak to Cecil, she went looking for him. Eventually, she came back on the phone and admitted she couldn't find him.'

'So now *he's* missing?'

'Very much so.'

'Well, I can't think that would upset Lucy very much,' declared Audrey, 'the way she was carrying on with Borrett in front of the poor man.'

'On the contrary,' said Jack, while surreptitiously feeding Spike a morsel of minced lamb, 'Bailey got the impression she was quite disturbed by the situation, and even more so when he told her of Bertie's death.'

'Does Bailey know she was one of Borrett's mistresses?'

'He does now and, being a dumped one, has added her to his suspect list.' Jack shook his head. 'That's the trouble with this case as far as I can see, Aud – one confession, plenty of suspects, but seemingly, no witnesses.'

'How about the couple on the narrowboat?' suggested Audrey. 'They moor it in the dyke don't they? Surely they saw or heard something.'

'No, because they weren't there. I called them while I was on patrol to check and found they were at the *Beauchamp Arms* in their narrowboat when it happened, and had since moved downriver to Reedham. I advised them to stay put there, well out of the way. Naturally, they were anxious to know what had being going on, so I'm going to meet them there tomorrow while on patrol, and update them.'

'Yes, well, just make sure you don't neglect your duties, Jack,' warned Audrey, collecting up their plates and stacking them in the sink. 'You must have felt shattered today.'

'Luckily, the fog persisted a bit, so I managed a short nap in the car before a late start.'

'Good.' Audrey was obviously still thinking as she started the washing up. 'So, what will happen to Lynsey now?'

'The police can hold her for twenty-four hours without a charge. Sometimes the Superintendent will authorise another twenty-four extension. Either way, by Monday morning she'll have been charged or released.'

'But probably charged?'

'I'm afraid so. Then she'll be before the magistrates for a hearing.'

'What then?'

'If the magistrates think there's a case to answer, being a murder charge, it'll be referred to the Crown Court.' It had been a long harrowing day and Jack felt himself starting to wilt. Excusing himself from the washing up, he picked up the newspaper and flopped into an easy chair. 'Whatever, love, it'll probably spell the end of her legal career ... unless I can find out what really happened before it ever comes to that.'

'Oh no,' sighed Audrey, 'not another investigation.'

But by now, Jack had yawned, the paper had slipped to the floor and she was only talking to herself.

*   *   *

Sunday morning's weather seemed to somehow mirror the morbid feel of the yard when Jack arrived early to take the launch on yet another day's patrol. Beneath skies covered by dark overcast, low stratus scudded across the flat marshes on the back of a chilly south-west wind, noisily vibrating the POLICE – DO NOT ENTER tape that surrounded the crime scene.

Parking well clear, he noted that both Borrett's Mercedes and the Watlings' car had been removed, leaving just one marked police car and a larger van belonging to the Scene of Crime Officers whose overalled forensic specialists were now painstakingly picking over the wreck of *Merlin Magic*. For both protection and security, the boat had now been warped back inside the wetshed alongside *Tugger*.

Giving a salutary wave to the lone constable on guard, Jack made his way to the launch, passing Admiral Ashfordby's *Curlew*, the only other boat still in the dyke, vainly tugging at her mooring in the squally breeze. Checks done on his launch, Jack wasted no time getting under way and heading for the main river where a BroadsBeat RIB lay at the head of the dyke, preventing other craft from entering. A chat with the two constables, and then he was off downriver, glad to be out on the wide waterway once more where the wind kicked the flooding tide into little white-capped tumblers. Here, life's values were soon restored.

Not to say conditions weren't just a little daunting for the few hire-cruisers already making their way westwards on the tide. By contrast, they seemed ideal for the two yachts thundering downriver, big mains'ls reefed, lee-rails under and doubtless heading for some congenial rendezvous at a waterside inn. As they passed, the crews gave the ranger cheery waves before leaving the launch in a welter of curling wakes and rattling blocks. At their mastheads, the burgees streamed straight out in the Force Five breeze that soon had them approaching the laboured passage of Reedham ferry.

This was the only vehicle-crossing over the Yare between bridges at Norwich and Yarmouth and the sole remaining chain ferry on the Broads. Clearly, circumnavigating this moving obstacle held no challenge for the yachts, as they passed either side of the rectangular vessel slowly clanking its way across the river with a cargo of three cars. The service had been operated for over half a century by the same family, who were also landlords of the adjacent Ferry Inn where boats moored and crews enjoyed a convivial drink at the bar as a prelude to the Sunday carvery. Motoring by, Jack was thankful that, no matter what tragedies struck, even in this small world, life carried on.

And life was certainly carrying on at Reedham's public staithe where more boats lined the quay. To Jack, this popular stopping place on the Southern Rivers was more like a little port than a Broadland village. Only twelve miles from the sea, the tides here ran fast, making the need for correct mooring procedure a necessity rather than a choice. Another obstacle to navigation was the railway swing bridge, no problem for low-decked motor-cruisers, but requiring a rig-down for yachts that misjudged its opening times. Clearly that was not going to be the case for the two now approaching its already opening span. As the hundred year old structure swung ninety degrees along the river, they passed through with a wave of thanks to the operator.

Jack would not be following them, because half-way along the quay he'd found the boat he was looking for, the long, slender hull of *Faith and Hope* with Charity Howden beckoning him from the afterdeck.

'Good to see you again,' she yelled as the launch came alongside.

'Yep, and good to see you both too,' replied Jack, as Marcel appeared on the foredeck to take his headrope.

'*Bonjour, Jacque.*' The Frenchman secured the line. 'We are so sorry to hear of the *tragédie* at the little boatyard.'

'Yes, you were lucky to be well out of it,' said the ranger as he climbed aboard.

'Lucky for us, but not for Mr Borrett, by the sound of it.' Charity glanced skywards to where a rain squall seemed bent on heading their way. 'Not a day for sunbathing, Jack, so let's go below where the kettle's already on.'

'Sound's good.'

Down in the saloon, the flower-patterned curtains, soft cushions and smell of polished woodwork, were as inviting as ever.

'So, you didn't know anything about the happenings at the yard until I called you?'

'No.' Charity shook her head. 'We'd moored upriver at the *Beauchamp Arms* for an evening meal. Later we shifted down here to Reedham.'

'What, in that fog? Why ever did you do that?'

'I'll explain later.' She handed Jack his coffee and sat down beside him. 'We were still in bed when you called to say that Bertie was dead. We couldn't believe it, but we got up and tuned into Radio Norfolk and heard brief details on the news. They said someone was helping the police with their enquiries, which sounded a bit ominous. They didn't say who, so we're hoping you might tell us.'

'If that is not breaking a ...' sitting on the couch opposite, Marcel was searching for the word.

'... confidence,' helped out Charity.

'No, it's okay.' Jack sipped his coffee. It tasted good, like the big cups of breakfast coffee they served in France. 'It'll be public knowledge anyway after tomorrow's court appearance, and I've no doubt at all it was the only talking point in the village yesterday, so everyone living thereabouts will know all the gruesome details by now.' He briefly explained his unexpected encounter with Lynsey Butterick and events thereafter, but without mentioning the other people involved.

Charity sat listening in silence and, when he'd finished, Jack could tell there was something she wanted to add. After sitting in thought for a full minute she finally said, 'You know, Jack, I think I can vouch for having seen that girl arrive at the yard.'

This revelation took Jack by surprise. 'You're kidding. You? How?'

'Because I was there on Friday night, on my own at the Cookcraft Yard.'

'But I thought you said you were at the Beauchamp Arms,' pointed out an increasingly baffled Jack. 'What on earth were you doing alone in the yard?'

'I wasn't there for an entirely "earthly" reason.' She gave a tentative smile, half humour, half embarrassment. 'I was ghostwatching.'

Jack put down his coffee. 'This whole business gets weirder by the minute.'

'Not really, Jack. I told you about the spirit of the murdered girl who's supposed to haunt the yard. Well, after our meal at the pub, and with the fog coming down so thickly, it seemed the perfect condition for a manifestation. Marcel was busy wiring in the new chart-plotter he'd treated himself to, and so I got on my bike and pedalled off down there in the hope of seeing the apparition myself.'

Across the saloon table, Marcel gave a resigned shrug. Jack, however, was keen for more details.

'What time was this, Charity?'

'It was probably just before midnight when the woman arrived. I'd been standing back from the sheds where I could keep an eye on the staithe, when I heard a vehicle arrive and then drive away. Very soon after that, there was the sound of footsteps coming up the track. I knew it couldn't be the spirit, and when the figure did appear out of the fog, I could tell it was definitely mortal.' Charity shrugged. 'In a way, I was disappointed. I was hoping for that murdered girl's ghost and instead I got a young woman, staggering along in modern jeans and dragging a suitcase behind her.'

'... and who also caught a glimpse of you in the fog.'

'Oh dear,' apologised Charity, 'I hope I didn't scare her.'

'She was certainly startled,' said Jack, 'but it was nothing compared to the horror she endured later. Did you see or hear anything of that?'

'No. I'd already seen the lights on in *Merlin Magic*'s saloon and guessed it must be Borrett on board. When the woman arrived, and knowing his reputation, I suspected why. I didn't want to be seen as some sort of voyeur, so I thought it best to clear off and cycled back to join Marcel at the *Beauchamp Arms*. Having just finished installing the GPS, he was itching to try it in the fog, so we motored to Reedham. It was quite an adventure, but great fun.'

'... and it meant you missed all that happened at the staithe,' added Jack with mixed feelings. 'So, you're absolutely sure you didn't see or hear anything out of the ordinary?'

She shook her head sadly. 'No, I'm afraid not. I wish now I'd stayed. I might have been able to help her.'

'... or at least be a witness for her defence. Nevertheless, you will have to report what you've told me to the police, Charity. If nothing else, you can confirm the time and the accuracy of Lynsey's story as far as you know it.'

'I'm not sure the police would regard me as a very good witness, Jack.'

'Why not?'

'Because I have my own theory of what happened, but one which they wouldn't even start to consider.'

'Which is ...?'

'That your Miss Butterick went into another dimension.'

*   *   *

Jack spluttered slightly as his coffee went down the wrong way.

'Another dimension! You mean she experienced some sort of time-slip? You surely can't believe that's what happened, Charity.'

She smiled back tolerantly. 'I assure you I do. Spirits can manifest themselves in many ways, Jack, such as appearing and disappearing forms, strange noises, moving objects, translucent images, poltergeists and, like this, time slips.'

'But what happened on Saturday night was real enough, Charity. A man's dead and there's a body to prove it.'

'Yes, I know, but dimensional anomalies with a mix of past and present have been experienced before and by very rational people. In fact, a well-known one occurred in 1973, quite close to here in Great Yarmouth.

Jack sat back and shook his head. 'Ghosts of once-living beings are one thing, Charity, but how can you have ghosts of material things? Like the old boat Lynsey says she was on.'

'Spectres of inanimate objects are by no means unknown, Jack. There are a number of theories as to why some events re-occur like this, but to me, the most feasible is that some events on earth are so significant or traumatic, that they imprint themselves on the ether itself. And then someone, like Lynsey, wanders into them and sees a replay of the original.'

'But if you're saying this was the old crime being replayed ... it wasn't, was it?' argued Jack. 'A hundred years ago, it was the girl who was murdered and the skipper survived, whereas, this time it was the skipper who was murdered and the girl was the one who got away.'

'I know, but I think, like the Yarmouth case, this was a rare example of the past colliding with reality, added to which, there could well be another dimension yet.'

'Yet another dimension?' frowned Jack. 'I'm hardly keeping up with the ones so far.'

Charity gave a sympathetic smile. 'I'm talking about reincarnation, Jack. It's another aspect of occult reasoning. Perhaps that poor girl of a hundred years ago returned as Lynsey, and this time with the knowledge to fight the forces of evil. By the same token, Borrett could be that old skipper in modern form and finally paying the price for his debauchery.'

'A hundred years ago, that skipper was hanged, so I think he paid the price then,' said Jack, unconvinced. 'But what about the boat and boatyard sheds? Lynsey says she saw no buildings and the boat she went on was nothing like *Merlin Magic*, but some old wooden boat.'

'I researched the original story in depth, Jack, and found that a hundred years ago when that occurred, there *were no* buildings at the staithe and the crime took place on the murderer's own fishing boat which, in those days, would surely have been wooden.'

'That's quite a theory, Charity,' said Jack puzzled and rubbing his forehead, 'but you're absolutely right when you say the police won't want to hear it.' He took a card from his wallet and handed it across. 'These are the contact details for Detective Inspector Bailey. He's a good man but, believe me, he deals only in cold hard facts. Tell him about seeing Lynsey, and even why you were there, but leave it at that.'

'And what do you think will happen then?'

'He'll probably send someone to take a statement from you.'

Marcel seemed uneasy. '*Jacque*, will the police want to speak to us both?'

'Possibly.' Years at Scotland Yard had made Jack suspicious of those who shunned contact with the police and he saw that anxiety now in Marcel Carbonne's eyes. 'Would that be a problem?'

'Not really. It is just that I had a little *affrontement* – how do you say? – confrontation, some time ago with your London police.'

'Let me explain,' said Charity, leaning across to reassuringly squeeze her boyfriend's arm. 'It was just under a year ago, Jack. We'd taken *Faith and Hope* into London via the Grand Union and Regent canals. We were moored in Kentish Town and went for a drink at a local pub. Unfortunately, some drunken local moron latched on to us and while Marcel was at the bar, he started coming on to me. Marcel came back and tried to warn him off, but he persisted and it ended up with the man on his back. Unfortunately, the landlord called the police and Marcel was arrested, charged with causing grievous bodily harm and taken to court.'

'Sound's like bad luck to me,' sympathised Jack.

'Yes, but we had some good luck too, because there were plenty of witnesses to say what really happened, and the magistrate let him off with a caution and bound him over to keep the peace for twelve months.'

'He must be close to having a clean record again then,' said Jack, 'but I can understand your concern, because the police always check out previous convictions when they're dealing with serious crime. Better that you tell them first rather than let them find out.'

'That sounds good advice,' agreed Charity, 'so should I tell Inspector Bailey when I call him?'

Jack thought for a second. 'No, let me. I'm planning to see him myself tomorrow morning. He's a good friend as well as someone I've worked with many times, so he'll listen when I explain the situation.'

'Oh, that's so good of you, Jack.' Charity beamed appreciation and Marcel added his own thanks.

'Yes, we are truly grateful.'

'Don't mention it.' Jack glanced at his watch. 'Time for me to get back patrolling. Thanks for the coffee. I'll be in touch after tomorrow.'

Five minutes later and he was in his launch, heading back upriver and with much more to think about than when he'd first taken this morning's break.

* * *

As it turned out, the rest of Jack's duty-day had been busy enough to avoid much further thought on the matter. Between Reedham and Cantley, a large yacht had fallen victim to the squally conditions and lay in the reeds with a broken mast. After helping to disentangle the rigging and get them shipshape enough to proceed on power alone, he'd then encountered a hire-cruiser with steering problems. A tow to a local boatyard had sorted that one and by then it was early evening and time to be heading back to the dyke where he found the police RIB gone, but still no visiting boats. Doubtless, word had already spread amongst the boating community about the sinister happenings at the old Cookcraft yard and that, for the time being at least, it was a place to be avoided. After securing the launch for the night, Jack made his way back down the moorings towards the wetshed where the police tape still vibrated noisily in the wind. All was eerily desolate, the forensic team having left, and the burnt-out remains of *Merlin Magic* even more sinister in the darkness of the wetshed. But this was an opportunity not to be missed. Jack pulled out his torch and ducked under the tape for a closer look.

In the still-fresh breeze, the blackened boat tugged and creaked at its moorings, as though in some pain at the indignity of its own ending. Jack studied the burned and buckled wheelhouse and the broken portholes. For a steel vessel, she had succumbed surprisingly easily to just the careless throwing of an oil lamp, and now the final destination of this once-fine boat would doubtless be the scrapyard. Like some stricken creature in its death-throes, the boat once again creaked against the quay while its contorted guardrails bent even more. Jack looked for the reason and saw they were holding the mooring lines securing the boat to the quay. Why? He looked closer and noted something that certainly begged a further explanation.

Time for that later though. Right now he had other plans. Above the whine of the wind in the rafters and the banging of a loose sheet of corrugated iron roofing, Jack could hear the bell of St Mark's calling the faithful to evensong. It reminded him that Audrey would be on her way to St Cuthbert's to prepare for its evening service. He pulled out his mobile phone and rang, hoping he'd caught her before she switched hers off. Thankfully, she answered.

'Hello Jack. You just caught me at the church gate. What's the problem?'

'No problem, Aud, but I'm going to be a bit late home.'

'That's all right, the sidesman's away this weekend, so I'll be taking longer to clear up.'

'Okay, I'll come straight to the church to pick you up.'

'That'll work fine, but can I ask what's delaying you?'

'Just a little snooping around the village. Seeing if there are some aspects to this whole sorry business that I've missed.'

'Oh, Jack ...'

But Jack wasn't listening. He was already making his way on foot along the track, at the end of which he turned right and headed for the extreme western edge of the village. Here, after just a little searching, he found what he was looking for.

George Granston's workshop had been difficult to spot, obscured as it was by a mature high beech hedge, no doubt planted many years ago to hide what would have been something of an eyesore in an otherwise pretty village. This alone would have deterred trespassers, but Jack was intrigued to find a far-newer high chain-link fence surrounding the whole unit. It seemed almost an overkill for the rather rundown-looking workshop, but doubtless there was valuable tooling and machinery within that needed protecting. Jack pressed his nose against the sturdy locked gate for a closer look.

The workshop itself was built of brick, slightly larger than a bungalow and with a metal chimney emerging from what was probably the foundry section at the back. GRANSTON FABRICATIONS, said the peeling sign beside the big sliding door at the front. All the windows were barred and the yard was littered with discarded oil drums and various bits of rusting metalwork. Clearly George Granston didn't share his wife's rather orderly approach to life, but untidiness didn't mean the man was a poor craftsman and, having seen all he wanted, Jack turned on his heel and made his way back into the village.

His objective now was St Mark's, but this took him past Admiral Ashfordby's home, lying as it did within easy walking distance of *Curlew* and church alike. Knowing the admiral, like Audrey, would be attending evensong, Jack paused at his gate for both thought and inspection. This quaint thatched cottage with small-paned windows and white-stuccoed walls, adorned with several hanging baskets and a creeping clematis, was probably the first and only home of their own that the admiral and his wife had ever lived in. After a lifetime of naval service around the world, Lady Ashfordby's early death meant their time together in this little corner of England had been sadly short-lived. Throwing himself into the life of the parish had probably been Sir Claude's way of coping with bereavement but, after several years of being alone, it stood to reason that he'd now be missing female companionship. With that thought, Jack turned and looked back towards the staithe before continuing on up the slight incline towards the church.

Here, the service was in full swing with the congregation singing a rousing hymn with gusto. For such a small community, the events of the last forty-eight hours must have been traumatic indeed, and no doubt the church had more worshippers than usual, some there for words of comfort and prayers for the departed, but some wanting to keep abreast of any gossip. Jack paused by the lych-gate to listen to the hymn and once more gaze in the direction of the staithe. Then he looked up to the fine pitched roof and round Norman tower, a theory fast-forming on at least one aspect of this whole strange business.

Should he stop and have a word with the admiral after the service? He decided against it, knowing from personal experience that churchwarden duties didn't end with the last hymn. Besides, he had a rather more speculative plan that might bring things to a head quicker than mere words.

With the last verse of the hymn ringing in his ears, and with a marching step, Jack descended once more to dyke, staithe and waiting car. Minutes later, he was on the road and heading for yet another church.

*   *   *

Chapter Twelve

Unlike St Mark's, the Fellows' church of St Cuthbert's had a square 14th century tower standing at the west end of the nave, its arcade arches and mounting clerestory, all serving to reinforce an impression of modest grandeur and stocky strength.

St Cuthbert's was also a larger church, which meant that Audrey's duties, at the end of evensong, took that little bit longer unless Jack was there to help her. On duty days, when he missed the actual service, he would walk to join her at the end, but today, being late, he drove straight to the church and arrived to find his wife already locking away the brass cross and candlesticks.

'Sorry for the delay, Aud, but I'm glad I took the time for a poke around the village. It gave me food for thought.'

'That's okay, Jack, I'm almost done.' She tried to supress her mild irritation as she asked, 'What exactly was it you needed to check?'

'Nothing specific, but even in my Yard days, I always found any crime-scene held its own secrets that just needed a bit of teasing out.'

'And did you "tease" any out tonight?' Audrey tried not to sound sarcastic. She'd always admired her husband's detective skills and firm principles of right and wrong, but this was yet another case she would really have preferred he didn't get involved in.

'A few. For a start, I'd like to know what's happened to the deck fittings on the late-Borrett's boat. It's been warped back into the wetshed now, but someone's taken all the quality cleats and fairleads off it.'

'You mean the ones Bertie used to import from Holland?'

'Yep, they were the newest bits on the boat and certainly worth a few bob.' Jack absent-mindedly straightened some hymnbooks. 'The SOCO team were busy on the boat all morning, so they must have been removed sometime late afternoon. If I had to point a finger, it would be at the Hinnerley brothers.'

'Quite possibly, Jack, but being valuable, it's just possible that Elsie *told* them to remove the fittings *before* they were stolen.'

'Yeah, you may be right. Perhaps George Granston's got them for safe-keeping in his workshop.' Jack looked around him. 'Anything I can do to help you now, Aud?'

'The kneelers still need straightening if you want a job.'

'Right.' Jack happily set about his task. He admired Audrey for taking on such an important role in the running of St Cuthbert's and appreciated the sense of peace and spiritual contentment he always experienced within its sacred walls. It was a harmony with the past he felt now as he went from pew to pew, sliding the colourful and varied kneelers back into their place beneath while, at the same time, marvelling as he always did, at the splendour of his surroundings. Above him, the archbraced hammerbeam roof spoke of the skill and dedication those fourteenth century builders had applied to their task while, at the side of the nave, the recumbent alabaster figures of a local knight and his wife marked the tomb of one who had served in the crusades. The hassocks themselves were works of art, but of the present, having been covered with tapestries sewn by members of the congregation and illustrating local scenes relevant to the parish. Audrey had spent many months completing one of the wherry Albion, while others had chosen such things as windpumps, wildlife and fish. It was the last cushion to be straightened, but Jack found himself simply gazing at it, as though this fine, but inanimate object was trying to tell him something. It depicted a golden sword, shining brilliantly in the form of a cross that Jack assumed was another reference to the interred knight.

'That kneeler seems to be taking a bit of straightening, Jack,' chided Audrey.

'Right ... sorry.' Jack eased it into position with his foot and joined his wife at the back of the church. 'It's just that it made me think of the Sword of Excalibur and all those wonderful Arthurian stories of Camelot. For some reason, something in those tales seemed relevant to Borrett's death.'

'I can't think of anyone less knightly than Bertie Borrett ... God rest his soul.'

'Neither can I, but the admiral's a knight, so perhaps it's that. No doubt the connection will come to me eventually.'

'Yes, well while you're waiting for it, Jack, perhaps you can just help me move this table, and then we'll be done.'

Soon the security system was reset and the church door locked. 'Sad,' commented Jack as they made their way down the shingle path to their car, 'that now even churches have to be protected from the wrongdoer. Goodness knows what the Knights of the Round Table would have thought of that.'

'They were probably too busy fighting other worse evils, Jack,' said Audrey, climbing into the car beside her husband. 'Let's face it, love, evil has always been amongst us and you and many others have made a career out of fighting it.'

'You're right, Aud, and, as we know from our own experience, nowhere, however idyllic, is immune to its curse.'

'Talking of which,' remembered Audrey as they pulled away and headed homeward, 'what gave you "food for thought" as you poked around the village after work?'

'Some points of interest – as Sherlock Holmes would say – but I need to check things out before taking them further.'

Audrey knew better than to push her husband for early theories. Instead, she contented herself with a further warning not to get too caught up in it all. 'I think you should at least touch base with the Broads Authority, Jack, and assure them your first priority is your ranger duties.'

Jack, however, wasn't really listening for, in Audrey last words, he'd suddenly realised just why thoughts of the Arthurian legends had pointed at a possible solution to one of Bertie Borrett's dark secrets.

* * *

'It's not like you to sit with your head in a computer, Jack. Anything special?'

Audrey had just watched *Mama Mia* for the umpteenth time, but uninterrupted by her husband's usual deep sighs and "not again" comments. When he'd asked to borrow her laptop, she'd welcomed the distraction, but now, with the TV switched off, she was intrigued to know just why the internet was holding his attention for quite so long.

'Actually, I've been reading accounts of people experiencing time-slips.' Jack went on to explain Charity's theory on the events at Cookcraft yard, only to be met with the wifely derision he'd expected.

'My goodness, Jack, it's come to that has it?' Audrey tried to suppress her scepticism. 'You're really clutching at straws if you're resorting to that claptrap.'

'I grant you, it's a far-fetched theory, Aud, but otherwise-very-sensible people have had some strange experiences.' He tapped the laptop's screen. 'Like this old case in August 1901 when Misses Moberley and Jourdain, two English spinster academics were visiting the Palace of Versailles in France. Trying to locate the Petite Trianon where Marie Antoinette spent much time, they experienced an atmosphere of heavy dreaminess, at the same time as encountering people in 18th Century costume including, possibly, the queen herself. Strangely, it was another week before the two ladies could even bring themselves to discuss it, but when they did, they found they'd both experienced the same feeling of depression and loneliness.'

'Yes, I read about that mystery in a magazine,' remembered Audrey, switching off the TV. 'Certainly intriguing, but I seem to recall one theory was that they'd simply stumbled across a bit of fancy dress play-acting.'

'... but which didn't explain how the ladies had managed to identify features shown on maps drawn in 1780, but no longer there in 1901,' added Jack.

'I expect that's because they'd studied the history of the area before their visit. There's always a rational answer, love.'

'Okay, so how do you explain an incident that happened far more recently and close to here.' Jack scrolled up another page. 'Charity cited this one, but I wanted to check the facts for myself.'

'Which are ...?' Audrey was making an effort to sound reasonably tolerant.

'That in 1973, a coin collector by the name of Squirrel heard there was a stationer's shop in Great Yarmouth that sold a certain type of transparent envelope used for displaying coins. He'd never been there before, but knew how to find it. When he arrived he noticed the street was cobbled and the shop freshly painted. Inside was very old fashioned, as was the girl who served him. But she had the envelopes he wanted and charged just "one shilling" for three packets. This was when Britain was just converting to decimal currency, and so he gave her a five-pence coin which at that time was the same shape, size and value as a shilling. A week later he went back to the shop for more envelopes, but found it modernised and staffed by a mature lady who had no knowledge of the girl he described. She also insisted that they had no envelopes of the type he'd previously bought there.'

'Really? Move over, love, and let me read it for myself.' Audrey scanned the account with interest before slowly taking off her glasses. 'Just some sort of hallucination, surely? That previous experience was probably only a dream he'd had.'

'That would explain it, Aud, except for the fact that Mr Squirrel *still had* the envelopes he'd bought that day. When they checked, experts confirmed that, although his were new, they dated back to the 1920s and were long out of production.'

'You mean actual objects can move between time zones?'

'So it would seem, Aud, and, if so, at the same time Squirrel was left with envelopes long out of production, that shop assistant from the other time period would have been left examining an equally ambiguous five-pence coin depicting the head of a monarch she'd never heard of. In other words, while Squirrel was having a brief encounter with the past, the shop assistant was having one with the future.'

'This is all too much for me, Jack,' groaned Audrey. 'And one thing you're choosing to ignore is that both those encounters you've related, took place in settings that are almost the same now as they were then. In other words, you're only talking about people who could have been in period costume, whereas your Charity is trying to say that even the old wooden fishing boat that Lynsey was on, was part of this so-called "dimensional anomaly".'

'Quite, but it seems *things* can be spiritual as well as people.' Jack closed down the laptop. 'In fact, I remember from my Scotland Yard days, the story of how a London Transport double-decker bus was haunting Cambridge Gardens in Notting Hill.'

'A bus?'

'Yes, a number seven actually that always appeared at about one-fifteen in the morning. It seemed to enjoy harassing motorists and, on one sighting, caused a car to hit a wall and kill the driver. Witnesses reckoned the bus simply vanished afterwards. The sightings started in the late 1930s and the last was in May 1990.'

'But why would a bus, of all things, come back in spirit form?'

'I have no idea, anymore than I do of many strange things that happen in this world, but reports of spiritual things are by no means uncommon. Through the centuries there have been hundreds of sightings of ghost-ships.'

'Like the Flying Dutchman, you mean? Surely, they're all just myths and legends made up by drunken sailors. You can't believe everything you hear or read, Jack?'

'No, of course not.' Jack put the laptop to one side,' but what *I am* saying is that the solution to some mysteries is way outside our normal conception of things.'

'Well, I don't think the solution to Lynsey Butterick's problems lie in the supernatural,' huffed Audrey, picking up the jumper she was knitting for their little grandson, 'and she certainly won't be able to use it as a defence in a court of law.'

'I think she'd pooh-pooh any such idea quicker than anyone,' agreed Jack, 'and I've told Charity Howden not to mention it to Bailey either.' He sat back in his armchair. 'That's not to say I won't. I've arranged to see him at Bethel Street tomorrow morning.'

'Am I right in thinking that a theory is hatching in that devious mind of yours?' asked Audrey suspiciously, but without looking up from her clicking needles.

'Only the odd jigsaw pieces, Aud, and it's still to be seen if they ever fit together. I need the bigger picture which, hopefully, Bailey might help with tomorrow.'

'It'll be too late to save Lynsey though.' Audrey paused to sort out a knot in her wool. 'Isn't she up in front of the magistrates in the afternoon?'

'Yep, but not in person. It'll be a virtual hearing, through a two-way video link between the courtroom and a specially designated room in the PIC where she'll sit.'

'Good heavens, how things change. So where's the defending solicitor?'

'Either in court in the usual way or sitting beside his client in the PIC ... though I rather think that Lynsey won't need one. If I know her, she'll be defending herself.'

'Is that wise? I thought the courts never encouraged anyone to act for themselves.'

'They don't, but she *is* a barrister, Aud, and well versed in legal argument. And, anyway, this won't be a trial. In serious crimes like murder, the magistrates, guided by a legal advisor, only determine whether there's a case to answer and then, if so, refer it up to the Crown Court.'

'So will she still be held on remand?'

'I sincerely hope not. These days, it's only those still posing a threat to the general public who aren't allowed out on bail.'

'But, presumably, that will be with conditions attached?'

'Oh, yes. She'll be given the date of her first Crown Court hearing, ordered not to make contact with any of the parties involved, and possibly have to report regularly to a police station.'

'So, will she be able to return to London?'

'Probably. In most cases like this, the police and courts like the accused well away from the crime scene.'

'But, if she's going to defend herself, how can she establish a case if she's away from the very area in which it all happened, and not allowed to make contact with anyone involved?'

'Good point, Aud. I don't know how she'll handle that one.'

'But you still think she's innocent, Jack?'

'Yes, I do.'

Audrey stopped knitting, put it on her lap and sat obviously considering something. Then, mind made up, she said, 'Jack, if the courts allow it, she'll have to come and stay with us so you can help her sort out this whole dreadful mess.' Then, obviously confident her suggestion was the right one, she resumed her knitting. 'From what you tell me, that young woman's going to need all the help she can get.'

* * *

Chapter Thirteen

In all his investigative work with DI Bailey, Jack had never taken credit for any of their successful outcomes, preferring instead for them to be stepping-stones on the detective's well-earned rise up the promotional ladder. What he had accrued, however, was a fair balance of goodwill and ready access to Bailey's office, confidences and thoughts. It wasn't a privilege ever to be enjoyed by a member of the public, but Jack's past police rank and experience made it possible, and especially now on this Monday morning, as he entered Norwich's Bethel Street Station and asked to see the DI.

'Jack. I knew it wouldn't be long before this case had you on my doorstep.' Bailey stood up to shake hands, shirtsleeves rolled up, tie loosened and seemingly glad of a break from the mountain of work before him.

'You know me too well, Bailey, but first things first ... how's the girl?'

'Miss Butterick? Hardly a "girl", Jack, but she's okay. According to the Major Investigation Team at Yarmouth, she's spent enough time in police cells as a barrister not to be too shocked by the reality of it all.'

'Good, and I'm hoping it won't be for much longer. Has she been charged yet?'

Bailey nodded. 'Yes, murder. No doubt a clever lawyer will later get that mitigated to manslaughter, but for the moment it's the top indictment.'

'But you won't oppose bail?'

Bailey sat turning a ruler over in his hands. 'No, I don't think so, Jack. We've checked and, as you'd expect, her record is completely unblemished.'

'Good. I hope before it comes to Crown Court I'll be able to prove her innocence.'

'You really believe she *is* innocent don't you?' Bailey shook his head in disbelief and tapped the bulging file. 'For crikey's sake, Jack, it's all there, as clear as can be.'

'I see a situation that's far from clear, Bailey. I want to find out what really happened in the yard that night, because I think so far we've only scraped the surface.' Jack took out a scrap of paper and handed it to the DI. 'Just to remind you, this is our address. I'd like you to get word to

Lynsey that this is the one she can give the court if they allow her bail and permission to stay locally.'

Bailey frowned. 'Is that wise? Normally we don't allow contact with any other parties involved, and you yourself could well be called as a witness.'

'I'm also the only friend she's got hereabouts, and she needs someone to fight her corner.'

'Okay, Jack, I won't oppose it, but I'm sure the court will.' Bailey pointed the ruler warningly. 'And don't be so sure she'll be free after this afternoon's hearing anyway. Just because I'm not going to oppose bail, doesn't mean the CPS won't.'

'I'm sure Lynsey knows how to handle the Crown Prosecution Service.'

'I hope so, for her sake. The Major Investigation Team reckoned she was well able to look after herself,' admitted Bailey, with the glimmer of a smile.

'Did her story change at all?'

The DI shook his head. 'Nope. Continued to insist it was a different bloke she saw go over the side of a different boat, but ...' he paused to flick open his notebook, '... now we do have a witness who can confirm seeing a young woman arrive at the yard at the time Lynsey said she did.'

'Charity Howden?'

Bailey nodded. 'She rang me first thing this morning. Apparently, she's already made your acquaintance.'

'That's right. She and her French partner, Marcel Carbonne, live on a narrowboat. Through work, I've got to know them quite well and they have a mooring in the dyke where Borrett died.'

'... but weren't there during the critical time, unfortunately,' bemoaned Bailey. He shut the notebook. 'But at least we do now have confirmation that the vessel she saw Miss Butterick board was Borrett's steel one, which rather blows the wooden fishing boat story right out of the water.'

'Perhaps not the best of expressions under the circumstances, Bailey,' chided the ranger, 'and let me correct you on one point – Charity only saw a woman's vague outline in the fog that night and didn't positively identify her as Lynsey Butterick.'

'No, but it all fits, Jack, and further rubbishes the "different man" bit as well.'

'Not necessarily.' Jack decided not to pursue that particular line. 'Just out of interest, Bailey, in her interviews with the MIT at Yarmouth, did she explain just why she chose to abandon a law career in London to come and act for the likes of Borrett?'

'Only that he was offering good money and it gave her the excuse she wanted to escape the London rat race.'

'I can understand that,' said Jack, 'but what puzzles me is why Borrett specifically wanted *her* to represent him. In the car, she assured me she's not that experienced at the bar yet, has never handled civil cases, never knew him previously and, as far as she knows, has never worked for anyone else who did. Have you come up with any ideas?'

'Only that, in retrospect, it does seem to hint of stalking. It seems the Hinnerley brothers had a photo of her when they went to meet her at Norwich Station on Friday night. She recognised it as one that had appeared in a national newspaper when she was involved in some criminal case in the city. She can only think that Borrett saw it, formed an unhealthy fascination, and got his PA solicitor to hire her for the solar farm battle he had on his hands.'

'Feasible, I suppose,' acknowledged Jack, 'but I can think of cheaper ways to pursue someone you fancy. Certainly Borrett was a bit of an oaf, but he wasn't stupid and must've realised he'd never get away with unlawful detention and probable sexual assault, especially of a barrister. As for Lynsey, she was obviously scared stiff and did what she did to escape.'

'It's one thing acting in self-defence, Jack,' argued Bailey, 'but using an oil lamp as a weapon to bash someone over the head, set their boat on fire and then shove them over the side, is taking things a bit far.'

'She insists she only pushed him out of the way and he stumbled overboard.' Jack frowned. 'And as for the oil lamp ... the so-called weapon ... have you found that?'

'Not yet, and we can only assume it went overboard with Borrett. Seeing as Lynsey Butterick admits the assault anyway, it's not one of my top priorities right now.'

'But haven't you thought it strange that there should be an oil lamp there in the first place? *Merlin Magic* was a relatively modern boat with electrics and most mod cons, so why did Borrett have an oil lamp on board at all?'

'Possibly for emergency lighting but, I suspect, used that night for a bit of romantic ambience.'

'I've never thought the stink of paraffin that romantic.' Jack turned his nose up and grinned. 'No, Bailey, until you find that lamp, I won't believe there was one ... on *that* boat, but there would have been on the old boat Lynsey said she was on.'

'Oh come of it, Jack!' Bailey leaned back in his chair and put his hands behind his head. 'You don't believe all that rubbish about different boats and different men, do you? Granted, the poor woman might have been in some sort of traumatic shock after her terrifying experience, but the reality is what actually happened. What other possible explanation can there be?'

'You wouldn't believe me if I told you.' Jack didn't elaborate further, but simply shrugged and said, 'There are many strange aspects to this case, Bailey.'

'Well, that's one thing we both agree on,' granted the detective. He tapped the already thick file in front of him. 'For one thing, Mrs Borrett's suspicions.'

'You've actually spoken to her since it happened, then?' Jack, settled a little further into his chair. 'When was this?'

'Yesterday. I went down to Providence Farm to take a full statement.'

'How was she?'

'Pretty good, considering. In fact, *very* good. I got the impression that now she's over the initial shock, losing Bertie was probably the best thing that had happened to her since marrying the bloke. Apparently, he had a long list of mistresses, including Lucy Watling and, she suspects, some woman in a village downriver.'

'What makes her think that?'

'Only the fact that Bertie had been shooting off in the yard's workboat at odd times.'

'But she has no idea where?'

'No, but he was always gone for a while.'

'Interesting,' Jack made a mental note, 'but coming back to the crime itself, did she say what she was actually doing at the boatyard so early in the morning?'

'Yes she did. Apparently, she was well aware of hubby's fascination for the young barrister and his intention of meeting her on board the boat on Friday night. Her plan was to go down early Saturday morning and catch them *flagrante delicto*.'

'And instead found a blazing boat and Bertie in the dyke ...' Jack's eyebrows half-rose, '... if she's telling the truth. Hard to think she was jealous of Borrett, Bailey.'

'Quite, but I don't think she *was* jealous as such. It was more a case of protecting her financial interests. Apparently their marriage was on the rocks and Bertie had made it clear he was filing for a divorce.'

'... whereas, if she got grounds for her own, the financial settlement would be more in her favour, which also means it wouldn't matter to her whether Bertie was alive or dead.'

'I'm not so sure,' said Bailey, picking up the ruler again and turning it over in his hands, 'because she also admitted knowing that Bertie was planning to cut her out of his will.'

'Ah, that puts a different complexion on things,' admitted Jack, 'because Bertie dead now means she'll inherit everything after all.'

'Exactly, but only by the skin of her teeth, thanks to Cecil Watling.'

'The missing PA?'

'The one and only. Apparently he should have had the new will finalised by now, but it seems he hasn't for other reasons.'

'Which are ...?'

'You might hear for yourself soon enough, because I've made further enquiries and asked Mrs Watling to come here this morning for an interview.' Bailey put down the ruler with an amused smile, as though he already knew the answer to what he was about to ask. 'Want to sit in on it, Jack?'

'The lovely Lucy?' Jack nodded enthusiastically. 'You bet.'

Spot on cue, Bailey's DC came into the office and said, 'Mrs Watling to see you, boss.'

'Good, show her up.'

* * *

Lucy Watling sat in the chair beside Jack and facing Bailey across his desk. Dressed in dark trousers and a white top, she certainly looked the picture of feminine innocence even though the nervous movement of her fingers and dark-ringed eyes indicated she was feeling anything but.

'I presume you've still had no word from your husband, Mrs Watling?' enquired Bailey.

Lucy sniffed and, despite rather theatrically dabbing under each eye with a tissue, answered 'No' with a definite catch in her voice.

'But he was Bertram Borrett's Personal Assistant?'

'Yes.'

'For how long?'

'About nine months.'

'And before that, he was a practising solicitor with a law firm here in Norwich.'

'Yes.'

'What made him make a career change?'

'Oh, he was just fed up with that sort of work and felt the need of something different.'

Bailey leaned a little closer across his desk. 'Mrs Watling, let me give you some advice. Whatever the outcome of this interview, it will help you ... and me ... enormously, if you are completely honest from the start. Now, let me ask you again ... *why* did your husband leave his former solicitor's job?'

Lucy cast anxious eyes towards Jack for reassurance and found none. Instead, she took a deep breath and said, 'There was a difference of opinion with the legal partners.'

'Quite a considerable difference, actually,' Bailey flicked open another file on his desk, 'to the extent that he was asked to resign. To save you the embarrassment, Mrs Watling, let me spell it out for you, because we visited your husband's old firm and had a chat. They explained how, at that time, he was handling personal injury claims and that you worked for the doctor supplying most of the expert testimony. What they eventually discovered was that you had been invoicing the legal firm for twice what the doctor was charging. The invoices required payment to a business name whose bank account you and Cecil had set up between you. Cecil would ensure his firm paid that amount to that account and you would make a payment to the doctor's account for his original charge.' Bailey sat back. 'Quite a nice little scam you had going there.'

'Well ... perhaps the accounting was ... well, perhaps a little unorthodox ...'

'Not "unorthodox", Mrs Watling,' interrupted Bailey, frowning, 'it was downright fraudulent. And you would have got away with it if the principal partner of Cecil's firm hadn't met the doctor involved at a social event, and complained about the high cost of his opinions. You were both lucky not to end up in gaol when the full scale of your embezzlement became known.'

'Yes, well, it was decided not to take any action.'

'Only if you paid back the full amount you'd stolen and both resigned immediately.' Lucy made no response to this and Bailey leaned forward again. 'Is that right, Mrs Watling?'

The reply was barely audible. 'Yes.'

'Good, we've got that straight.' Bailey sat back once more. 'And so, your husband then took the job as Bertram Borrett's PA?'

'Yes, because we needed the money and somewhere to live. Although Cecil hadn't been called before the Law Council and struck off, the word had got around and he was blacklisted from any other law firm. We heard Bertie ... Mr Borrett ... needed someone, Cecil applied and got the job.'

'I can imagine it was very useful for "Bertie" having a bent solicitor working for him,' said Bailey, 'but, unfortunately for your husband, Cecil, it was even better having one with a promiscuous wife.'

'What do you mean by that?' asked Lucy with the false indignation of one who already knew the answer.

'Just what I said. I had a long chat with Mrs Borrett yesterday and she made no bones about the fact that you'd been having an affair with her husband. She said half the village knew too.'

'Perhaps we did have a casual fling,' admitted Lucy with a little sniff, 'but that ended some while ago now.'

'A couple of weeks ago, actually,' reminded Bailey, glancing at his notebook, 'and since then your husband Cecil has lost his job and you're both being slung out of the cottage that went with it.'

Lucy blinked twice. 'What exactly are you saying?'

'I'm saying, Mrs Watling, that both you and your husband had a motive for murdering Bertram Borrett.'

That at least had the effect of making the lady sit upright in her chair. 'You're not serious. Why would I want to murder ... anyone?'

'Possibly for a number of reasons, the most likely being revenge.'

'Oh, I soon got over that business.' Lucy gave a little gesture with her tissue as though she were waving away a distracting fly. 'Cecil and I managed to iron out our marital differences and were all set to begin a new life.'

'Yes, that's what worries me,' said Bailey, fixing the lady through narrowed eyes, 'because it seems that you and your husband getting your act together usually results in someone else ending up that much poorer. Why, for instance, had your husband been sacked?'

'Just Mr Borrett flexing his muscles again. He wanted the cottage for his new lady lawyer, so she'd live near enough to Providence Farm to come running whenever he wanted her ... and, I bet, not just for legal advice.'

'Quite possibly, but, according to Elsie Borrett, it was because her husband had discovered certain irregularities in one of his bank accounts.'

'I honestly don't know anything about that,' pleaded Lucy.

'That remains to be seen,' said Bailey, sitting back in his chair, 'but what *is* clear is that both you and your husband had ample motive to murder Bertie Borrett.'

The colour drained out of Lucy's face. She blinked nervously and sat forward as she stammered, 'M ... murder ... us ... of course not.'

'Why not? With you and your husband's past history, any court case would've seen you both heading for a custodial sentence. Avoiding that might well have made a supposed drowning accident in the dyke, well worth while.' Bailey sat back. 'Did either you or your husband previously know Miss Lynsey Butterick?'

'No, we'd never heard of her before Bertie ... Mr Borrett asked my husband to secure her services.'

'Do you know why Mr Borrett asked for her specifically?'

'No. From what Cecil told me, he was just asked to contact her and make her a generous offer.' Lucy made a brave attempt at indignation. 'My Cecil was only doing his job, Inspector. He'd never murder anyone. He's just not the type.'

'I'd know that better if I could talk to the man,' stressed Bailey. 'So, where is he, Mrs Watling?'

'I don't know where my husband is, or why he left,' admitted Lucy with another little sniff.

For a few seconds, Bailey closed one eye, as though studying this flirtatious lady through a telescope. 'No, Mrs Watling, I really don't think you do.'

Feeling slightly off the hook, Lucy decided now was a good time to fight back.

'There are others though, who would have liked to see Bertie Borrett dead. It was obvious he had big plans for that London lawyer, so I believe her when she says she had to fight him off and push him overboard to get away. But what about the grieving widow herself? She's got a fancyman of her own, so having that louse of a husband dead works just fine for her. But one thing I can assure you of is that Bertie Borrett would never have taken Cecil to court on money issues. Believe me, the last thing he'd have wanted was anyone looking into his business affairs.'

'Which is why the police are now sealing your husband's office as we speak, and putting a legal hold on all Mr Borrett's transactions. Tomorrow I'll be bringing a police auditor to Providence Farm and he'll go through everything with a tooth comb.' Bailey nodded towards the door. 'You can go now, Mrs Watling, but don't leave the area without my permission.'

'But ... but ... I was hoping to, perhaps, have a little holiday abroad very soon.'

'To presumably join your husband?'

'I told you ... I don't know where he is.'

'Yes, well if you find out, Mrs Watling, don't hesitate to let me know.' Bailey flicked shut his file. 'Failing that, I'll see you again tomorrow.'

* * *

'Cheers, Jack.' DI Bailey raised his glass. 'So, what did you make of Lucy Watling?'

Detective and Ranger were at the *Adam and Eve*, a flint-built public house with curved Dutch gables, standing adjacent to the similarly constructed walls of the Cathedral Close and opposite the Norwich Law Courts where both men would be attending Lynsey's afternoon hearing.

'Bit of a mixture, really.' Seated at a corner table in the lower bar, Jack frowned slightly. 'Certainly, she knows more than she's letting on and I'm sure she has a strong suspicion of just where husband Cecil is right now, but I think she might have been telling the truth when she admitted not knowing *why* he'd cleared off quite so suddenly.'

'That's what I thought,' agreed Bailey. 'Certainly she's pinning her hopes on joining him soon ... wherever he is.'

'Well, you've scuppered that idea,' grinned Jack, 'but I got the impression it came as a complete surprise to find out that Bertie Borrett had sussed their scam. My guess is that right now she's cursing a husband who's blown it and left her to face the music.' Jack glanced around to check if their meals were coming, but also to ensure they weren't being overheard. He lowered his voice. 'The thing is, Bailey, there are several characters back there, including Cecil Watling, with motive enough to kill poor old Bertie, so how can you still be so adamant that Lynsey Butterick is your guilty party?'

'Because she admits she was responsible, Jack, and furthermore, from what I've heard of Cecil, I think Lucy Watling was correct when she said her husband wasn't capable of committing murder. And why would he bother anyway if he was all set to do a runner? Likewise, I rule out Lucy because, if she thought they'd got away with the scam, she didn't have a motive either.'

'... except revenge at being dumped,' reminded Jack. 'I actually saw that happen, and I can asure you Borrett didn't spare her feelings.'

'Yes, but it appears she was reconciled with Cecil soon after, so surely that would've softened the blow.'

'The blow I saw her subjected to in the car park would take some softening, I can tell you.'

'How sad,' muttered Bailey, insincerely. 'But how about her revelation that Elsie Borrett had a lover? Do you know anything about that?'

'Possibly ...' Their meals arrived and Jack waited until the waitress was well clear, '... but I need to check things further before I stick my neck out.'

Bailey knew better than to press for details. 'Okay, Jack, but perhaps I'll find out more myself when I'm back at Providence Farm tomorrow.'

'Perhaps,' grunted Jack while tucking into his steak and kidney pudding, 'and while you're in that area, I suggest you give the Hinnerley brothers a good grilling.'

'Why? You think they may be involved?'

'I think they're involved in *something*. They're the local no-goods who finally found their niche working for Borrett. Now their boss is curling his toes up, I suspect they're helping themselves to anything worth a bob or two from the yard.' Jack told Bailey about the missing fittings from *Merlin Magic*.

The DI paused for a mouthful of lasagne. 'I had a police guard on the boat for as long as forensics were checking it, but I'm investigating murder, Jack, not petty thieving. If Mrs Borrett wants to report a theft, we'll deal with it. Otherwise, my team has more important work to do.'

'... unless those fittings were somehow connected to Bertie's death.'

'I can't see how, but if you've any thoughts, Jack, I'd like to hear them.'

'Nothing specific yet, Bailey, but I think you'd be well advised to get a full background check on the victim. Borrett was a scrap-metal dealer down in London. Nothing wrong with that, but it took a lot of money to buy Providence Farm and I'd be interested to know if he had any previous.'

'It's already being done,' assured Bailey, finishing his meal and pushing away the plate. 'Hopefully, we'll be getting the gen, if any, by tomorrow.'

'Good.' Jack waited while the waitress cleared the table and brought the coffees they'd pre-ordered. 'There is another thing you might check out with the Met when they get back to you. You remember I mentioned Charity Howden's live-in boyfriend on the narrowboat?'

'Yep, a Frenchman called Marcel Carbonne wasn't it? What about him?'

'Well ...' Jack explained Carbonne's run-in with authority and subsequent charge and court case.

'But you say he was let off with a warning?'

'That's right. The magistrate accepted that it was self-defence and the case was dropped, but I know Marcel's worried it might look bad in your investigation, so it would be good to get that sorted from the start.'

'Always best,' agreed Bailey, writing the details in his notebook. 'I'll get that full case record as well.'

'I'll be interested to know what it throws up and also what you find in Cecil's office tomorrow. I'm on duty, so perhaps we can meet up at the boatyard for a chat.'

'Sound's good,' agreed Bailey, stirring sugar into his coffee, 'though it won't be as pleasant a venue as this.' He looked about him. 'Is this really the oldest pub in Norwich?'

'Apparently so. It was first referred to in 1249, and said to be a watering hole for the men building the Cathedral, though this building standing today dates from the 17th century. It's got form though. This lower bar we're sitting in used to be the cellar, and they discovered the remains of a medieval monk when they were renovating it in the 1970s.'

'Did they now? And what was a monk doing in a boozer anyway?'

'The Benedictine's owned the place actually,' explained Jack. 'They ran the Great Hospital, just down the road. How one of them came to meet his end here, we'll never know, but perhaps it's his ghost that still haunts the place.'

'Well, he has good taste, I'll say that for him.' Bailey smiled and sat back. 'Why does every old building have to have a ghost story?'

'Perhaps it's because people experience things in them that they can't explain.' Jack took a sip of coffee. 'Like Lynsey Butterick's odd business. I've even had a paranormal explanation put forward for that.'

The DI paused, with his coffee cup halfway to his lips. 'Say that again.'

Jack explained Charity Howden's time-slip theory.

'So, now you're telling me my only witness is some sort of phantom-freak.' Bailey shook his head in despair. 'This case gets stranger by the day. You surely don't believe that rubbish do you, Jack?'

'No, though perhaps I'm not as ready as you to dismiss it out of hand. But what I do believe is that the answer to this whole business is far deeper and sinister than is first apparent.'

'It's already weird enough for me,' groaned Bailey, 'so when you have your solution, let me know. In the meantime ...' he glanced at his watch, gulped back the remains of his coffee and stood up, '... more earthly matters in this dimension, beckon. Come on, Jack, let's see if Lynsey Butterick is granted bail.'

* * *

ADAM · EV

Chapter Fourteen

'This is a bit different to the Magistrates' Courts I used to give evidence in, Bailey.'

After checking through security on the ground floor of this modern building, Jack and the DI were upstairs, sitting in the spacious main concourse outside Courts One and Two. It was the latter where prisoners on remand, like Lynsey, were to appear, either in person or by video link. An exact time couldn't be given for Lynsey's hearing, but she was eighth on the list, and a friendly court usher had promised to advise them when it would be time to go in. It wasn't difficult for Jack to identify the defendants awaiting their hearings, or the efficient-looking defence lawyers, clutching bulging files and scurrying about between courts or in and out of interview rooms.

'Yeah, I can imagine. It's certainly less intimidating for defendants these days, but we wouldn't want to revert back to the old Dickensian atmosphere.'

'Perhaps not,' conceded Jack, having felt more anxiety from patients in a dentist's waiting room than amongst some of the accused around him.

'Thinking of times past,' said Bailey, by way of conversation, 'did you know, prior to the building of these courts in the eighties, archaeologists found the remains of a Norman house. They preserved what was there and then built the courts above them. They even found an inside loo, which was very rare in those days. Pretty smelly, I should imagine, because it relied on the rise of the river level to flush it. The public can still look round the site on Heritage Open Days, so you ought to bring Audrey along.'

'I'm sure she'd be fascinated,' said Jack, absent-mindedly, because his attention was now taken by the opening of a door to one of the side rooms. Inside was a small booth containing a desk, chair and microphone in front of a video screen. A smartly dressed man could be seen standing up and gathering some papers together. 'What goes on in there, Bailey?'

'Defence solicitors direct video link to their clients in the PIC. Pre-hearing briefings and discussions ... that sort of thing.'

As the solicitor left the booth, he smiled and held the door open for the next user, a rather portly man of average height and thinning red hair, who simply pushed past him without eye contact or words of thanks. And then the booth door was firmly shut.

Contemplating the arrogance of some people and feeling the need to stretch his legs, Jack decided to take a walk down to reception where he'd seen some old remains displayed behind glass. It was on his way back, as he stopped to have a quick look inside the café, that the quiet general hubbub of hushed voices was disturbed by the slamming of a door. Jack looked round and saw that same man, having left the booth, now pacing up and down with a very flushed face. Obviously, not all had progressed as he would have liked. By the time Jack regained his seat, the usher had come out of Court Two to invite them in.

They went through the double doors into the courtroom, but not before the agitated lawyer from the booth had barged wordlessly in ahead of them and taken his seat at the defending solicitor's desk. As he flicked through some papers taken from his leather briefcase, Jack and Bailey took their places in the public seats at the back. The court was bright and well lit and Jack studied its layout.

Some things were much the same as in his old Scotland Yard days. On the bench sat the three magistrates. In the centre, and flanked by her slightly older male and female assistants, the chairperson, a lady who Jack judged to be in her early fifties. Just below them was their legal advisor, the justices' clerk, an efficient young woman in a smart trouser suit. Between her and the public seating were the lawyers, the Crown Prosecutor on the right and defence solicitor on the left. Next to the latter was the dock, separated by a glass screen, but today empty, its function replaced by the large wall-mounted video screens set either side of the court on which could be seen a young, tired-looking offender with his solicitor in the King's Lynn PIC. His case had just ended with a referral date to the Crown Court and now the clerk was standing and fingering a remote control. Instantly, that image was replaced by one of the Great Yarmouth PIC and the figure of Lynsey Butterick, sitting calmly behind a desk and microphone.

To Jack, she looked a very different Lynsey to the one he'd last seen that Saturday morning, just days ago. Now her blonde hair was gathered in a ponytail and gone were the jeans and tee-shirt, replaced by a smart blouse under a dark blue jacket. Doubtless, her familiarity of court procedure was working in her favour, but Jack still detected a slight nervousness in the way she turned a pen over and over in her hand.

The hearing began by the clerk standing facing the screen and asking

Lynsey to confirm her name, date of birth and address. She replied clearly, giving her address as a London one in the borough of Southwark.

'You are here today,' continued the clerk, 'to answer a charge of murder, in that on Saturday morning ...' she gave the date, '... you murdered one Bertram Borrett. Do you plead guilty or not guilty?'

'Not guilty.'

'These are the magistrates who will be hearing your case,' said the clerk, fingering the remote and bringing a small depiction of the bench, the full sized image of which Lynsey would be seeing, into one corner of the court screens.

'Good afternoon, Miss Butterick' said the chairperson, making virtual eye contact with the defendant.

'Good afternoon, ma'am.'

'And this is the Crown Prosecutor,' continued the clerk, using the remote to relay the appropriate images to the PIC, 'and this is Mr Rotherby-Jones, who will be representing you.'

'No he won't.' There was a stunned silence broken by Lynsey herself . 'I spoke to Mr Rotherby-Jones a short while ago and made it quite clear I would be representing myself at this hearing.'

'Ma'am,' said the defence attorney, standing up and addressing the bench, 'you will be well aware that Miss Butterick is indeed a qualified barrister, but you will also be aware of the inadvisability of anyone acting for themselves in a court of law.'

'Quite so,' agreed the magistrate. She turned to her screen view of Lynsey. 'Miss Butterick, are you determined to defend yourself in this matter?'

'Yes, ma'am. Very determined.'

The magistrate turned to the clerk, who already had the word-of-law at her fingertips. 'No-one can be forced to have professional representation, ma'am. It's every defendant's right to act as their own defence if they so wish.'

'And so, as a barrister, I rather think Miss Butterick regards herself more than eligible,' said the magistrate with a smile. She turned to the lawyer in court, still standing, somewhat aghast. 'There you have it, Mr Rotherby-Jones. It seems your services are herewith dispensed with.'

'Ma'am,' said the lawyer through gritted teeth, before giving a small bow and storming out of the court.

'Dispensed with all right,' said Jack in a smiling quiet aside, before the Crown Prosecutor stood to give a full and detailed account of the circumstances leading to Lynsey's arrest.

'Yes, thank you,' said the magistrate when the prosecutor had completed her brief. She then turned for a quick consultation with her assistants on either side before turning back to Lynsey's screen image. 'Miss Butterick, we have decided you do have a case to answer and, as a barrister, you will be well aware that this is one that will have to be heard in the Crown Court. Therefore we are remanding you in custody until then.'

Well prepared as ever, the clerk stood and announced the date, one month hence.

'Is that quite clear, Miss Butterick?' asked the magistrate.

'Yes, ma'am, but I am requesting that I be released on bail until that hearing.'

The magistrate frowned and looked to the Crown Prosecutor who stood up. 'Ma'am, the police have indicated they have no objection to bail, but the CPS feel it would not be advisable, owing to the seriousness of the charges.'

'Ma'am, as I will be representing myself,' spoke up Lynsey, 'I need to be able to organise my defence, and for that I need my liberty in the interim.'

The chairperson raised a questioning eye at the clerk and there was a delay as the legal advisor picked up a heavy volume and spent a few moments reading silently from a chosen page, before facing the bench once more and detailing legal precedents.

After a few minutes' discussion with her assistants, the chairperson faced Lynsey again. 'We need more time to come to a decision, so we will retire for a short break.' And, with that, everyone in the court stood as the three magistrates filed out through a door to the right.

Within ten minutes, the words 'All stand' warned of their return. Agreement reached, the chairperson addressed Lynsey once more. 'Miss Butterick, we have listened to your request and, though we cannot encourage anyone to undertake their own defence, we grant you bail to appear before the Crown Court on the day you have been given.'

'Thank you, ma'am.'

The clerk rose once more and faced Lynsey. 'Is the address you gave earlier, the one you wish your bail to be registered to?'

'No. I shall be remaining in Norfolk in order to have access to my defence witnesses.'

'What address will that be then?'

Lynsey read out Jack's name and address.

Now it was the turn of the Crown Prosecutor to get to her feet. 'Ma'am, we cannot allow this.' She consulted her file of notes. 'Mr Fellows will likely be a witness during the trial and, as you are well aware, one of the conditions of bail is that the defendant has no contact with any witness.'

'He'll be a witness for my defence, if anything,' countered Lynsey, 'added to which, Mr Fellows is an ex-Detective Superintendent of the Metropolitan Police and, as such, the person I would like to conduct investigations on my behalf.'

'The defence lawyer has to have equal access to the case as the prosecution,' advised the clerk, 'and therefore this application should be judged in that light.'

After another quick conference, the magistrate gave her judgement. 'Miss Butterick, the circumstances we have before us are indeed exceptional and our response to your request must be likewise. You will be allowed to stay at the address given, but you must advise us if you decide to change that. Additionally, we still require that you have no contact with any others connected to this case except with the permission of the police. Mr Fellows, however, will be allowed to act for you and have such contact. You are therefore released on bail herewith.'

'Thank you ma'am.'

And with that, the clerk switched off the link to Great Yarmouth and Lynsey's hearing had finished.

* * *

'This is amazing.' Lynsey paused from throwing Spike another stick to gaze again at the slow-moving river and still reedbeds stretching either side. 'It's a world away from where I've been the last couple of days.'

Audrey nodded sympathetically. 'I can imagine that, you poor thing.'

After the court hearing, Jack had driven straight to Great Yarmouth and collected Lynsey from the Police Investigation Centre at Gorleston. She'd emerged a little paler, but very relieved at her release, and full of gratitude for all the support being given by the Fellows. Driving homeward, Jack had made a conscious effort not to discuss the case and instead had given her the chance to quietly unwind as she watched the unfolding Broadland scene for the first time in daylight. Having been welcomed by Audrey, she'd revelled in a shower and enjoyed a home-made meal before jumping at Jack's suggestion of them all taking Spike for his evening walk. Now the Border Collie was leading them along the narrow bank towards the old skeleton mill on the river's bend.

'You did the right thing staying, Lynsey,' said Jack, noticing the change that had already come over the young lawyer since her release.

'Yes, I know I did. In some ways it would have been easy to scuttle back to London, but here's where I'll find the answers to this mess I've got myself into, and besides, there's no way I would give Miles the pleasure of saying "I told you so".'

'That must be Rotherby-Jones, the man who wanted to defend you this afternoon?'

'Yes. He's a fellow-barrister in the same chambers as me. Given half a chance though, he'd like to share more than office space.'

'But you don't feel the same,' guessed Audrey, picking up the dismissive tone of Linsey's words.

'No, not at all. He's been chasing me for a year now and said he'd go to any lengths to stop me coming here. What he never realised was that *he* was one of the reasons I wanted to leave.'

'Obviously not someone to be put off easily,' said Jack, taking Spike's stick and throwing it back along the path. 'I presume he just took it upon himself to act as your defence this afternoon?'

'Yes, which is typical of the man. Against my better judgement, I stupidly contacted him to ask for some clothes to replace the ones I'd lost in the boat fire. Being Miles, he straightway drove them up himself and arrived at the PIC on Sunday afternoon. He wanted to see me, but I refused a meeting, and told him to just leave the clothes with the duty officer, which probably sounds dreadfully ungrateful but, if you knew him like I do, you'd understand.'

'From what I saw of him, I understand completely, but he obviously subscribes to the theory that anyone who defends themselves has an idiot for a client.'

'Very much so ... and he might be correct,' she added with a sigh, 'but, apart from not wanting to be beholden to him in any way, I also saw that by defending myself I could push for bail and stay in Norfolk, thanks to your kind hospitality.'

'It's the least we could do,' said Audrey as they reached the old mill. 'Both our daughters have left home, so we've plenty of room to put you up.' In the west, the early summer sun would soon be dipping towards the horizon, its weakening rays highlighting a marsh harrier soaring above in search of supper. It was time to turn back. 'You've had a rotten introduction to the Broads, Lynsey, so it's about time you saw how beautiful and therapeutic they can really be.'

'Yes, friends of mine in London hired a cruiser here last summer and just fell in love with the area. Looking at their photos, I could see why, and so, with Borrett's offer of work, it seemed fated that I should take the job and sample Broadland for myself.' She gave a sad little smile. 'Ill-fated, as it turned out, but looking at this view right now and experiencing the peace, beauty and tranquillity it evokes, I still can't bring myself to regret it.'

'And I hope you never will ...' Jack gave a reassuring smile back, '... especially when we've sorted out this whole rotten business.'

'Thanks, Jack ... and you too Audrey, for all you're doing.' They moved off again as Spike forged ahead. 'You don't know what it means to have you on my side ... someone believing in me, because I'm not sure DI Bailey does.'

'Oh, I don't know, Lynsey. He's a man who always keeps an open mind, and I suspect even he's beginning to realise that there's more to this than meets the eye.'

'... and if anyone's going to find out what that is, it'll be my husband,' added Audrey, with a long-suffering look behind a proud smile. 'If I know my Jack, he'll have found the truth before very long, and then you'll be able to put it all behind you and go back to your chambers in London.'

But Lynsey shook her head. 'I'm not so sure. Over the last year or so, I've been becoming increasingly disenchanted with the law. That's another reason I took this job up here with Bertie Borrett.'

'But I thought being a barrister must be one of the most glamorous of professions,' persisted Audrey.

'It is, unless you're a defence lawyer, when some judges and prosecutors view you as not much above the criminals you're defending. Luckily, I don't really mind what anyone thinks of me as long as I get justice, but the trouble is, it doesn't pay much either. Most of my work was done on Legal Aid for minimum fees, which you have to wait an eternity to receive. People think barristers are rolling in money, but I can assure you I'm not. Being from a humble background, I don't have the luxury of private income and, quite honestly, I was finding it pretty difficult to make ends meet.' Lynsey paused to watch a great crested grebe pop to the surface with a small fish in its mouth. 'In reality, the only lawyers who make real money are those specialising in civil cases.'

'... like Bertie Borrett's solar farm dispute? Presumably, he was making it worth your while to drop everything and come up here?'

'Yes indeed,' she freely admitted. 'The package was certainly tempting, especially as he'd paid me several thousands in advance.'

'Really? That was very generous of him wasn't it?'

'In some ways, yes, though a proportion of fees paid in advance isn't unusual. What was illogical though, was that he should want me to represent him at all, a lawyer with virtually no experience in such cases.'

'I think we know the answer to that,' said Audrey, meaningfully. 'He was obviously taken with your looks, even though he'd never met you.'

'Thought about in retrospect, none of it makes sense. When Miles spoke to me this afternoon by video link before the hearing, he said I must have been mad to go on that old fishing boat with a man I'd never met.'

'So, did you discuss the case with him then?' asked Jack.

'No, but he seemed to have all the relevant details. I can only assume he'd got them from the CPS.'

'Is that normal, without direct instructions?'

'Not really, but if Miles gets something into his head, he becomes pretty determined.'

'So it would seem,' said Jack thoughtfully as he watched Spike, tail wagging wildly, snuffling down a rabbit hole. He nodded towards the river. 'Well, I'm back on duty on the Yare again tomorrow, so I suggest you have an easy day, Lynsey. Why not take yourself off for a long walk with Audrey and see if you can recall anything else, however insignificant, that might throw some light on it all.'

'I've been thinking of nothing else since it happened, Jack, but perhaps being in this wonderful environment will help.'

'Let's hope so.' What Jack didn't say was that it had already helped him. There was still a long way to go, but already the germ of a theory was beginning to take hold.

* * *

Chapter Fifteen

Tuesday morning found the Southern Rivers grey and mournful. Setting off on his patrol, Jack hoped it wouldn't prevent Audrey and Lynsey carrying out their planned ramble to the boardwalk and viewing platform overlooking Barton Broad, followed by a leisurely lunch at Neatishead's White Horse Inn. Some good fresh Norfolk air was what that city girl needed to rekindle her fighting spirit, but she needed ammunition too and that was his job.

So far, he hadn't provided anything other than surmise, but tonight he hoped he might just find some answers to at least one part of the mystery. Before that was the meeting he intended to have with Bailey. Though the DI still regarded Lynsey as his prime suspect, Jack knew he had many more lines of enquiry yet to investigate. It would be interesting to hear what the audit of the Providence Farm office produced, and also the results of the DI's own interview with the Hinnerley brothers.

These and many other thoughts were all turning over in Jack's head as he cruised upriver on the flood, intending to return after midday on the ebb. On this midweek day, the river was mercifully lacking in other traffic. It did however, provide one gladdening and rare sight in the form of a grey seal, far from its North Sea home, but seemingly enjoying a sojourn on smoother waters as it dived and rolled just below the surface. It disappeared completely as Jack cruised slowly past its last seen position, but when he looked astern, there was its be-whiskered head and two bright eyes, staring after him as though cheated of company and unsure as to whether to follow the launch any further upriver.

For Jack, the decision was rather more elementary and, with no further distractions or problems en route, he was well past Cantley by the time the flow started to slacken. He was scanning ahead for a wider stretch of river in which to turn when his mobile rang.

'Morning, Bailey. How are things going?'

'Slowly. I'm at Providence Farm at present, and will be for an hour or so yet. Any chance of a quick meet at the crime-scene about two pm?'

Jack checked his watch. 'That would work well. I'll be there. Any news to report?'

'Some.'

'I look forward to hearing it.'

Jack rang off and continued looking ahead for the best place to swing the launch around. He knew this river well and recognised the feature just coming up on the port side. Bringing the launch to dead slow so as to keep down his turning circle, he studied it more intently while wondering just why he had never considered this possibility before. It was something else he would need to explore very soon.

That would be another day though, as now he needed to be heading back. With the wheel of the launch hard over and the revs back up, he swung around in a tight one-eighty that took him once more downriver towards the village dyke and his meeting with Bailey.

* * *

Easing down the dyke and passing the parish moorings, he came across *Faith and Hope*, back on its berth, but with no sign of its liveaboards. Further on he passed Admiral Ashfordby's *Curlew* and continued on to the boatyard where the figure of Bailey was just emerging from behind the main shed. The detective smiled and waved. 'Chuck us your lines, Jack, and I'll make you fast.'

'Thanks, mate.' While the detective managed two turns and a tangle on a couple of quay-posts, Jack shut down the engine and grabbed his lunch bag. 'Hop onboard, Bailey. Catering's limited to coffee, I'm afraid, but at least it's hot.' He poured two mugfuls from the flask and handed one to the DI who was settling himself down in a corner of the open cockpit. 'So, what's happening?'

'Not as much as I'd like, but I've got my DC and the auditor still up at Providence Farm going through Cecil Watling's papers. Earlier on, I had a diver down in there ...' Bailey indicated just astern of the launch, '... looking for the oil lamp Lynsey used to hit Borrett.'

'And ...?'

'... no sign of it.'

'Doesn't surprise me. How about the Hinnerley brothers? I thought you were going to meet them here for a chat.'

'That was the plan. They were told to be here first thing, but they never showed.' Bailey turned up the collar of his wax jacket and took an appreciative sip of his steaming coffee. 'I tried to call them to say they'd now be enjoying the hospitality of the station, but no reply as yet.'

'Always a sign of guilt for something, Bailey.'

'Guilt for what? You got any theories, Jack?'

'Some, but they're still a jumble of bits and pieces. It's a case of putting them together but, unlike a jigsaw, I'm missing the big picture on the box lid.'

'Tell me about it,' groaned Bailey, staring despairingly up the dyke.

'I will once I've checked something out.' Jack warmed his hands around his mug and glanced up to the skyline above the village where the tower of St Mark's Church stood aloof. 'I'll be nosing around up there tonight.'

'For what?'

'Oh, just some answers, talking of which, did the Met get back to you with any gen on Borrett's past?'

'Yes, though not a lot to go on. Plenty of suspicion, but no charges. Seems they linked him to several metal thefts, but couldn't actually nail him.'

'Hmm. It would be interesting to know just which jobs they suspected him of being involved in. Any chance of something more specific, Bailey?'

'Why not,' replied the DI in a strained, sarcastic voice. 'I'll call them again first thing tomorrow. I haven't got much to do, so it'll help pass the time.'

'Yeah, sorry ...' Jack knew all too well the overwhelming volume of any senior detective's workload, '... but I think it might be important. If nothing else, it might explain where Borrett's wealth came from, though whether it's connected to his death remains to be seen.'

'I'm beginning to wonder what's connected to what around here,' grumbled Bailey, before pointing to Charity Howden's narrowboat just a few hundred yards down the dyke. 'Scotland Yard also sent me the details of the little trouble they'd had with the French chap off that one.'

'Marcel?' Jack shrugged. 'I just wanted you to confirm his story that he clouted a bloke who was badgering Charity.'

'... which is basically what happened,' confirmed Bailey, frowning, 'but it was more than just "a clout", Jack. Seems he broke the fellow's jaw in two places and put him in hospital for a fortnight.'

'Really? He's a fit-looking lad all right, but I'm surprised he could be that violent.'

'So was I. While the diver was doing his stuff, Marcel wandered down the dyke to see what was going on, which gave me the opportunity to have a direct word with him about it.'

'And what was his explanation?'

'Only that he'd had some training in martial arts and rather let his emotions get the better of him.' Bailey paused to flick a mosquito from his sleeve. 'He's certainly a likeable chap, but obviously someone well capable of assaulting Borrett and dumping him in the dyke.'

'But hardly likely,' said Jack. 'For a start, he doesn't have a motive and has every reason to keep his nose clean. He and Charity are a devoted couple, only just in the neighbourhood, and seem happy to live a simple life afloat.'

'It's immaterial anyway, as he says he was on their narrowboat at the *Beauchamp Arms* that night until Charity arrived back on her bike in the early hours.'

'Are there any witnesses to confirm his story?'

'I sent a PC to interview the landlord, who said they'd eaten at the pub that night and that he'd actually spoken to Marcel, who was indeed fitting a chart- plotter. He noticed the boat wasn't there the following morning, so I presume they went on to Reedham as they said.'

'Have you interviewed Charity yet?'

'Not here, but I did have a brief chat while she was cleaning at Providence Farm. Inevitably, she brought the discussion round to her ridiculous slip-in-time theory and all that rubbish.' Bailey sat back and contemplated his empty cup. 'In spite of that though, it's difficult to see how either of those two can be involved. She's slightly away with the fairies, and he's a typical Frenchman and as laid back as they come.'

'That's a fact, is it?'

'What is?'

'That he's French.'

'Oh yes. I checked his passport myself. He's a bona fide French citizen all right.' Bailey frowned slightly. 'What makes you ask that, Jack? Do you have doubts?'

'No, just something said.' He shook away trifling thoughts. 'So, how have you left things?'

'Only that I've told them they'll have to give DNA swabs to my DC so we can eliminate them completely.'

'Has everyone else been tested?'

'Yep, all except our lovely Hinnerley brothers and we'll get theirs just as soon as we can.'

'Any results yet?'

'No, they'll take a few days and I'm not too hopeful when we do. The forensic boys couldn't find much in Borrett's boat, what with it being burned and half-submerged, but it'll be good to check what we do have.' Bailey looked further down the dyke to where *Curlew* stirred at her moorings. 'That sailing boat belongs to Admiral Ashfordby, doesn't it?'

'Yes. Have you spoken to him yet?'

'No, but I know he's been having a battle with Borrett over the solar farm project, and he did seem very attentive to Elsie, who I reckon is also holding something back.' Bailey handed his cup back to Jack. 'I know it doesn't make sense that someone of his rank and age should be having a fling with the victim's much-younger wife, let alone commit murder, but he was down here that morning at the same time as Mrs Borrett. He said he'd seen the blaze from his cottage, was worried about his boat, and came down here to investigate.'

'Except I walked through the village Sunday evening and found that you can't see the boatyard from his place.'

'Perhaps he just saw the glow from the flames ... unless you've other ideas.'

'Possibly, but I'll know whether I'm right or wrong after tonight.' Jack screwed the top back onto the flask and stowed away the lunch bag. 'In the meantime, thanks for keeping me in the picture and sorry I've not been more forthcoming.'

'I expect you've got your reasons, Jack, but there is a favour you can do *me* now.'

'Go on.'

Bailey indicated up the hill in the direction of Providence Farm. 'I'll be going up there later to see if they've found anything, but first I want to have another word with Lucy Watling. I'd like you to hear what's said, but it would be stretching things a bit for you to join me there. I'd bring her down here, but the boatyard's all locked and bolted so, okay if we use this launch?'

'Of course. I can spare another hour.'

'Great.' Bailey got straight on his mobile.

* * *

'Thanks for coming, Mrs Watling. I hope it wasn't too tiring.'

After Bailey's call, Lucy's appearance had taken some while, explained by the fact she'd had to come from Providence Farm on foot. Now, sitting in the launch with the DI and Jack, high-heeled boots thrown to one side, she massaged sore feet obviously unused to walking and certainly in such inappropriate footwear.

'I don't know why you couldn't have had a chat with me up there, seeing as our car's been impounded by your forensic people. I've got better things to do than tramp around these God-forsaken lanes.'

'I'm sure you have,' Bailey replied insincerely, 'but I want to talk to you about things you might not want others to know.'

'So, why's *he* here?' she asked with a cursory nod to Jack.

'These rivers and dykes fall under Mr Fellows' jurisdiction, and he's helping with the technical aspects of this case.'

It was an answer, vague as it was, that seemed to satisfy Lucy. 'All right. So, what is it you want to talk about that's so private?'

'Just how much you knew of the embezzlement your husband was indulging in at Providence Farm.'

'I don't know what you mean.'

'Yes you do, Mrs Watling. I told you last time we met, of Elsie Borrett being aware of some dubious transactions being made on her husband's overseas account just days before his death. That was the reason you two were going to be thrown out of your cottage and be left penniless.' Bailey leaned back against the cockpit coaming. 'In my book, that's motive enough to want Borrett out of the way.'

Lucy stopped massaging her feet and sat bolt upright with feigned indignation. 'I hope you're not suggesting again that my Cecil had anything to do with Bertie Borret's death?'

'It's difficult to suggest anything right now, seeing as your husband has disappeared from the scene.' Bailey eased his tone just a little. 'Have you heard from him since we last spoke, Lucy?'

She shook her head. 'No.'

'Or have any idea of where he might be?'

'No ... no idea. I wish I had.'

'Ah, well there we might be able to help you,' confided Bailey, leaning a little closer. 'You'll be glad to know, Lucy, that yesterday we managed to trace your Cecil's movements since he drove to this boatyard in the dead of night.'

'Really?' Lucy clearly felt that sarcasm might now be her best defence. 'That was clever of you.'

'Not really. First, we made enquiries with the local taxi firms and tracked down the driver who'd collected him from this very yard that same night. And guess where he took him?'

'Go on ....'

'Heathrow Airport.'

'Heathrow!' Now it was Lucy's turn to sit forward. 'You mean he was ...'

'... skipping the country. Are you saying you knew nothing of this?'

'No, I didn't ... the bastard.' Lucy's hands were screwing into tight fists. 'I suppose he was getting a flight to Spain?'

'Why Spain, Lucy?'

'Because he'd ... because I believe he had certain financial interests there.'

'He certainly did – an offshore account, to be exact, and one fed by funds from Bertie Borrett's own account in Holland.'

'I don't know anything about that.'

'Yes you do, Mrs Watling, and my guess is that you were expecting to join your husband in Spain any day now, to enjoy living the rest of your life off those funds.'

'How could we if, as you say, Bertie had already cottoned on to the whole thing?'

'Which is what Elsie Borrett thought as well,' continued Bailey, 'but even a ruthless operator like her husband wasn't quite sharp enough to catch out the likes of yours. You see, our auditors have been busy all morning in Cecil's old office and it wasn't that difficult to follow the money-trail of Cecil's activities. It was all pretty enlightening.'

'Are you going to tell me?' asked Lucy, unsure as to whether she wanted to know or not.

Bailey nodded. 'Your Cecil was a faster operator than perhaps even you realised. Once he knew that Borrett was on to him, he acted with lightning speed and immediately transferred over a million euros from Bertie's Dutch account to one in Spain he'd set up without his boss knowing. Although in Borrett's name, Cecil, of course, had made himself a signatory to that account, meaning he then had immediate access and control of that money. It was quite a coup.'

'But one which you seem to have successfully exposed. I suppose now, he and that money are all going to be brought back here.' Lucy's dreams of a comfortable Iberian future seemed to be disappearing as fast as her confidence.

'We would if they were still there,' explained Bailey. 'Unfortunately, all that money in your Spanish account was transferred again the day before Borrett's death.'

'Transferred ... transferred where?'

'To a Chilean bank account.'

'Chile ... you mean South America?' asked an increasingly confused Lucy. 'Why on earth would he transfer it there?'

'Because that's where Cecil is now. We checked on his flight out of Heathrow, Mrs Watling. Your husband didn't go to Spain. Instead, he took the early morning LAN flight to Santiago.'

Lucy closed her eyes and shook her head. 'I really didn't know.'

'No, I don't think you did, because your dear Cecil made sure that this time you wouldn't be sharing the fruits of his endeavours.' Bailey gave her a meaningful look. 'He's dumped you, Mrs Watling, and left you with nothing.'

She brought out a tissue and this time they were genuine tears. 'So, where does this leave me?'

'Right here, because I might still need to talk to you again about Bertie Borrett's murder.'

'B ... but I told you ... I had nothing to do with that?'

'You could have. He treated you badly ... remember?'

'If either of us did it, it would have been my husband.' A little flame of bitterness had by now crept into her voice. 'Perhaps Bertie caught him here doing his scarper and Cecil killed him to get away?'

'Perhaps that *is* what happened,' conceded Bailey. 'Perhaps you do know more than you're letting on.'

'I damned well don't. I'm just bloody furious.'

'Yes, well go back to your cottage, make a cup of tea, and think things over,' advised the DI.

Lucy dejectedly pulled on her boots and ten minutes saw her teetering back along the boatyard track towards a home she would soon be losing and a life supported by she-knew-not-what.

* * *

'Was I a bit hard on her, Jack?' Bailey sat back again as the launch bobbed a little in the freshening afternoon breeze.

'No, I don't think so. She's a manipulative woman and it'll do her good to see what it's like to be on the receiving end.'

'Manipulative, but I don't think murderous, Jack.'

The ranger shrugged. 'Who knows what passions beat in a woman's heart, but I think you're correct – her bitterness against Borrett was being sated enough by seeing Cecil taking him to the cleaners.'

'Which still leaves Lynsey Butterick well in the frame.'

'Not if I can establish the real truth behind it all.' Jack disappeared briefly into the cabin to start the engine before returning to the cockpit and Bailey. 'Like I said, after work tonight, I'm going to be doing a little more investigating of my own.'

'Yes, well don't dig too deep,' warned the detective. 'The last thing I need is some extra off-the-record sleuthing gumming up the works.'

'Better than extra-terrestrial, Bailey,' said Jack with a grin, 'but you can help right now by casting me off.'

'Will do.' Bailey leapt ashore, unhitched the mooring lines and handed them to the ranger. 'Have a good afternoon's patrol, Jack, and keep me advised of anything you find out. I'm sure you know what you're doing.'

Cruising slowly back down the dyke, Jack was wondering just how accurate Bailey's last statement really was.

* * *

It was well after six that evening by the time Jack had completed his patrol, secured the launch and filled in the paperwork. That left more than two hours yet until sunset and the night solitude he wanted for his investigation. It was time he spent by driving into Loddon for a walk along the Chet, followed by food and drink at the pub close by the staithe. Having already phoned Audrey earlier in the day to say he would be very late home and not to worry about a meal, he now called her once more. 'Hi, love. How's it going?'

'Fine thanks, Jack. Lynsey took Spike for his evening run earlier and enjoyed the calming effect of the river, especially as she'd been a bit upset earlier.'

'Really? What about?'

'Oh, while we were having lunch, that barrister chap rang again pestering her to meet up. She pulled no punches and told him in no uncertain terms to back off and leave her alone, which didn't go down too well. There were words and it ended with her being as upset as he was.'

'The right thing though,' assured Jack. 'I certainly didn't warm to the chap and she's got enough problems on her plate without having to cope with angst-ridden suitors. Lynsey's strong, though. She'll sort it.'

'I think she's pinning her hopes on you finding evidence for her defence quickly though, Jack. Do you think you'll discover anything new tonight that will help?'

'I hope so, Aud. At least it might clear up two mysteries in one, which I'm certain are connected to Borrett's murder.'

'Yes, well, just take care of yourself, love. We all need you home safe and sound.'

'So do I.'

Hours later, fed and watered and anxious to pursue his idea, Jack was just a half mile from the village, with the elevated form of St Mark's Church already stark against the stormy moonlit sky. He stopped the car. Was it his imagination or were there subdued lights already flickering in the chancel and graveyard?

He switched off the engine and got out and, as he did so, there came the crack and flash of two gunshots right at the base of the tower.

'What the ...?' He was back in the car in a second and speeding those last eight hundred yards to the church.

The lychgates were open when he braked to a halt outside. Up the path leading to the church door was a battered pickup. As Jack approached, he saw a young man lying motionless in a pool of blood beside the driver's open door. His neck and left shoulder were almost blown away and the other arm was outstretched with the letters H-A-T-E tattooed across the clenched fingers. Further on, face down in the shingle, was the body of another youth, his blasted yellow tee-shirt, blood-red. Even worse, standing over him with a still-smoking 12-bore shotgun, was Admiral Sir Claude Ashfordby.

'Admiral ... put it down.'

The ex-flag officer glanced up as though only vaguely recognising the ranger, but continued to stand immobile and very clearly in shock. Jack took the weapon, broke it open and ejected two spent cartridges. 'What happened?'

'I ... I'm not sure.' The admiral stumbled a few paces to where a bench seat overlooked the graveyard. 'I heard two gunshots as I was walking up the hill here. I ran to see what it was and found those two like that. The gun was beside one of them. I picked it up and ...'

'... I arrived.' Jack sat down beside him with a comforting hand on his shoulder. Already, he could see how black the scenario looked for this elderly man. 'Admiral, do you know who owns this gun?'

The answer took it a shade blacker. 'Yes, it's mine.'

Jack whipped out his mobile, pressed three nines and, within fifteen minutes, two police patrol cars, blue lights flashing, sirens blaring, were screeching to a halt at the gate.

* * *

'I should have known better than to let you go sleuthing around on your own.'

DI Bailey stood before St Mark's porch and shook his head. Following hard on the heels of the first policemen responding to Jack's call, paramedics had soon confirmed there was nothing to be done for the two victims, other than pronounce them dead. Instead, they'd taken the admiral into the quiet of the church and given him treatment for shock. Meanwhile, the police had called headquarters and strung the all-too-familiar police tape across the lychgate. Another fifteen minutes had Bailey and his DC arriving. After a quick briefing from Jack, the DC had disappeared into the church for a preliminary statement from Admiral Ashfordby, while Bailey gave further orders to his men.

'Usual routine. Make sure nothing's touched before the SOCOs get here and one of you keep an eye on the old boy inside.' Bailey surveyed the carnage down the church path. 'So, you reckon this all happened just a minute before you arrived, Jack?'

'Unfortunately, yes ...' Jack glanced at his watch, '... talking of which, you didn't waste any time getting here yourself.'

'That's because we were still close by. After a full day at Providence Farm we decided to stop off for a pub-meal on our way home and now I wish you'd done the same, Jack. I know you said you were coming back here tonight to confirm your suspicions, but I didn't realise they included murder.'

'Neither did I, I can assure you. There'd been strange lights seen in this church on several nights lately, which naturally fostered tales of spooky happenings. I wanted to see for myself.'

'I didn't think you were into ghost-hunting.'

'I'm not, but a number of us had noticed the admiral becoming very tired of late, and assumed it might be due to some autumn romance. But he's churchwarden here and, being as conscientious as he is, I knew he was worried about all these lead thefts. St Mark's couldn't afford CCTV, leading me to suspect the old warrior was running his own night watch. I came here tonight to check that angle and ...' Jack explained again the sequence of events after arriving back at the village.

'Well, if he was after the lead thieves, he certainly found them,' said Bailey grimly, looking towards the bodies. 'The Hinnerley brothers, I presume?'

'Yep. The one by the pickup is Horace and the one halfway down the path is Alfie. I'd say they were both trying to escape from whoever was threatening them.'

'It certainly seems that way,' agreed Bailey. 'And you think they were here to strip the church of its lead?'

'A glance in here will soon answer that,' said Jack, leading the DI to the open back of the Hinnerleys' truck where a miscellany of hammers, crowbars and other crude tools lay beneath ladders projecting out over the cab top.

Bailey turned over some of the equipment. 'All the gear for the job, but if they were here for a bit of lead-gathering, they chose a strange time to do it. We know for a fact that all the other thefts were done in the early hours of the morning, not at this time.'

'There might be a more sinister reason why this one was set earlier,' speculated Jack, 'but some of those other thefts certainly tie-in with what little we know of the Hinnerleys' movements. There was one quite close to here on the night of the public meeting, another a week later, and yet another on the night of Borrett's murder. The Hinnerleys picked Lynsey up in this vehicle instead of Borrett's Merc, and told her they had some job to do, which could well have been heisting lead off a church roof. We know Borrett was in the scrap metal business in London before moving up here, but it's hard to think he'd risk being involved for a few measly grand's-worth of lead. A more likely candidate to me is George Granston.'

'Granston? Who's he?'

'A local metal-worker with a fabricating shop in the village and, more significantly, a foundry. I had a snoop around there myself the other night, but couldn't see much. It's fenced up like Fort Knox, and certainly merits a visit.'

'Right,' agreed Bailey, tossing a hammer back into the truck, 'we'll check him out if you think he might be connected, though with the body count now at three, I don't want to get hung up on lead thieving.'

'My hunch is that Granston might be connected in some way to all these murders,' maintained Jack. 'Something suspicious is definitely going on in that workshop of his.'

'So, why would he want to murder Borrett?'

'Who knows, but he did have a working deal going with him, and my experience is that when dirty money's involved, it always ends with a fallout for those involved.'

'You could be right, Jack. I'll have words with him.' Bailey glanced again at the bodies of the Hinnerley brothers. 'I was hoping to get something out of those two, until your admiral decided to give them a full broadside.'

'Except that when you get his statement, you'll find he *didn't* do it, Bailey.'

'What, even after being caught in the act with his own weapon? Come on, Jack, it all stacks up.'

'He was on his way here tonight for another all-night vigil, that's for sure, but he was still a hundred yards down the road when he heard the shots, came to investigate, and found the Hinnerleys dead.'

'... by his own gun. You told me he admitted that.'

'Yes, but he didn't fire it. Admiral Ashfordby's an honourable man, Bailey. Those two were shot in the back running away. The admiral would never commit such a cowardly act. It goes against all his principles.'

'He's not commanding fleets at sea now,' argued the DI. 'He's in his eighties, in a rage at hooligans bent on relieving his beloved church of its lead roof so, in the heat of the moment, he gives them both barrels. He might've killed Borrett too.'

'You surely don't suspect the old seadog did that one?'

'Why not? He had ample motive. We know he couldn't stand the man, was in an almighty dispute with him over this solar farm business and, to cap that, the old chap could well have been having an affair with the victim's wife.'

'We only suspected that might be the case because he appeared to be very friendly towards Mrs Borrett and was burning the midnight oil somewhere. Now we know it was here.' Jack guided the DI into the seclusion of the church porch. 'Look, Bailey, there are a number of other factors which I'll explain ...' At this point, the forensic team's van drew up at the lychgate, '... but not now, because you're going to have your hands full here for a while.'

'I certainly am, but come to Bethel Street tomorrow, Jack, and we'll discuss it then. I've had more info on Bertie Borrett's dubious past which you'll be interested to hear.'

'I'm sure I will,' agreed Jack as he left Bailey briefing his SOCO team.

Somehow, he almost knew what the extra information would yield.

* * *

'Shootings! Oh my goodness.' In the Fellows' lounge, Lynsey cradled her glass of brandy. 'Where's this all going to end?'

'With the truth, I hope.' Arriving home with his news of the latest incident at St Mark's, Jack had poured generous tots for Audrey and Lynsey and an even larger one for himself. Now, sitting in the comfort of his armchair, he could only shrug and explain. 'Bailey had no option but to take the admiral in on suspicion of the double murder, but I'm guessing the old boy will be released tomorrow.'

'Let's hope so.' Audrey was feeling both sympathy and relief. 'At least we've found out the real reason he was getting so tired, poor man. And to think we suspected he might be having a fling with Elsie Borrett, when all the time he was just looking after St Mark's. And now he's under arrest.' She shook her head sadly. 'A gentleman like Admiral Ashfordby shouldn't be spending even one night in a cell.'

'No, it's not something I'd recommend,' agreed Lynsey earnestly. 'I'm still a barrister, Jack, even if my own circumstances aren't the best at present, so if there's anything you think I can do to help the admiral ...'

'Thanks, Lynsey. Let's hope it doesn't come to that, but I know Sir Claude would be grateful for your offer.' Further discussion was halted by the ringing of the phone in the hall. Jack went to answer it and, when he returned, his face was a mixture of confusion and worry. 'This case gets more bizarre by the minute.'

'Why, who was it?' asked Audrey.

'Bailey. He decided to go straight round to the Granston's home tonight to check a few things.'

'And ...?'

'... and George wasn't there and hadn't been for several days and nights. According to Margie, he went to his workshop early on the night of Borrett's murder and she hasn't heard from him since.'

'Good heavens. Presumably, she went to look for him?'

'Yes, but he wasn't there. She wasn't unduly worried to start with because, she admitted, things had been a bit strained between them lately, and that George sometimes spent the odd night away.'

'Really? Where?'

'She didn't know. He just said it was business and not to worry.'

'Well, it's been more than an "odd night" this time,' declared Audrey, 'so why on earth didn't Margie report him missing?'

'Her explanation to Bailey was that she suspected George of having an affair and simply didn't want the embarrassment of admitting it. But I think an additional reason might be that she didn't want to involve the police for fear of putting George into the loop as a suspect for Borrett's murder.'

Audrey put down her glass. 'Well, he's in it now and, by the sound of it, that could also include tonight's killings.'

'Except, they were done with Admiral Ashfordby's gun,' pointed out Lynsey, 'and the admiral's going to have a hard time proving he didn't just take out the Hinnerleys as part of his vigilante operation.'

'Not if it could be proven that someone else had got their hands on it beforehand.' Jack turned back to his wife. 'Aud, do you remember telling me how shocked Margie looked that time when you rejoined her in the church?'

'Yes. Like she'd seen a ghost.'

'More like something sinister stored in the vestry cupboard,' suggested Jack. 'You said she'd gone there to find a vase. What if she'd found a shotgun instead?'

'Certainly, that would be the very last thing she'd expect to be confronted with,' agreed Audrey. 'I can imagine a gentle soul like Margie being pretty shocked if that's what she found. So what you're thinking is that ...'

'... Admiral Ashfordby, keeping nightly watch on the church, had decided to take his shotgun with him, if only for protection if he caught thieves intent on stealing lead from the roof. He's churchwarden with keys to the vestry cupboard, so I'm surmising he stored it there, thinking no-one else would find it.'

'... but not allowing for the fact that Margie Granston would borrow the vicar's keys and find it lying there.' Audrey nodded sadly. 'Makes sense, Jack, except why didn't she tell me about it at the time?'

'Because she probably recognised it as the admiral's and didn't want to get him into more trouble. Remember, at that time, we all suspected the old boy of having an affair with Mrs Borrett and possibly even using the church as a clandestine meeting place.'

'Perish the thought,' regretted Audrey, penitently. 'To think that all he was doing was bravely defending that which he held dear.'

'So, what you're saying, Jack,' confirmed Lynsey as she followed Jack's forensic reasoning, 'is that this Margery Granston, after finding that gun, told no-one ...'

'... except her own husband who, after Borrett's murder, might well have foreseen that any questioning of the Hinnerleys could disclose their lead scam operation. It's not difficult to imagine him luring them to St Mark's on some pretext and then taking them out with the shotgun, confident the blame would fall on its owner, the admiral.'

'But how could anyone connive to have a lovely old man like Admiral Ashfordby sent to gaol on false charges?' asked Audrey.

'Very easily, Aud. Margie and George Granston were an ill-matched couple, and Charity Howden said she thought he had no time for his wife's church work. That being the case, he might well have had little patience for the churchwarden who encouraged her to spend time there.'

'He'd need keys to get into the church and vestry cupboards though.'

'But we know that Margie had borrowed the vicar's set, so George had ample opportunities to cut copies in his workshop.'

Audrey shook her head. 'Poor Margie. If that's all true, she'll be devastated. I'll give her a call first thing tomorrow.'

'Well, when you do, ask her if it really was the gun she found in the vestry cupboard that day.' Jack finished his drink. 'With her husband on the run, I can imagine she might now be a bit more forthcoming.'

'And certainly in need of some friendly support,' added Audrey, 'but in thinking of George as a suspect, Jack, don't forget he's not the only one who's disappeared.'

'I know ... Cecil Watling, the bent lawyer, is another one, but we know he's in South America now and well out of the frame for the Hinnerleys, but still very much a suspect for Borrett's and with the strongest of motives.'

'The more I hear, the more I wonder if there's anyone who *doesn't* have a motive except me,' said Lynsey with hope in her voice. 'Surely DI Bailey must be having doubts by now.'

'I'm sure he is,' agreed Jack, 'and you'll probably find out for yourself tomorrow. That was the main reason he rang. With all the mess at St Mark's, he forgot to say he wants you to come to Bethel Street with me.'

'Really? For what reason?'

'Something to do with other evidence coming to light at Providence Farm when they were searching there today.' He forced a smile. 'I'm sure it's nothing to worry about.' He went to the sideboard and poured himself another brandy, hoping his words carried more conviction than he actually felt.

* * *

Chapter Sixteen

'If this whole business has taught me one thing, Jack, it's an awareness of how differently you see law enforcement when you're on the receiving end.'

They were driving into Norwich, with Lynsey feeling the apprehension of any defendant about to be put through the rigours of interrogation.

'Yes, I can understand that.' Jack turned and caught his passenger's anxious glance. 'But you really shouldn't give up the law, Lynsey. With this behind you and the ability to see things through an accused person's eyes, you'll have a wealth of experience few of your contemporaries will ever know.'

'Lucky them.' They were entering the city limits now with fields and trees giving way to housing and light industry. 'But you're right, Jack. Certainly, lawyers would show a lot more empathy towards their defendants if they'd experienced a short stretch in custody themselves.' She turned her head away with a sigh. 'Miles Rotherby-Jones for a start.'

'He's a prosecutor, so sympathy's probably the last emotion he wants to foster,' reasoned Jack, his wry grin quickly giving way to a frown. 'Aud mentioned he called you again yesterday?'

'Yes, pleading, as usual, for me to return to London and to let him handle my defence, but I can't think of anyone I'd trust less.'

'The sooner he realises that the better.' Although nearing the end of the morning rush-hour, there was still a fair amount of traffic winding its way into the city and Jack slowed as they caught the tail-end of the queue ahead. 'Let's hope he has enough work in London to occupy his mind elsewhere.'

'That's the trouble, Jack, the infernal man's not there. He's *here*, staying in a hotel in Norwich, and pestering me to at least have a "no-strings-attached" meal with him.'

'You're joking!' Jack pulled away as traffic flowed once more. 'He really is a pain, isn't he? And, strangely, for a snubbed suitor, he's being incredibly attentive.'

'Obsessive, I'd call it. He's just trying to wheedle his way back into my life.' She gave a derisive sniff. 'Something that will *never* happen.'

'Very wise, but I wonder ...' Jack drove on, eyes on the road and thoughts on this latest development, '... if him staying local could actually work to our advantage.'

'I can't see how. What are you thinking?'

'Oh, just a little scheme I've got turning over in my mind to reveal the truth in this odd affair.' Jack pointed ahead to where the mighty steeple of Norwich Cathedral rose above the encircling city. 'Almost there.'

'Unfortunately.' She gulped. 'I guess I'll soon be finding out just what it is DI Bailey wants to see me about.'

'Probably just some loose ends to tie up.'

They continued to the city centre, parked in The Forum underground car- park and walked the short distance to Bethel Street police station.

* * *

'Thanks for coming, both of you.' DI Bailey nodded his two visitors into chairs opposite. Beyond his screened office, detectives busied themselves with a mountain of enquires and investigations, but in this sanctum, tension sat silent and brooding. He turned to Lynsey. 'You're probably wondering why I wanted to see you again so soon.'

'Yes. I can't think there's anything I haven't already told you in my defence.'

'That's what we hoped, Miss Butterick, but apparently we were mistaken.'

'How do you mean?'

'I mean that yesterday, as you probably know, we spent the day at Providence Farm going over paperwork in Cecil Watling's office.'

'Mr Borrett's missing PA.'

'Yes.'

'But, someone I never met.'

'... and are unlikely to, seeing as he's now on another continent. But thankfully, Mr Watling did leave a lot of papers in his files that have given us food for thought.' The DI opened the case file that seemed to have fattened considerably since Jack's last visit. He pulled out a printed sheet and held it up. 'Like this, for instance.'

Lynsey frowned at the single-sheet printout, trying to read its content and somehow sensing it bode her no good. 'What is it?'

'It's a draft, Miss Butterick ... the draft of Bertie Borrett's new will.'

Jack leaned closer. 'Presumably the one Elsie suspected he was making. Was she correct?'

'Very much so, and it went even further than she feared.' Bailey laid the draft down in front of him. 'Borrett didn't leave her so much as a sherry glass, and instead, bequeathed his entire estate to someone else.'

'A mistress?'

'We can only assume so.'

Lynsey was impatient for the facts. 'So, who was this undeserving, but very fortuitous person?'

Bailey nodded across to the young lawyer before him. 'You, Miss Butterick.'

'Me!' Lynsey leapt out of her chair and put steadying hands on Bailey's desk. 'But that's impossible.'

'I assure you, it's not. We still don't know what other little piles of loot Bertie Borrett had tucked away, but Providence Farm and the boatyard themselves probably come to well over £2.5 million.' Bailey allowed just a second for this to sink in before leaning forward. 'Are you saying you knew nothing of this, Miss Butterick?'

'Of course I didn't. Two and a half ...' Lynsey sat down again and ran fingers agitatedly through her hair. 'I'd never ever even met Bertie Borrett ... only talked to him on the phone, so why on earth would he leave me a small fortune?'

'Why indeed, but I'm sure we'll find the answer to that one along with everything else.' Bailey sat back in his comfortable chair. 'I think you'll agree, Miss Butterick, that this gives you a more than ample motive for speeding his end.'

Lynsey soon had an answer that one. 'Except that's only a draft, Inspector, which hasn't been formalised yet. It isn't worth a penny to me, so why would I commit murder for nothing in return?'

'Ah, but there our victim was a little ahead of the game,' continued the detective. He slid the draft closer for them to see. 'Perhaps Bertie had some premonition of events to come. Whatever, as you can see there for yourself, he actually signed and dated this draft and then got Cecil Watling to witness it.'

'So,' intervened Jack, 'what looks like a draft is actually ...'

'... Bertie Borrett's legal last Will and Testament,' completed Lynsey with a voice still echoing disbelief.

'Exactly.' Bailey shrugged. 'I suppose congratulations are in order, Miss Butterick. You are now a very wealthy young lady.'

'For what good it might do me.' Lynsey shook her head. 'It's obvious where all this is going, Inspector. What you've got there is the motive you've been looking for to compound my guilt.'

'I'm glad you admit how damning this looks,' said Bailey, slipping the will back into the file and closing the cover with ominous finality, 'unless you can come up with a better explanation.'

'I wish I could, Inspector, but right now I'm as baffled as you are suspicious.'

'Well, let me know if you do,' said Bailey with mock patience. 'In the meantime, you've become a very rich young lady.' He pressed a button on his telephone, answered in person by the female DC. 'Jenners, find a quiet room for Miss Butterick to have a cup of coffee. I just want to have a few words with Ranger Fellows here before he goes.'

* * *

With the office now to themselves, Jack blew out his cheeks. 'That was certainly an unexpected revelation, Bailey.'

'Yep, to me too, but it does pretty well seal the case against her.'

'Only if she knew she was Borrett's beneficiary before he was murdered,' argued Jack. He shifted in his chair. 'I was watching her face when you dropped that bombshell and I'd stake my pension she was as surprised as I was.'

'She's a barrister, Jack. Play-acting's part of her job.'

'I think I know this girl well enough now to recognise when she's being genuine.' Jack glanced around and lowered his voice. 'There could be another solution.'

'You have one?'

'Possibly.'

Bailey sighed. 'Okay, let's have it.'

Jack explained, and it was the DI's turn to raise eyebrows. 'Feasible, I suppose, but we'll know for sure when I have the data.'

'... talking of which, how about that extra info from The Yard on Borrett?'

'Yep, they emailed me all their gen.' Bailey took a printout from his file and scanned its content. 'It seems they were pretty sure he was dealing in other metals besides scrapped cars.'

'Such as?'

'Gold, predominantly, from a bullion robbery on a security company twelve years back.'

'Yes, I vaguely remember that one. From what I recall, none of the bright stuff was ever recovered.'

'Correct, and wherever it is now, at today's prices, it'll be worth a cool twenty million.'

Jack gave a low whistle. 'Certainly enough to keep Bertie Borrett in style, and for others to want to kill him.'

'Like other gang-members feeling cheated of their share, you mean?'

'Exactly. Were there many of them?'

'As far as it's known, only two others in the actual gang. They'd been helped by a couple of security guys who were soon identified and banged up for ten years apiece.'

'So, they'll be out now.'

'Yep, but both going straight. We checked them out and they had cast-iron alibis.'

'Which leaves the actual gang-members ... were they caught?'

'Only the probable leader, a well-known villain called Fred Calstock, who they reckon planned the whole thing. He got life.'

'And, presumably, none of them squealed?'

'No. The insiders were obviously kept in the dark and Fred died in gaol a few years ago without ever spilling the beans.'

'But The Yard suspected Borrett?'

'Very much so, and they took his scrapyard and London home apart looking for evidence.'

'But didn't find any?'

Bailey shook his head. 'Not so much as a nugget, so no charge could ever be brought to bear.'

'A wily lad was our Bertie,' acknowledged Jack. 'How about the rest of the gang?'

'They reckoned there was only one other involved – Calstock's son, Gerry, who simply disappeared off the face of the earth before The Yard could run him down. He's been missing ever since.'

Jack stroked his chin. 'Interesting, but not surprising. Knowing now that Borrett had bullion to dispose of has simply confirmed my suspicions.'

The DI had seen that look before. 'Okay, Jack. Go ahead and give me your thoughts.'

'Okay, but only the aspects I'm pretty sure about at present. It's based on the main problem any villain or fence has after a big job.'

'Disposing of the loot?'

'Exactly and, in this case, nearly a tonne of marked gold bars. Not the sort of thing Borrett was going to be able to sell on a stall in Petticoat Lane.'

'So, you reckon he ...'

'... bought a boat and boatyard with the sole plan of shipping it overseas to Holland where it could be distributed throughout Europe.'

Bailey seemed sceptical. 'Pretty risky, Jack. It would only take one rummage by the Dutch Customs to find a couple of bars stashed below and his game would be up.'

'Not for the likes of Borrett who, we've already seen, was pretty adept at avoiding the forces of law and order. No, the key to his gold export business were the Dutch boat-fittings he was importing to England.'

'In other words, the import business was just a front.'

'More than a front, Bailey, it was the means to an end. Borrett's boat wasn't the best maintained in the world, but it did boast shining brass fittings. I assumed at the time they were just examples of his imports, but now I'm sure they were something else.'

'You mean ...?'

'That's right ... gold. You remember he'd formed a working arrangement with George Granston and his foundry in the village.'

'... which we assumed was simply to retail the Dutch fittings.'

Jack nodded. 'Exactly, but it went far deeper than that. Granston was, in fact, moulding the gold into deck fittings, which Borrett then had installed on *Merlin Magic*, before sailing them across to Holland, where they were swapped for the brass fittings ostensibly being imported back.'

'... while, the gold ones he took over would be melted down and sold off world-wide,' said Bailey, following Jack's reasoning to its conclusion. 'A simple scam, but certainly feasible. So, what brought this ingenious racket to light?'

'A number of things. When I first saw Borrett's boat, I noticed the shiny fittings had been secured with badly scarred nuts and bolts. That seemed particularly careless and I came to the conclusion it must be due them being replaced more than once, though at that time I didn't consider the broader picture. Then, the day after the murder, I found the boat's deck fittings gone. I suspected the Hinnerleys of simply thieving them, which I think they did, but for far greater reward than simple boat gear. And then, that evening, I went to help Audrey clear up at St Cuthbert's after evensong and noticed a kneeling cushion and the tomb of a crusader. That made me think of Excalibur's sword and the Arthurian legends, though I wasn't sure why they seemed so significant to this case.'

'I still can't,' admitted Bailey. 'Mediaeval knights and their Round Table seem a long way from what we're trying to sort out here.'

'I know,' continued Jack, 'and I was still trying to make the connection myself when Audrey mentioned "touching base" with my headquarters.'

The DI shook his head. 'I still don't get it.'

'It was that one word ... "base". Then I realised it was the connection with the name Borrett had given his boat.'

'*Merlin Magic*?'

'Exactly. Merlin was a famous character from the Arthurian legends. He's variously described as a wizard or sorcerer, but also as an alchemist and you know what they did?'

'Remind me,' muttered Bailey, finding this thread ever-more obscure.

'They turned *base* metals into *gold*, Bailey, which, in his own way, was the very thing Borrett was doing. In fact, he tried to be just that bit too clever in using a play on words for the name of his boat, because he set me on the trail of his scam.'

'You could be right,' conceded Bailey, 'but, if you are, where's the rest of the gold still stashed? Or do you think most of it's now on the continent?'

'It might be, but I doubt it. Borrett's had that yard and boat for less than a year and, in that time, couldn't have made more than a dozen trips across to Holland. A bar of gold weighs a little over twelve kilograms, which would just about account for a full set of fittings per trip. That means there are still about twenty-eight bars left to ship. I have a hunch where they might just be, but give me a day or so to pursue some further enquiries.'

'I know better than to ask what those are,' accepted Bailey with a grin, 'but how does all this fit in with what's happened since? If the Hinnerley brothers really did nick those fittings and they were gold, then they didn't get to enjoy their ill-gotten gains for long.'

'I rather suspect they were murdered *because* of that theft,' explained Jack, 'and by someone who didn't want them telling tales about what they knew.'

'George Granston, possibly? He's still no-where to be found, which opens up other possibilities, Jack. He's about the right age, so how about him being the long-lost Gerry Calstock?'

'He could be. Did the Yard have a mugshot of Gerry?'

'No. Apparently, unlike his dad, he'd never had any previous they knew of.'

'Pity.' Jack stroked his chin. 'George Granston might also provide the answer to another open question.'

'Which is?'

'Mrs Borrett's lover. You remember Lucy Watling telling us Elsie had some fella on the side, who we later assumed was dear old Admiral Ashfordby. Now we know it was some other nocturnal activity that was sapping the old boy's energy, so who then is Elsie's fancy man?'

'Could be Granston,' agreed Bailey. 'We know he had a business relationship with Borrett, so perhaps he had an even more intimate one with his wife.'

'According to Granston's wife, Bertie had told George that Elsie was having an affair,' recounted Jack. 'Perhaps it was more than Bertie *telling* him ... perhaps he was *confronting* him as the third party.'

'Would he be that bothered, Jack? Everyone knew Borrett was the biggest adulterer for miles around.'

'In my experience, womanisers are the most possessive when it comes to their own wives,' said Jack. 'But I agree, there are many aspects of this business that don't make sense and a lot of loose ends we need to tie up. But, when we do, I suspect they'll all ultimately lead back to Borrett and the old Cookcraft yard. But, talking of dear old Admiral Ashfordby ... what's happening with him?'

'Released on police bail this morning.'

'Good. Did he have any more to tell you about the shooting?'

Bailey shook his head. 'Nothing more than he told you. Admits it was his gun which he'd been keeping in the vestry cupboard with the idea of catching any thieves stealing lead from St Mark's.'

'... and, instead, someone else, who knew it was there, used it to take out the Hinnerleys and make it look as though it was the admiral.'

'You could be right, Jack, because, like you, I can't believe he'd shoot someone in cold blood – he's not the type – but, until we find a more-likely candidate, he has to stay top of my suspect list.'

'I think I'll be able to supply you with a few more candidates before we're through,' said Jack.

'Well, good luck if you can, but I'll need to be kept informed, Jack. I'm going to let you have a pretty loose rein here, because my guess is that the solution to all this will depend a lot on what you find out at your end.'

'And what the results are at *your* end,' added Jack. It was time to push his advantage. 'I know you're busy, Bailey, but I'm going to need a little more data from different agencies in London.'

The DI gave a long-suffering sigh as he opened his notebook. 'Which are ...?

Jack gave the details and Bailey jotted them down. 'Right, that shouldn't take too long, but remember, I'm going to need hard evidence if I'm to bring charges. Fancy theories are all very well, but it'll need something more solid to convince the CPS.'

'I've got a plan for that too,' said Jack smugly, 'but first let me see what the next few days produce and then I'll reveal all.'

'I can hardly wait. In the meantime, make sure Miss Butterick stays out of trouble. I've stuck my neck out way too far for you already.'

'Yeah, and I'm grateful ... but just one more favour?'

'Go on.'

'I want to see Admiral Ashfordby.'

Bailey grimaced. 'Part of his bail is that he won't have contact with any witnesses ... and you are *it*, Jack.'

'I know, but he promised me a sail in his boat, so I want to take him up on it, if only to get his mind off what's happened.'

The DI gave the shrug of a man almost beyond caring. 'Okay, have a day on the river with the old boy. Who knows, you might even get a new lead.'

'I'll try,' promised Jack as the DC returned to see him and Lynsey out of the station.

'Please do,' muttered Bailey to himself as he settled back to his own mountain of work.

* * *

Chapter Seventeen

'Well, with your new-found wealth, I ought to get *you* to buy lunch.' They were driving homeward now with Jack trying to inject a little levity into the situation.

'Probably a good idea,' responded Lynsey who, for someone just told she'd inherited a fortune, seemed seriously subdued. 'I get the feeling that DI Bailey still intends me to be eating prison food very soon, so I ought to indulge while I have the chance.'

'Oh, I don't think things are as dire as they seem,' comforted Jack, without explaining any of his conversation with the DI, 'but perhaps we will skip lunch. I have a couple of phone-calls I need to make.' They were in open country again, heading back into the heart of Broadland with circumstances very different from the drive in. 'And you really had no idea that Borrett had made you the sole beneficiary of his will?'

'None at all. I can only assume he did it purely to spite Elsie.' She turned to face Jack. 'Whatever his devious reason, I can assure you I'm making no plans to spend a penny of that money. That rough draft, with just Watling's signature as witness, is so tenuous, I haven't the slightest doubt that Elsie will contest it ... and so she should!'

'I think that depends on whether she knows where it came from. Knowing Bertie Borrett as we do now, that money probably has very dubious origins and the last thing Elsie might want is for the law to start asking awkward questions. You might well find she prefers to let things lie.'

'Well, I'm not the sort who could let a woman who's put up with Bertie Borrett all those years, be thrown out of her home. I know what it's like to be short of money and without a man around.'

'Your family must have been very proud when you qualified as a barrister.'

'There was only my Mum and, having been ill for a while, she died very soon after I was called to the bar, so I was never able to repay her for all she did for me.' Lynsey wiped a tear from her eye, before continuing ruefully, 'She wouldn't be very proud of me now, would she Jack?'

'Oh, I don't know. I'm sure she'd admire the way you're handling the situation. After all, none of it's your fault.'

'I'm not sure if I am handling it.' She gave just the glimmer of a smile. 'It's you, Jack, who's doing all the spadework.'

'That's what an investigator's for. Remember, that was one of the reasons the magistrates allowed you to stay with us.'

They were off the main road now, coasting down the quiet country lanes towards the Fellows' village and home. Jack braked as a pheasant ran across the road in front of them, its panicky gait causing Lynsey to laugh out loud as it disappeared into the hedge and safety. 'How lovely to live a pace of life where you have time to give way to the wildlife. In London, they hardly stop for people.'

'There are some here I might be tempted to flatten,' confessed Jack with a smile, as they moved off once more. 'Your pompous Rotherby-Jones for one.'

'Quite. It's the thought of people like him who make me more determined than ever to settle down in Broadland ... if I'm ever able to lead a normal life again.'

Jack knew she was forcing herself to be positive and he was just as keen to encourage it. 'You will, Lynsey.' He glanced up at a sky now bright and clear. 'Have yourself a nice walk with Audrey and Spike this afternoon. I'm hoping I might see the admiral.'

* * *

'Did you manage to get hold of him, Jack?' Audrey looked up from the kitchen table where she'd been laying lunch for all three of them.

'Yes, and I'm glad I did. He seemed a bit low when he first answered, but brightened when I suggested an afternoon out on *Curlew*.'

Audrey looked pleased. 'I'm sure it'll be the very medicine he needs after a night in police custody. Just your call alone probably lifted his spirits. When things are black, hearing a friendly voice can make all the difference. I know Margie Granston sounded glad to hear mine when I rang.'

'I'm glad you called her,' said Jack, as he cut himself a piece of cheese. 'So, how is she?'

'As you'd expect – not good,' Audrey took the pan of soup off the hob, 'and there's still no sign of George.'

'And, does she have any idea of where he might be or why he disappeared?'

'Not really although, of course, she can't help feeling it must have something to do with Bertie Borrett's murder.'

'... and, possibly, the Hinnerley brothers as well,' reminded Jack. 'Did you ask her if it was the gun she discovered when she was looking for that vase in the vestry cupboard?'

'Yes, and you were correct. She knew it must be the admiral's, as he was the only other person, other than the vicar, to have a key to it. She felt she couldn't say anything to me, a virtual outsider, before talking to him about it.'

'Which she never got the chance to do, presumably,' surmised Jack. 'But did she mention it to her husband, I wonder?'

'I don't know, I didn't ask her, but she probably felt the need to confide in someone and, if so, it was probably George.'

'Hmmm. But did she give you any more details of what George was actually doing the night Borrett was murdered?'

'Only that he said he had to go to the workshop to complete an order. That was the last time she saw him.' Audrey took some rolls from the bread bin and put them in a basket on the table. 'I think what really worries her is the suspicion that George has a lady-friend.'

'Understandable,' said Jack, taking a roll and putting it on his plate, 'but has she any grounds for suspecting that?'

'Oh, just the secretive way he'd been acting. Telephone calls he wouldn't discuss, days and the odd night away, without giving a reason ... that sort of thing.'

'And did he give Margie any explanation for his change of behaviour?'

'Not really. She just said his unpredictable moods and grumpiness seemed to start after he'd been forced to sell his beloved boat which was his pride and joy.'

'Who actually bought it?'

'He didn't tell her. By that time they weren't communicating too well and he didn't like her prying.'

'That's strange, I thought things had looked up since he started selling Borrett's fittings?'

'Only financially, but not regarding their marriage. The day before he disappeared, he was apparently away all day.'

'And Margie didn't know where?'

'No, which just confirmed her suspicions that George had fallen for someone else.'

'Did she have any particular name in mind?'

'Nothing she could have proved but, of course, Elsie Borrett was always a likely contender. Everyone suspected she had a man on the side and, now we know it wasn't the admiral ...'

'... husband George could well be the one. I wonder ...' Jack put down the water jug he was about to fill from the kitchen tap. 'Don't wait for me, love, because there's a call I need to make right now.' He left the kitchen for the hall, just as Lynsey came in to join them for lunch.

Audrey could only shrug her shoulders the way she had so many times before.

* * *

'Right, Jack, with the breeze on our tail, we'll be able to run up the dyke on jib alone.'

It was a glorious afternoon now, the deep blue of the sky reflecting in the slightly ruffled water and the greens of the surrounding Broadland scene made all the more vivid by the unbroken sunshine.

'Just the therapy we need, Admiral, after all that's happened,' enthused Jack as, up on the coachroof at the base of the mast, he raised the small triangular foresail.

'Absolutely.' At the tiller, Sir Claude, Breton yachting cap square on his fine head, and white beard stark against the dark navy of his guernsey jumper, hardened one of the jibsheets and sat back, a picture of contentment. 'We'll be on the main river soon, Jack, so stay up there and standby the main halyard.'

'Aye aye, cap'n.' Another minute and they were nosing out of the dyke and onto the Yare, where the admiral briefly brought them head to wind. 'Right, hoist!'

There were several lines to be heaved on this gaff rigged river cruiser, but with the peak halyard secure, Jack could finally make his way back down into the well of the cockpit and relax. The breeze was a gentle southerly and now they were heading downriver, the tan mains'l full and an arrowhead of water already curling back from the old boat's bow.

'She's going well, Admiral.'

'Yes, always been a joy to sail.' He glanced aloft to where his personalized burgee fluttered at the masthead. 'Should've got misself afloat weeks ago, but things ...' His voice trailed off with recollections of less-happy times.

'They've been eventful weeks, Admiral. Ones which none of us could have predicted.'

'You're right there, but I can't deny I've behaved like a bit of an ass. Chap my age, should've known better.'

'You did what you thought best for your church,' said Jack, anxious not to break the atmosphere of healthy acceptance, 'but I'm afraid the police will never be sympathetic to any vigilante operations by the public.'

They were following a bend in the river with the yacht heeling slightly in the now-quartering wind. Sir Claude eased his mainsheet and *Curlew* sluiced through the water just a little faster. 'No, I know, but the theft of church lead is one of those crimes that cost a hundred times more to correct than to prevent.'

Jack followed his skipper's action and adjusted the jibsheet slightly. 'Did you suspect the Hinnerleys as being the ones doing all that thieving?'

'I had a good idea, what with their record and the fact that they were seen going out in that truck of theirs late on the night lead was stolen from a church. No proof though, so, I decided to mount a nightly watch and catch the devils in their work. I had the gun there just for personal protection in case they cut up rough if I tried to carry out a citizen's arrest.'

'But it never came to that.'

'No, the blighters turned up well ahead of the time the other thefts had taken place. Would've caught them red-handed early morning, but at that time I was only half-way up the hill when I heard the shots.'

'Fired by whom, I wonder?' asked Jack, rhetorically. 'Obviously by someone who knew where to find your gun and had access to the church.'

'Exactly. Been wondering that one misself and can only come to one conclusion.'

'George Granston?'

'Has to be, Jack. His wife had the vicar's keys, so it wouldn't have been difficult for him to make copies.'

'And he's been missing since Borrett's murder.'

'All a bad business.' The mains'l was luffing slightly again and he sheeted in. 'Never had any time for Borrett, as you know, but the blighter didn't deserve what he got in the end.'

'On the night of the murder, I remember you saying you spotted the fire in the boatyard from your home,' reminded Jack. 'But that wasn't strictly correct was it, because you can't see the old yard from your cottage.'

'No, bit of a fib that one.' The admiral stroked his white beard. 'Truth was, I was up at St Mark's on my night-watch, but I couldn't tell them that could I, for fear of giving the game away?'

'I guess not, but the truth always wins out in the end,' said Jack.

Curlew herself seemed to be rejoicing in this first sail of the year, the slight creak of her rig and the surge of water down her varnished sides, the only sound to break the peace of the day, until a clanking around the next bend announced the proximity of the Reedham Ferry. As the ungainly vessel came in sight, the admiral aimed *Curlew* for the gap at its stern, sailing past so casually that he had time to glance at his watch. 'Fifteen-twenty. Good. Bridge'll be opening shortly and we can keep on downstream to Breydon.'

'Great.' Jack was genuinely pleased. He was enjoying this brisk sail as much as his skipper. Soon, they were gliding past Reedham's long quay where he recalled the last time he was here was the Sunday morning after Borrett's murder when he'd stopped for a chat with Charity and Marcel on *Faith and Hope*.

They'd earlier spoken briefly to Marcel before setting off. The Frenchman had been busy painting the narrowboat's topsides in the fine weather, but explained that Charity was at her job at Providence Farm. He said they hoped to be off cruising the following day.

Bridges would not be something that would hamper the narrowboat's low hull, nor the high mast of *Curlew* this afternoon, for ahead, the swing bridge was indeed opening and a minute had them speeding through the gap on the ebbing tide.

Soon they were passing the entrance to the New Cut and continuing down the Yare, bearing away with a freer wind and watching their wash create Mexican Waves in the reedbeds lining the banks. The admiral was easing the mains'l out again and Jack correspondingly slackened his jib sheets. Several miles ahead, the structure of Polkey's Drainage Mill poked just above the marshes, beautifully restored and marking the half-way point of their remaining run to Breydon. The river ran reasonably straight until there, perhaps a good time to ask a few more questions. 'Lucy Watling, Admiral ... where's she living now?'

'Still in the cottage she used to share with that crooked husband of hers.'

'Really? That's very understanding of Elsie, considering that the pair were all set to embezzle her and Bertie.'

'That's Elsie for you. Generous to a fault.' The admiral shrugged. 'Personally, I'd have given the madam her marching orders, but Elsie somehow feels that, in a way, Lucy's as much a victim of Bertie as she is.'

'That's more sympathy than her vanishing husband's shown her.' The river was curving slightly southward now and Jack prepared to sheet in again. 'Presumably, she's heard nothing more from him?'

'No, not a whisper as far as we know ... hello, what's this?' The admiral was squinting ahead along the opening reach to where a pair of boats lay close together near the north bank.

'That's *Spirit of Breydon*,' said Jack, identifying the large, powerful Broads Authority launch that patrolled the fast-flowing tidal reaches of the lower Bure, Yare, and Breydon Water. 'Looks as if a hire-cruiser's in trouble.'

With their fast progress, it didn't take long before they were level with the boats and the admiral steering around the cruiser that was now backing away into mid-stream and obviously preparing to continue its journey. At the stern of *Spirit of Breydon*, one of her regular crew was waving the holidaymakers off and shouting, 'Have a good trip and don't let this spoil your time on the Broads.'

Jack glanced at the admiral who was already starting to harden the main. 'We'll go about, Jack, and find out what's happening ... ready about ... lee ho.' He put the helm hard over to port and then *Curlew* was turning in her own length and coming through the wind with a rattle of loose blocks and luffing sails, before settling down on the port tack to head the way she'd come. Now the wind was just slightly ahead of the beam, but the admiral was allowing the sail to continue luffing and the boat to merely creep along on jib alone. It was slow sailing, but a few minutes had them back abeam the Authority launch. 'Right, Jack, let fly your sheets.' With the power gone from the jib also, *Curlew* slowed yet more, her way neutralised by the ebbing tide as she stopped just feet from the other vessel. Jack knew both rangers on board, one of whom was peering over the launch's other side. 'Problem?'

'Yes, and not a very nice one either.' The second ranger was dropping fenders for the yacht to come alongside. 'We could do with your help, Jack. Can you come aboard?'

Jack glanced towards the admiral who nodded in reply. 'No problem, but this is a lee-shore, so kick my bow off as you go, and I'll keep sailing up and down this reach.'

'Right ho!' Jack did as ordered and then he was onboard *Spirit of Breydon* and *Curlew* was already sailing away back upriver. 'Okay ... what's up?'

'Body of a man.' The senior ranger indicated the hire-cruiser, now downriver. 'They spotted it in the reeds and gave us a call. Luckily we were close and came straight here.'

'Have the police been informed?'

'Yep. BroadsBeat are on their way, but they told us to retrieve the body.' He gave an apologetic smile. 'He's going to be heavy, Jack. Can you give us a lift?'

'Sure.' Jack went to the side and looked down at the lifeless figure in dark reefer jacket, face-down, his arms and legs moving in eerie unison with the river's heave. 'I'll take his midships and you two get his legs and shoulders.'

They grabbed the sodden corpse and hauled it on board into the launch's open well. One of the rangers straightened his back. 'Phew, people are a lot heavier dead than alive.'

'Especially when they're as waterlogged as this one.' Jack wiped his hands on his trousers. 'Back in The Met, we used to get a small bonus for recovering bodies from the Thames.'

'... but all we get is extra paperwork,' moaned the *Spirit*'s skipper with grim humour. He glanced down at the sad bundle his colleague had just turned over. 'I wonder who this poor beggar is?'

'I can tell you that,' answered Jack, staring at the bloated but still recognisable features of the corpse. 'His name's George Granston.'

* * *

'Our pathologist reckons he's been dead at least a week, Jack.' On the other end of the line, Bailey gave a weary sigh. 'In the water all that time, apparently, but even so, it wasn't difficult to ascertain cause of death as a broken neck before he went in.'

'Certainly not suicide then.' Jack was sitting upstairs in his study, a welcome glass of brandy in hand as he came to grips with the day's events. 'So, if your doc's correct in his timing, Granston probably died the same night as Borrett.'

'Which kind of eliminates him as a suspect.'

'Afraid so,' agreed Jack, taking a sip of the amber liquid, 'but, by the same token, it also takes Lynsey further out of the frame.'

'I'm beginning to lose count of frames, let alone suspects,' groaned the DI. 'If the death toll goes up anymore, we'll be talking genocide instead of murder.'

'I know what you mean, but this does rather fit in with my new view of things,' encouraged Jack.

'Views ... frames ... theories.' Bailey seemed glum to the point of despair. 'When you've cobbled them together into some sort of case, Jack, let me know, because I don't mind admitting I'm getting stumped.'

'Don't worry, I will. In the meantime, I made a few telephone calls of my own before you rang, and tomorrow I'm off to hopefully tie up yet more loose ends.'

‘Well, good luck, because any day now the Chief Constable’s going to be putting me back on traffic duty.’

‘It’ll never come to that,’ assured Jack, ‘but I’m still going to need help from you if we’re to break this one.’

‘If I can, I will,’ promised the DI. ‘I just want to get to the bottom of this whole rotten business a.s.a.p.’

Don’t we all, thought Jack, as he hung up and went down to join Audrey and Lynsey in the conservatory.

* * *

Chapter Eighteen

'Good to see you again, Jack. Long time since we patrolled together.'

It was the next afternoon and Ranger Harry Bentley had just brought the Broads Authority RIB alongside the Burgh Castle quay.

Jack hopped aboard. 'And you, Harry, and thanks for fitting this in.'

'No problem. I'm on the Waveney today anyway, checking on reported illegal eel-nets.'

'Any luck?'

'Some. We hauled up a couple and found one without a licence disc, so that's been confiscated. I dropped the fisheries chap off with it just before lunch.'

'That's good.' As they sidled away from the moorings, Jack settled down beside the inflatable's pilot console and looked aft to where the walls of the old fort were still just visible. Two millennia earlier, Hanorovian mercenaries here had guarded what was then a great estuary, against attack by marauding Saxons. Different times, different troubles, thought Jack, as the scene slid back to the 21st Century and a state-of-the-art lifeboat moored close by the large boatyard from which it had just emerged from a major refit. Then that too had disappeared astern as they headed upriver.

'So, I guess this has to be connected to the Borrett murder and all the other deaths since?' From past experience, Harry Bentley was well aware of his colleague's liking for investigation.

'I'm afraid so, Harry. All pretty baffling, but I'm hoping the Waveney might produce some answers.'

'I guess you won't have found much sympathy for Borrett from other river users.' Harry eased up the rpm as they reached the 6mph limit. 'Buying the old Cookcraft yard and then closing it down didn't win him many fans.'

'No, but everyone deserves justice. Did you ever meet the man?'

'Just once, and I managed to resist his charm,' replied the ranger, pulling a face. 'I caught him speeding down the New Cut in *Tugger*, the old yard workboat.'

The New Cut had been dug in the 1830s as an attempt by Lowestoft to break Great Yarmouth's monopoly of harbour dues for vessels transiting from the North Sea to Norwich, but what interested Jack was why Bertie Borrett would have been using it. 'When was this, Harry?'

'About a couple of months ago.'

'Any idea where he was heading?'

'No, I didn't ask and I doubt he would have told me if I had. He was pretty bolshie as it was, at being held up and having his details taken.'

Jack could imagine. Speeding boats were a constant problem on the Broads, not least because they eroded the waterway's fragile banks. Most offenders were inexperienced holidaymakers on their first boating adventure, often unaware of the limits or how to keep to them. In these cases, a friendly warning from the ranger usually sufficed, though their details would be taken and a second violation treated more seriously. 'Had he been caught before?'

'Just once ... in his big steel motor boat. I gather Mr Borrett regarded the by-laws as an irritation that applied to everyone but him.'

'Well, neither he or *Merlin Magic* will be speeding again Harry.' From the winding Waveney approaching St Olaves, it was almost possible to see the line of the New Cut straight-lining back to Reedham. 'Where, exactly, did you stop him?'

'Not far from where we are now ... at the lower end of the cut, just before the Haddiscoe Bridge. I seem to remember that he pointed ahead to St Olaves and said he hadn't far to go, so I guess that might have been where he was making for.'

'Good, that works in well with my suspicions. If it's okay with you, Harry, I'd like to have a snoop around when we get there, particularly the island.'

"The Island", was a triangle of land in the Haddiscoe marshes, its southern base fringed by the Cut itself, and the other two sides by a sweeping curve of the Waveney. Across its lower half ran the main Beccles to Great Yarmouth road. As they neared the 5mph sign, Harry reduced power. 'Looking for what, exactly?'

Jack explained.

'Hmm.' Harry stroked his chin. 'I think I might know the very one you're talking about, but we'll soon find out.'

Sure enough, they were already at the first public moorings of St Olaves and, before long, riverside bungalows and boatyards were slipping by.

'Finger's crossed, Harry.' The bow-string girders, balustrades and parapets of the old bridge were now in sight and it wouldn't be long before Jack knew whether his hunch was correct or not.

* * *

An hour and three-quarters later, and they were back at Burgh Castle, running with the last of the ebb tide as they approached the moorings. Harry Bentley slowed the RIB and scanned ahead. 'Where's best to drop you?'

'My car's in the boatyard, so ...' and then Jack was surprised to see the long lean shape of *Faith and Hope* moored alongside the fuelling jetty, '... can you lay me alongside *her*, please?'

'No problem.' As they passed the narrowboat's large saloon windows, figures on the inside looked up and waved and then Harry was spinning the RIB round to stem the tide and fetch up right by the open steering position at the stern. Jack stepped onto the steel deck, pushing the RIB off as he did so. 'Many thanks, Harry. A good day's work.'

'You're welcome. Glad we found what you were looking for.'

It was Marcel who emerged first through the narrow stern door. '*Jacque*, it is good to see you.'

'Same here, Marcel ... an unexpected pleasure.'

By this time, Charity had joined them. 'We're just about to have an early-evening drink, so come and join us.'

'You've talked me into it.' He followed them down into the long, narrow confines of the boat.

'There's somebody here you'll recognise, Jack,' said Charity, over her shoulder, as she led them for'ard to where a rather large strawberry-blonde, wearing a dusky pink trouser suit, reclined on one of the saloon couches.

'Elsie Borrett!' Jack was somewhat taken aback. 'What are you doing here?'

'Enjoyin' gettin' away from it all, love.' The widow moved over and tapped the vacant space beside her. 'Come and sit yourself down, darlin' and take the weight off yer feet.'

'We needed to refuel and decided it would do us good to spend a bit of time away from the village after all that's happened,' explained Charity from the open galley. 'I was cleaning for Elsie yesterday and told her we were planning to take *Faith and Hope* out today. I could tell immediately that she envied us ...'

'... and so they invited me to join 'em,' carried on Elsie, 'and here I am. To tell you the truth, love,' she said, patting Jack's knee, 'what with Bertie's demise and all the police enquiries, Providence Farm's the last place I wanna be right now.'

'I can understand that,' agreed Jack, 'but I thought you didn't like boats.'

'I don't, normally, but this one ...' she swept her hand over the narrowboat's interior, '... is lovely and cosy.' It certainly was. Although the late afternoon air was already becoming chilly, here in *Faith and Hope*'s saloon, with its large windows and double bow doors, it was still pleasantly warm enough to steer Elsie's thoughts into other channels. 'Oi, where's that other bottle of Chardonnay I brought onboard?'

'Will you share it with us, Jack?' asked Charity, bringing the chilled bottle from the galley.

'Love to, but ...' Jack held up his hand, '... I'm driving home from here, so I can't.'

'Well, I know you wouldn't say no to some tea.'

'Thanks. That would be great.'

'Well I ain't drivin' nowhere,' declared Elsie, jumping up and fetching corkscrew and glasses from one of the saloon cupboards. 'Sun's below the yardarm, ain't it Jack, so no time to waste.'

'Here, let me,' offered Marcel, taking the corkscrew and bottle. 'I can see Elsie, she is keen to have her little tipple, as she calls it,' he teased as he poured. In the warmth of the boat's interior, he was wearing only shorts and singlet, emphasising broad shoulders and muscular, tattooed arms. Feeling decidedly over-dressed, Jack shed his own jacket as Charity placed a mug of tea by his elbow.

'Right, 'ere's to much happy cruisin' for this lovely boat,' toasted Elsie, her glass held high.

'Yes, and here's to a happier future for you,' said Jack, making a token raise of his cup in response. 'You've certainly had a rough few days.'

'A rough few decades, more like.' Elsie took a generous gulp of her wine. 'I don't mind tellin' you darlin', life with Bertie Borrett was no picnic.'

'Well, that's all over now,' reassured Charity. She turned to the ranger, obviously hesitant to raise another unsavoury subject. 'Is what we've heard correct though, Jack ... that George Granston has been found in the river?'

'I'm afraid so. Yesterday, just above Polkey's Mill.'

'Poor Margery.' Charity shook her head. 'And so much tragedy in one village.'

'One crime often triggers another ... and then another,' explained Jack. 'A sort of domino effect.'

'Well, no-one's goin' to cry over those Hinnerley brothers gettin' their just desserts,' said Elsie. 'Never did like those two little towrags.'

'I believe Admiral Ashfordby was found at the scene, gun in hand.'

Charity was living up to her name and not passing further comment on the dead. 'Is he still in custody?'

'No, released on bail,' answered Jack, while choosing not to mention his own pleasant sail with Sir Claude the previous day. Instead, he nodded towards Marcel. 'I hope your interview with DI Bailey wasn't too onerous.'

The Frenchman smiled. 'No, he understand my own little confrontation with the police in *Londres*.'

'We're grateful for your help on that one, Jack,' added Charity.

'No problem. Have you had any more interviews with the police?'

She shook her head. 'No. Inspector Bailey's DC came to take DNA swabs from both of us for elimination purposes, but that was all.'

'She took one from me as well,' added Elsie, raising her glass. 'I told her it would probably show ninety per cent alchohol.'

Jack gave a polite chuckle. 'All just standard police procedure.' He turned to the others. 'But tragic events like this are extremely upsetting, even to those not directly involved. You say you felt the need to get away from the yard – are you planning on finding another mooring?'

'Well, that's part of the reason for today's trip,' explained Charity. 'I don't want to leave poor Elsie in the lurch at such a sad time, but staying there is a bit too close to the memories of all that happened.'

'So I told 'er, you go and find yerself another berth, love, and get livin' again.' Elsie shrugged and smiled. 'That's what I plan to do.'

'But I'll still be housekeeping at Providence Farm,' assured Charity, 'because Elsie has kindly offered to come and collect me on my cleaning days.'

'More for company than anythin',' admitted the widow. 'It'll be no trouble, darlin'.'

'But "trouble" is what I'll be in if I'm late for supper,' laughed Jack, standing up and slipping his jacket back on. 'Thanks for the tea, Charity.'

'Not at all.' She followed him out onto the afterdeck, obviously keen to voice a thought. 'Jack, I'd love to meet your wife, so why don't you both come out for a trip with us on *Faith and Hope*? It would be one way of saying thanks for all the support you've given Marcel and me.'

'That would be lovely, but Lynsey Butterick is staying with us right now.'

'Ah yes ...' Charity's eyebrows rose in understanding, '... DI Bailey's main suspect. Poor girl. What a rotten time *she's* had.' Then she smiled with another suggestion. 'Well, why don't you bring her along as well. It would be good to meet her ... and under better circumstances than last time.'

Jack smiled. 'What, in this dimension, you mean?'

'Very definitely.' Only two words, but Jack suspected there was an agony of decision behind them.

'You mean you've given up on your time-slip theory?'

'I'm afraid so, Jack, especially when there have been more murders since with no paranormal explanation.' She looked sheepishly down at her feet. 'I really wanted my theory to be true and the photo of Lynsey that Bertie kept locked in his study to be the image of the murdered girl from all those years ago. But I realise now it was all my fanciful imagination.' She looked up, her face bright with new purpose. 'So, with Marcel's encouragement, I've decided to put the spiritual world behind me and concentrate on more earthly things ...' she glanced over the marshes to the west where a pair of swans were just winging their way, '... like the wonderful wildlife all around us.'

'Very wise.' Jack gave her shoulder a reassuring squeeze. 'You'll be all the happier for it, Charity. And Lynsey will love a trip on this boat, though she is still subject to bail conditions, so I'll need to clear it with DI Bailey.'

'Well, give me a call when you've got the okay, and we'll set it up.'

'I will, and thanks again for the tea.'

'Our pleasure.'

Walking to his car, Jack pondered on all he'd seen and discussed this worthwhile afternoon. The time for action was fast approaching. Before starting the engine, he called Bailey on his mobile.

'Hi, Jack. What's happening?'

'Progress, Bailey, but I need to ask you something. Can we meet over a drink somewhere this evening?'

'Good idea, because there've been some interesting developments at my end.'

'I look forward to hearing them. What's the best time and place for you?'

'I'm at the Crown Court right now. How about the *Wig and Pen* at six-thirty?'

'Sound's good. See you there.'

* * *

Norwich Crown Court sits in the same complex as the Magistrate's Court and probably equi-distant from the *Adam and Eve* and the *Wig and Pen* public houses. This early evening, the latter was busy with young city workers enjoying laughter and a bit of socialising before heading to wherever their hearth and home lay. From his own London days, Jack knew that the busy buzz of a communal gathering could be as discreet as a locked room. Certainly it was more pleasurable as, drinks in hand, he made his way towards the corner table, nicely enclosed on two sides by wood panelling and on the other two, by chatting couples.

'Thanks, Jack. Cheers.' Bailey took his first sip and stretched his legs under the table. 'So, your trip yielded fruit?'

'Very much so. Only a skeleton of circumstances at present, Bailey, but it won't be difficult for us to put the meat of substance on them.'

'Okay,' the DI sat back. 'Let's try.'

'Right.' Jack leaned closer and explained all he'd discovered that same afternoon.

When he'd finished, the DI's eyebrows rose expressively. 'That's certainly an important find, Jack. You sure it's the one?'

'Positive.'

'Okay, we'll check it out. How about the rest though ... isn't that being a bit speculative?'

'Certainly, but when lots of irregularities suddenly start making sense, you begin to form conclusions.' Jack sat back. 'Okay, that's my slant ... what have you found out?'

'Some pretty significant stuff, actually.' Bailey gave a full rundown on all that had transpired.

Jack gave a low whistle. 'You're right ... that data puts a whole new twist on everything. And there's no doubt about it?'

'Not unless you want to question the exactness of the Forensic Science Laboratory.'

'Seeing as they're the best in the world, I don't think so. What else have you got?'

'This.' Bailey threw a file onto the table between them. 'Have a read. I think you'll find something there to catch your eye.'

Jack scanned through the thick document. 'This *is* interesting, Bailey, and certainly it points us in the right direction.'

'Right, but do we have a case yet?'

'Not for the murder, we haven't.' Jack looked thoughtful. 'I think we'll need to engineer some shock tactics to get the reaction we want.'

'Any suggestions?'

'Yes, I have actually, but it'll require some slack on your part regarding Lynsey Butterick's bail conditions.'

'Blind eyes can be turned, Jack, if the results justify the means.'

'I'm sure they will. Oh, and now what I'm going to ask, might seem a bit macabre.'

'Try me.'

Jack spelled out his request.

'You're right, Jack, but if you really reckon it's necessary ...'

'I do, Bailey.' He handed the file back to the DI. 'I think this just about clinches it.'

'So do I.' The DI stood up. 'Sorry I can't buy my round, Jack, but things to do. Give me a call when it's all set up.'

'I will. A lot to sort, so give me forty-eight hours.'

The two men went their separate ways, Bailey to collect his car from the Crown Court, and Jack to collect his from the small park across the road, but calling the admiral on his mobile as he walked.

'Ashfordby.'

'Admiral ... Jack Fellows here. Look, I'm planning a little operation where I'll need your help. Can you do something for me?'

* * *

Chapter Nineteen

'Jack, this is absolutely wonderful.'

Lynsey Butterick stood at the stern of *Faith and Hope*, her hair blowing freely in the easterly breeze as the narrowboat made its slow passage upriver.

Beside her, Jack was pleased to see the strained look gone and, in its place, the biggest of smiles lighting up her face. 'Glad you're enjoying it, Lynsey.'

'I just love it.' She glanced across to Marcel, long brass tiller in hand, casually helming them along the river's way. 'Thank you so much for inviting me.'

The Frenchman smiled back. 'You are very welcome, *Lynzee*. It is our pleasure.'

She waved her hand over the encircling reedbeds of the lower Yare. 'This is just the sort of scene I envisaged while cooped up in my dusty London chambers.'

'No-one can say you've had an easy ride getting here ...' Jack turned to face her, '... so I'm glad you're not disappointed.'

She paused to take in the seemingly limitless expanse of flat marshes and, above them, the huge cloudless Norfolk sky, but when she turned back, there was just a shadow of worry in her eyes. 'The only cloud on my horizon right now, Jack, is that, having found my idyll, circumstances might yet conspire to separate me from it.'

'Don't worry. I hope very soon we can do something about that.'

'Tea up!' It was Charity's cheerful call that had broken the slightly melancholic mood, as she emerged from below with a tray of steaming mugs and a plateful of Audrey's delicious buttered scones. She put it on the cabin roof. 'Help yourselves.'

'Thanks.' Jack took a mug and scone before peering down into the boat's interior. 'How's Audrey doing down there?'

'Fine ... totally at home.' Charity gave another of her cheeky smiles. 'I reckon you might talk her into a life afloat yet, Jack.'

'That'll be the day ...' already the steering platform was becoming rather congested, '... but I think I'll join her down there and continue the campaign.'

'Good idea.'

It was only two days since Jack's last meeting with Bailey at the *Wig and Pen*, a time in which he'd contacted Charity to suggest this day for the offered trip. And so they had all met in the old Cookcraft yard after lunch and set sail early afternoon.

The weather was fine, but after an unusually late frost, the day remained chilly despite the mild easterly wind off the North Sea. For Jack, finishing his tea with Audrey in the saloon, it would be warm as well as companionable. He found his wife sitting contentedly on one of the couches, gazing through the windowed double bow doors as the Yare unfolded silently ahead.

'This really is perfect, Jack. Is Lynsey enjoying it too?'

'Very much so. I think it's going to be difficult to get her down here out of the fresh air.'

'A bit too fresh for me though.' Audrey gave a pretend shiver. 'The sun's lovely through these big windows, but is it going to last?'

'Not if the forecast's right. They reckon the visibility will start dropping late afternoon.'

Audrey glanced at the brass bulkhead clock. 'In other words, quite soon.'

'I'm afraid so. Just before I came below, I noticed signs of mist already starting to form in the marshes.'

'Oh, well ...' Audrey glanced outside to where the Cantley factory was sliding past, '... I expect we'll be mooring here?'

'No, not yet, Aud.'

'So, where is our actual destination?'

'Good question.' The response was from Charity who had joined them. 'I know Jack's got something in mind but, as yet, he's keeping it to himself.'

'Not for much longer though.' He glanced towards the stern. 'Do you know, Charity, I've never handled a narrowboat. Do you think I could have a go?'

'Of course.' She stood aside to let him pass. 'In fact, I'm sure Marcel could do with a break, so go and take the tiller.'

'That would be great!'

Back at the stern, Lynsey was chatting to the Frenchman about life afloat on the canals. She turned to the ranger as he joined them. 'Had enough of women's gossip, then, Jack?'

'Something like that, but Charity reckoned it would be okay for me to try a trick at the helm. That okay with you, Marcel?'

'But of course. Here, take it.'

The feel of the long tiller wasn't unlike a sailing boat and Jack immediately felt at home, conning this long boat along with the engine purring beneath his feet and only the slightest wash to mark their four mph progress.

'Bravo ... the man, he is a natural,' pronounced Marcel with a flourish. 'I shall go below and leave you to it.'

'What a charmer,' said Lynsey with a grin when they were alone. 'And what a wonderful life he and Charity share together.'

'Yes, they must be pretty compatible to live in such a confined space for months on end.'

They were past Cantley now and Jack was looking ahead to where the Yare took an almost ninety degree turn to starboard. On either side, the marshes stretched onward, but with patches now obscurred by blankets of pearl-like mist.

Lynsey wrapped her arms around her body. 'It's getting clammy.'

'That's because the warmer, moister east wind is drifting over a still-cold surface, and the result is ...'

'... fog.'

'Exactly.' Jack glanced astern to where the Cantley silos were already becoming ghostly images while ahead, the bend in the river was fast approaching. He turned to face Lynsey and said quietly, 'I might not get another chance to see you alone before things happen.'

'Things ... happen?' There was a suspicious anxiety in her voice. 'What are you talking about Jack?'

'I'm talking about the scenario I've set up and which you'll soon be part of.' By now they were turning to follow the river's meander with the entrance to a narrow dyke appearing just to port. 'Some of it's going to be uncomfortable and a bit unpleasant, but trust me. This is all a means towards finding the truth amongst a morass of bitterness and deceit.'

'Believe me, I want to know the truth more than anyone.' She swallowed nervously. 'I trust you totally, Jack.'

'Good.'

And then he was throttling back the engine to dead slow, pushing the tiller hard over to starboard, and swinging them straight into the strange dyke that led to who-knows-where.

* * *

'*Sacre bleau, Jacque*. Where are you taking us?' Marcel had appeared back on the steering platform with impressive alacrity. His voice was friendly enough, but clearly he feared for the safety of his precious narrowboat. 'Never will we be able to turn back in such a thin waterway.'

Sure enough, the dyke they were idling down was very narrow with boats moored to the bank either side, but Jack hastened to reassure his host. 'Don't worry, there's a turning space at the end and, anyway, I thought we might moor up at the public staithe to have a break.'

'If you think it a good idea with this fog settling in.'

Jack didn't answer, but concentrated on helming until the end of the dyke was in sight. He indicated the tiller to Marcel. 'Here, you'd better take her to moor up while I help Charity with the lines.' They'd arrived at a pleasant dead-end with grass banks and surrounded by trees. The public mooring was empty of boats and Marcel brought them skillfully alongside.

Charity had entered the for'ard well via the bow doors and, as the narrowboat kissed the bank, she was ashore, head-rope in hand and already securing it to a handy mooring post. Jack stepped ashore from the aft end and soon the stern line was also made fast and the engine shut down.

In the resulting silence, and with the descending fog muffling all other sound, the staithe seemed utterly peaceful, with no working boatyard and just a few ducks to stir the limpid water. Lynsey was taking in the scene but, rather than being entranced by it, her expression instead was one of suppressed anxiety.

'Are you okay, Lynsey?' Jack had just checked his mobile phone, but now he joined her back on the after deck.

'I'm ... I'm not sure.' She looked around again, her gaze ever more haunted. 'You know, Jack, I could swear this is the spot where I boarded the old wooden boat.'

'I'm sure it is.' He turned to face the track leading to the main road where a Mercedes car was just turning in and parking close by the staithe.

* * *

By this time Audrey had come up from below to join the others on the after deck. She peered towards the car and its disembarking passengers. 'Isn't that Admiral Ashfordby?'

'And that's Elsie with him,' added Charity, slightly bewildered. She turned to Jack. 'What's going on?'

'Bit of a cheek, I admit, but I've invited some others to join us.'

'You could have told me, Jack.' She seemed somewhat put out and Audrey could only agree.

'Really, Jack, this isn't good enough. You should at least have asked.'

'I know,' said Jack putting up his hand for peace. 'I confess this is all a bit underhand, but it is important, I promise you.'

'Important for what?' asked Charity, before noticing a third person climbing out from the rear seat of the Mercedes. 'And, good grief, isn't that Lucy Watling as well?'

'Afraid so.' By this time the car group had reached *Faith and Hope* and Jack was glad of the momentary distraction.

'Well, ain't this quite a gatherin'?' greeted Elsie as she dumped a box of clinking bottles onto the narrowboat's deck. 'This looked like it might be some party, so I thought we'd better boost the ship's cellar.'

'Wind's in the east, Fellows. Fog's coming down,' observed Admiral Ashfordby, indicating the ghostly precipitation already starting to enshroud the staithe. 'Reckon we ought to talk about this somewhere warmer and drier. Permission to come aboard, ma'am?' he asked of Charity.

'Er ... well ... yes, I suppose you'd all better.'

Admiral and widow climbed aboard followed, perhaps a little unenthusiastically, by Lucy. As she hauled herself up onto the after deck, she fixed Jack with reproaching eyes. 'I understand this was your idea?'

'Yes, it was, Lucy, and very shortly you're going to find out why.'

Her reply was a withering look as she made her way below.

Charity lingered for one last shot at the ranger. 'I know I said the-more-the-merrier, Jack, but this is a bit much.'

He nodded guiltily. 'You're right, but all will soon be clear. I needed to get everyone together and your narrowboat seemed the ideal venue.'

She relented slightly. 'Well, if it will help clear the air, I'm sure it'll all be worthwhile.'

In fact, the air was already becoming a little stuffy in the overcrowded saloon by the time Jack joined them, so much so that Marcel opened the bow doors allowing himself and Charity to sit outside in the for'ard well, while Elsie explained the circumstances of their arrival. 'It was dear Claude himself who called me to say we was havin' this get-together and could I drive us 'ere,' she bubbled, fetching the corkscrew from the built-in sideboard and handing it and a bottle outside to Marcel. ''ere, love ... do us the honours.'

By this time Lucy had managed to squeeze herself a seat on the same couch, but Elsie had other plans. 'Get us some glasses, girl. They're in the cupboard at the bottom there.'

Lucy duly obliged, though not with the best of grace. 'I hope someone's going to tell us just why we've been hauled out to this God-forsaken spot.'

Jack could see the same question mirrored in the faces of the other ladies seated facing each other. Elsie was busy topping glasses with red or white wine, Lynsey was clearly trying to grasp what was actually happening and Audrey was doubtless planning just what she was going to say to her husband when she got him home.

'We're here,' he began, standing in the open doorway between galley and saloon, 'to solve a mystery.'

'Mystery?' Marcel held out his glass for a helping of red. 'But why this *subterfuge, Jacque*? Why not just tell us what it is you want to do. We would have been happy to oblige.'

'But not all of you.' Jack took an offered glass. 'It's always been my experience that a little intrigue brings people in and, if I'd explained my reasons for this gathering, some of you might not have been here now.'

'Well, we are, Fellows,' said the admiral, 'so the sooner we get on with this, the better.'

'Right, I told you we were here to solve a mystery, but perhaps I should have said "mysteries", because there are two here to be sorted, even though they are inextricably connected. The big one, of course, is who killed Bertie Borrett?' Jack cast a quick glance towards Elsie, but the widow already seemed too well-anaesthetised with wine to react adversely to any hurt this subject might cause. 'And the other is how the crime could be committed in one place while the person accused ...' he nodded towards Lynsey, '... swears she was in another.'

'If you believe her,' snorted Lucy behind the shelter of her wine glass.

'Well, I thought *I* did,' spoke up Charity from the for'ard well. 'I had the theory that she'd passed through ...'

'... a dimensional time-slip,' completed Jack, 'but I think even Charity has had second thoughts on that idea. However, that still leaves us with Lynsey's story of a strange wooden boat, and that would certainly be more believable if we could see it for ourselves.' By now Jack could feel a slight vibration coming through the souls of his feet from the narrowboat's flooring. He knew the cause – it was the throb of a slow-turning, powerful diesel engine coming down the dyke. 'Well ... here it is.'

He didn't need to draw anyone's attention to the shadow passing the saloon windows. It was the hull of an old wooden fishing boat.

From the corner of his eye, Jack could see Lynsey Butterick clasping a hand to her mouth in horror.

*   *   *

For once there was silence in the narrowboat's saloon as all watched with varying reactions the sight of this old vessel coming alongside the opposite bank of the dyke. Finally, it was Admiral Ashfordby who spoke up first. 'Good grief ... it's Granston's old boat.'

'Indeed it is, Admiral, and the same boat Lynsey was lured onto the night of the murder.'

'You're right,' confirmed the girl herself with trembling voice. 'That's the one.'

'And very much of *this* world,' sighed a slightly-embarrassed Charity. 'But what's it doing here now?'

As if in part answer, uniformed figures appeared on deck – police officers, who soon had the fishing boat secured alongside. From the square wheelhouse, a figure in civilian clothes hopped ashore and came striding around the end of the dyke. Jack went up onto the narrowboat's deck to meet him.

'Beautiful timing, Bailey. You couldn't have done it better.'

'Thanks to the lads from BroadsBeat.' Bailey handed Jack a sealed envelope before sniffing the saturated air. 'I thought this fog might slow us down, but the old scow got us here on the money.'

'Yes, even *I* didn't plan for this weather, but it sets the scene better than we could've hoped for.' Already beads of condensation were forming on their shoulders. 'Let's get below. There's more than one person down there who wants to know just where this whole pantomime is leading.'

*   *   *

'I think Jack Fellows has already explained the reason we've got you all here together.' Bailey stood in the galley doorway facing a saloonful of bemused faces. 'That boat ...' he nodded towards the apparition-come-to-life, '... was used as part of a well-thought-out scheme that ended in murder, but I'm going to let Jack himself tell you how.'

'Let's start with what we all know as fact,' began the ranger. 'I know

Elsie won't mind me saying that Bertie Borrett had a lot of enemies, some as a result of his amorous adventures outside marriage.'

'Tell me somethin' I don't know,' muttered the widow. She pointed her wine- glass at Lynsey. 'And the latest one was 'er.'

'Bertie had certainly formed a fixation for Miss Butterick,' agreed Jack, 'to the extent that he'd taken her on as his legal advisor, paid her money and set up a late tryst on his boat the night she arrived. Except there was someone else who was also besotted with Lynsey, someone who firmly intended she would never stay in Norfolk.'

'This is news to me, Fellows,' said the admiral. He looked around. 'Is this blighter with us now?'

'Not yet, Admiral, but he soon will be.' As if on cue, the sound of a car was soon followed by two lurching headlight beams illuminating the swirling, thickening vapour, as a smart BMW came up the track and parked beside Elsie's Mercedes. A slightly rotund figure emerged, pulling on a full-length black coat as, scowling, he made his way towards the narrowboat.

To Lynsey, this surprise was as unwanted as it was unexpected. She cast Jack an almost-accusing glare before answering everyone's unspoken question with three words. 'Miles Rotherby-Jones.'

* * *

After an abortive attempt to plant a kiss on Lynsey's cheek, the barrister took a seat in the saloon, coat still on and clearly intending his visit would be a short one. 'I trust there's a good reason for you instructing me to meet you here, Bailey,' he muttered, while brushing some loose grass off the bottom of his pinstripe trousers and onto Charity's saloon carpet. 'I assumed this would at least be a discreet discussion.' He scanned the assembled gathering. 'Instead, it seems I'm appearing before half the village.'

'Don't worry, this won't take long,' replied the detective with more menace than reassurance. Rotherby-Jones huddled lower into his coat, the collar turned up as though to shield him from lesser mortals. For her part, Lynsey had joined Charity and Marcel out in the for'ard well, rather than meet his gaze.

Jack didn't waste any time getting back to the business in hand. 'I'd just been explaining how someone was very keen indeed that Lynsey here should not stay in Norfolk very long.' He fixed his eyes on the newcomer. 'That "someone" was you, Rotherby-Jones.'

The barrister shrugged. 'I was dead set against her coming here, I grant you. She had the makings of a wonderful career in London, so why should she throw it all away on some mad dash to the sticks?'

'But it went far deeper than that, didn't it? You'd been wanting an intimate relationship with Lynsey for months and knew that if she settled here, your chances would be pretty-near zero. And so you conspired to scare her off Borrett and have her running back to London and into your arms.'

'That's ridiculous,' protested Rotherby-Jones. 'I haven't the foggiest idea what you're talking about.' He went to stand up and leave. 'I'm not going to sit here and be cross-examined by some minor official ...'

'If you want to hear what's going to be said about you, I suggest you hang around for just that bit longer,' advised Bailey.

Rotherby-Jones paused for only a second before sinking back onto his seat. 'Very well, but make it quick.'

'I'll try, because your input was relatively simple. What you did was contact someone here and ask them to concoct some scheme to scare the living daylights out of the woman you purported to love. That person was more than happy to oblige, because they saw this strange request as giving them the chance to do something they'd been intending for a while – murder Bertie Borrett.'

'Are you saying *I* was involved in his murder?' Rotherby-Jones' question carried just a touch of anxiety.

'Not "involved", but certainly instrumental.'

'This is incredible,' broke in Lynsey. 'I really don't like this man, but I still can't see him having the wit or stupidity to pull off something so bizarre.'

'He didn't,' continued Jack, 'but, believe me, the one who did was more than capable. Let me explain how it was done.'

'I wish you would, darlin',' said the widow, 'cos I'm losing the plot before we even start.'

'I'll keep it simple, Elsie. As the admiral pointed out, that boat out there was the one originally owned by George Granston, which he had to sell when his business started to run into trouble.'

'Which was about the same time we moved into the village,' remembered Elsie. 'Lucky for him, my Bertie's import business helped him out.'

'Quite, but what you probably didn't know, Elsie, was that it was your late husband who bought the boat from Granston.'

'Can't have,' protested the widow, 'Bertie never owned that boat.'

'I can assure you he did. I checked with our registrations office and they recorded the change of ownership.'

'So, why didn't I know about it?'

'Because Bertie wanted it kept a secret. You see, he had big ideas for that boat which certainly didn't include you ... but I'll come to all that in a bit. What is more relevant to Lynsey's frightening experience is that later, someone else also had plans for it.'

'Who?' asked the admiral.

'I'll get to that in good time, Sir Claude. First let me explain the plot as far as Rotherby-Jones here was concerned.'

'... which is that I simply wanted Lynsey to realise she'd made a big mistake and come back to chambers,' almost pleaded the barrister.

'Yes, and the plan that was hatched would have certainly done that,' agreed Jack. 'Let me give you my slant on things and you tell me how close I am. I'm guessing that the day before he was murdered, unknown to Bertie, the fishing boat was brought to this dyke, which lies parallel to the village dyke and only a few miles away. Lynsey had never been here before so, arriving late at night, she would never know the difference. The Hinnerley brothers were tasked with collecting her from Norwich Station and bringing her here. The fog that formed that night only added to Lynsey's total lack of awareness of just where she was. She would go onboard and meet the bearded man she thought was Borrett and who would make threatening sexual advances towards her. The plan was that she'd escape and retreat, disillusioned and disgusted, back to London.' He turned back to Rotherby-Jones. 'So, how close am I?'

The barrister gave a begrudging nod. 'Near as dammit ... spot on.'

'Good.' Jack shrugged. 'Having fulfilled his role, that bearded man was then to have taken the boat back to the marina where Bertie kept her.'

'Which was where?' asked a somewhat-sobered Elsie.

'The one on the island down by St Olaves. I found it there a couple of days ago and knew my suspicions were correct. What you do need to realise at this stage,' continued Jack with a glance back towards the barrister, 'is that, as far as Rotherby-Jones was concerned, this was just a scheme to scare the living daylights out of Lynsey Butterick and send her back to London. What he didn't know was that the instigator of the plan was, in reality, using it as a background for murder.'

'You're damned right I didn't know that,' agreed the barrister. He turned an appealing face towards the company. 'For goodness' sake, it was just a joke ... a prank ... to make the girl I love see some sense.'

'... which almost put "the girl you love" in gaol for life, you idiot,' said Lynsey bitterly, as she came into the saloon. 'You really are a bastard aren't you?' She raised the glass of red wine she was holding and threw it straight into Rotherby-Jones' face. 'Have a drink on me, Miles, because this is the last we'll share together.'

'Oh, I say ... steady on ...' he stood up, wiping himself down with a silk handkerchief, '... right, I get the message.'

'At last!' Lynsey slumped down with the others.

Rotherby-Jones petulantly made his way towards the galley and exit, but couldn't resist one last passing shot. 'If you come to your senses and change your mind, I shall be back in our chambers.'

'No chance,' said Lynsey, shaking her head at the sheer gall of the man.

'But I do suggest,' warned Bailey, 'that when you get back to your law books, you look up "obstructing the course of justice", because you might just be needing it.'

Rotherby-Jones gave them all one more withering look and was gone. 'Good riddens,' sighed Lynsey, as his BMW disappeared down the fog-shrouded track.

'Amen to that,' agreed Jack.

'Didn't like that chap one bit,' stated the admiral, 'but how did you get onto his nasty little scheme?'

'Just detective's intuition really.' Jack sat back down with the others. 'What first made me suspect him was the fact that he knew more than he should about the night. Lynsey told me she hadn't discussed it with him and yet, when he spoke to her on video link from the magistrates' court, he told her she "was stupid to go on that old fishing boat". How did he know that, other than being party to the whole thing? Add to that, his obsessive pursuit of Lynsey here, plus another factor I'll come to later, and I knew he must be involved somehow.'

'Good thinking, Jack, but that only solves *one* mystery, doesn't it?'

'Who killed Bertie Borrett being the other and most important.' Jack glanced at the assembled group and their expectant faces. 'Okay, if you're prepared to hear things that some of you would rather not, I'll tell you.'

* * *

Chapter Twenty

'Before we ask *who*, it would be best if we knew *why*,' said Jack.

They were all seated in the saloon, cradling mugs of tea, except Elsie, who continued to imbibe, though now the wine had given way to Napoleon brandy – perhaps not a bad choice with the light getting dimmer and visibility even worse in the thickening fog.

'Bertie Borrett had been a scrap metal dealer in London when he married Elsie here,' continued Jack, 'but it wasn't long before he'd branched out into other less legitimate pursuits.'

'He was a no-good'n from the start really,' expounded Elsie. 'Always in trouble even as a lad, from what I heard, with petty thievin' and chasin' the girls. I hoped to change 'im and get 'im law-abidin', but I guess yer can't change bad blood and he couldn't wait to become a villain proper.'

'An ambition fulfilled when he went into partnership with a well-known London crook called Fred Calstock,' continued Jack. 'The crowning glory of Calstock's career in crime was a gold bullion raid on a security warehouse in London. Two staff from the firm had given them help and inside information, Calstock and his son Gerry were going to do the actual job and, we can suppose, Bertie was going to fence the stuff afterwards.'

'But, presumably, it went wrong,' guessed the admiral.

'No ... if anything, it went too well,' answered Bailey. 'There was more gold than even they expected – just under a metric tonne – but they still managed to load it into their truck and, we're sure, eventually, to Bertie Borrett's scrapyard for disposal onto the black market.'

'Forty bars, to be exact,' pointed out Jack, 'which must've been a daunting prospect even for the likes of Bertie.'

'I knew him gettin' mixed up with that Fred Calstock spelt bad news,' said Elsie. 'I remember that gold 'eist and wondered at the time if my Bertie was somehow involved. He was never the same old Bertie after that.'

'But a potentially very wealthy Bertie,' stated Jack, 'because he got to keep the whole lot.'

'The inside help at the security firm spilled the beans when the Yard interviewed them,' explained Bailey, 'and it wasn't long before Fred was in Number One Court at the Old Bailey, being handed down a life sentence. In his case, it meant just that, because he died in The Scrubs a couple of years ago.'

'What about the other one ... his son, Gerry?' asked the admiral.

'Ah, he was the cleverest of the lot, because he managed to give the Yard the slip and disappear off the face of the earth,' revealed Jack. 'But I'm betting the one thing he could never accept or forget was that Bertie Borrett had the two-thirds share of gold that should rightly be his. What we now know is that Gerry Calstock was determined to track down Bertie and get it back. But, in the meantime, Bertie himself hadn't been idle, having sold his scrapyard and moved here to Norfolk for a couple of very good reasons.'

'He told me it was for our 'ealth,' said Elsie.

'He may have been right, but not in the way you thought.' Jack gave the widow a reassuring smile. 'No, he hoped to perhaps cut his links with London and buy himself some anonymity in Broadland away from the man he knew must be out to hunt him down.'

The admiral gave a hefty scoff. 'A pretty forlorn hope, I would have thought, in this day and age.'

'Quite. I'm sure his hunters were scanning the internet almost daily for any mention of Bertie Borrett. They must have finally hit the jackpot when Bertie got caught for drink-driving and his name in the papers.'

'... which is probably why he took the Hinnerley brothers on,' added Bailey. 'Ostensibly, they were to drive him around but, knowing his cover was surely blown, he also needed minders to watch his back.'

'The main reason he chose here though, was its ease of access to the North Sea and a way of taking the gold, undetected, to Europe.' Jack went on to explain the whole boat-fittings scam in detail.

'I thought there must be something fishy there,' said Sir Claude. 'Those imported fittings were nice, but not worth enough to finance a lucrative business.'

Jack smiled. 'They certainly weren't as "nice" as the fittings he took out. Unfortunately for Bertie though, his old past was catching up with him fast. Fred Calstock's children had not only located him, but had sussed the racket and were all set to get back what they considered theirs before any more was shipped abroad.'

'"*Children*"?' queried Audrey, picking up the plural. 'I thought you said Fred Calstock had just one son – Gerry – but now you're saying he also had ...'

'... a daughter , and she was here as well to extract the revenge she felt her father was owed.'

'Here?'

'Oh, very much so.' Jack scanned the assembled group. 'In fact, she's in this cabin with us right now.'

All eyes went unfailingly to the figure of Lynsey Butterick sitting quietly in the corner.

* * *

'I knew there was some other reason for her bein' here!' exclaimed Elsie. 'And all the time I thought my Bertie was chasin' her, it was her what was after him ... and 'is gold.'

'What are you talking about?' demanded Lynsey, sitting bolt upright now and all set to defend her corner. 'My father wasn't a crook ...' she hesitated, unsure, '... at least I don't think he was. I never even knew my father.'

'That's what you're telling us,' joined in Lucy.

'Yes and it's the truth.' Lynsey tossed her head towards her latest accuser. 'But what about you? We all know you were sleeping with Bertie Borrett, and that you and that missing husband of yours are out-and-out crooks, Mrs Watling ... or should I call you "Ms Calstock"?'

'You cheeky little bitch ...' shouted Lucy, standing up.

'All right ... all right,' ordered Jack, holding up a calming hand, 'let's keep it civilized shall we?' He turned to the widow. 'But you were correct on one point, Elsie – Fred Calstock's daughter *did* deliberately have an affair with your husband for the sole purpose of finding out where he'd hidden the gold.'

'So Lynsey's correct,' reiterated Charity. 'Fred Calstock's daughter must be Lucy Watling here.'

'I don't know why I'm standing here listening to this,' huffed Lucy, making her way towards the door. 'You don't know anything about me.'

'But we do,' said Jack, putting up a hand to stop her leaving, 'and it's enough to know that, although your morals aren't of the very best, they're not bad enough to commit murder.'

'Of course they aren't.' Placated, Lucy sat down again before rethinking her words, '... I mean, of course *I didn't*.' She turned to Jack. 'So, if it isn't me, who really is Calstock's daughter?'

'It has to be Lynsey after all then, doesn't it?' answered Charity.

Jack shook his head. 'No, it doesn't actually.'

'Then who is she?'

'She's you, Charity.'

'Me! You are joking aren't you, Jack?'

'No, sadly I'm not. DI Bailey here did a check of marriage records at Somerset House. The one recording your marriage to Mr Howden gives your maiden name as Charity Calstock.'

'So what?' Charity paused only seconds to recover her wit. 'Are you seriously suggesting that, having a wonderful partner like Marcel here, I'd make love to the likes of Bertie Borrett?'

'Yes, you would if the rewards were great enough ... which they certainly were. You knew Borrett for the womaniser he was and, having got that cleaning job at Providence Farm, you were certain it wouldn't be long before he made advances towards you ... which he did. That's how you knew he had a photo of Lynsey locked in his study, a fact known only to the police after they did their search.'

Charity shook her head sadly. 'You're mad. Marcel and I love each other.'

'Yes you do,' agreed Jack, 'but not as lovers. Yours is a different kind of love.'

'How do you mean?'

'I mean it's the love which exists between brother and sister.'

'What?' There was an audible gasp from the others, but it was now Marcel who spoke up. 'What is this, *Jacque* ... some kind of little joke? Are you saying I am this 'arry Calstock. *Sacre bleau*, I am French as you well know, and Charity, she is English.'

'And so are you.'

'This is *absurde*.' He took his passport from a breast pocket and threw it on the table. 'ere, please examine. I am a subject of France.'

'Indeed you are,' accepted Jack, 'but it's how you obtained that passport that's important.'

'Are you saying his French accent is all phoney then?' asked the admiral.

'No, not totally.'

'I think you'd better explain.'

'I think I had. Okay, let's go back to just after the bullion robbery over twelve years ago. Fred Calstock has been sent to prison, but his son Gerry has managed to vanish. Where and how? You gave me the answer yourself, Marcel.'

'I did?'

'Yes, two days ago when I was on this very boat. It was warm and you were wearing just shorts and a singlet, showing off, not only your fine physique, but also something else.'

DI Bailey stepped forward. 'Roll up your right sleeve, Carbonne.'

Marcel shot his sister a questioning look, but Charity merely nodded before lowering her eyes. As he slowly obeyed, all eyes took in the tattoo displayed just above his elbow. It was an emblem in the form of a flaming grenade.

The admiral popped on a pair of reading glasses. 'Looks pretty innocent to me, Fellows.'

'Yes indeed,' agreed Jack, 'but behind it lies a formidable organisation, a system that, through the years, has allowed countless men to obtain new identities.'

'You mean ...?'

Jack nodded. 'That's right – the famous French Foreign Legion. Look at the facts. Gerry disappeared for ten years. Legion contracts are for five, so I'm guessing he did a full two. They teach you French and, in that time, he grew to speak it like a native.'

'But is his passport genuine?' asked Lynsey.

'It is indeed. You see, when a man joins the legion, they order him to choose another name. This works to both their advantages – he achieves the anonymity he's probably seeking and, if anyone from his old life tries to make contact, the legion merely say they know of no man of that name. That's one of the perks of serving, but an even bigger one, if you achieve an honourable discharge, is that you finally get a French passport, but in your *legion name.*'

As he spoke, Jack noticed Bailey almost imperceptibly key his mobile. Then the DI stepped forward. 'Gerald Calstock, I'm arresting you for the murder of Horace and Alfred Hinnerley and also for the murder of George Granston.' He turned to Charity. 'And Charity Howden, I'm arresting you for the murder of Bertram Borrett. You're not obliged to say anything but ...' Bailey read the full caution and, as he did so, all heard footfalls on the steel deck as two burly constables came on board while, beyond the saloon windows, headlights and blue flashers speared the foggy gloom. They stopped just short of the narrowboat. The detective nodded towards them. 'Time to go.'

Charity took one despairing look at Marcel, but her brother merely drew himself up to his full height. For a second, Jack thought he was going to fight, but the look in his eyes was a mixture of pride and regret, rather than violence. '*Le Legion Etrangere*, it was my home ... the perfect life for me ... I should never have left it.'

'No you shouldn't, but the quest for gold has been the downfall of many a man ... and woman.'

Brother and sister paused for just a few seconds, taking one last look at the boat that had been their home. Then the constables, followed by Bailey, were ushering them up on deck and out into the darkness. Doors slammed, the police car backed away and turned and then they were gone.

'Lordy, I need a stiff one.' Elsie pulled a bottle of vodka from her box. 'I think we all do.'

'Marcel and Charity ... brother and sister ... would you believe it?' Lynsey shook her head in disbelief at the sudden change in her circumstances. 'When did you first suspect it, Jack?'

'Perhaps, just a little vaguely, quite early on. I was on this boat chatting and Marcel mentioned that Charity had had a love of boats since she was a little girl. How would he know that?'

'Well, she might have told him if they really were lovers,' suggested Audrey.

'Yes, and that's what I more or less accepted at the time. But then other little suspicions started creeping in when I learned of the bullion robbery and the fact that Fred Calstock had a son *and* a daughter. It wasn't difficult to check Charity's maiden name, but we knew we'd scored when the results came back of the DNA profiles ordered by Bailey as part of the enquiry. Those buccal swabs showed sufficient genetic evidence to confirm a biological relationship between Marcel and Charity and that they were indeed siblings.'

'But what about all that business of her being a paranormal investigator?' asked Audrey. 'What was all that about?'

'Probably just an excuse for her to nose about at strange times and ask searching questions,' reasoned Jack, 'but it also allowed her to advance a counter argument when Lynsey started insisting the circumstances of her experience were different to the crime-scene.'

'A pretty cunning pair between them,' accepted the admiral, 'but when did you first link them to Borrett's murder?'

'Ah, we have Lynsey's dear old Miles to thank for that. You see, when the enquiry started, Marcel told me he'd once been in trouble with the police over an assault incident in London. In retrospect, I think he was trying to avoid any undue suspicion by coming clean from the start. Bailey obtained and showed me the original case file, but the name wouldn't have meant anything to me if Rotherby-Jones hadn't turned up here playing knight-errant.'

Lynsey's eyebrows rose. 'You mean Miles took part in his case hearing?'

'That's right ... as his defence attorney. Now, there are nearly sixteen thousand barristers practising in the UK, so such an unusual name appearing in two different, but connected, contexts had to be more than suspicious. Marcel was bound over for a year, so the courts would need to keep track of his whereabouts in that time. That's how Miles knew Marcel was in Norfolk and, when he needed someone here to do some dirty work, decided to contact his old client – one of his few successes as a defending barrister – and call in a favour.'

'... by asking him to somehow scare me into returning to London.' Lynsey shook her head. 'Even so, I'm surprised at Marcel agreeing to such a daft idea. Being a wanted man, I would've thought he'd avoid any chance of brushes with the law.'

'Yes, but don't forget he had a bona fide French identity now. More important though, and what Miles didn't realise, was that Marcel and Charity had another agenda. Those two had found out where the gold was hidden and decided it was time to eliminate Borrett. Now they also saw that if they engineered Lynsey's scare cleverly enough and committed the murder the same night, they'd also have a ready-made suspect to take the blame.'

'Me?'

'I'm afraid so.' Jack reached across to the large envelope Bailey had given him. 'Lynsey, I'm going to ask you to look at a photograph of a man. It's not very nice, but I need to know if you recognise him.'

He slipped a large print from the envelope and, ensuring the others couldn't see it, held it in front of Lynsey. She grimaced slightly, before nodding her head.

'Yes, I do. It's the man who held me captive on the boat over there and who I pushed over the side.'

'Good.' Jack put the photo back in the envelope. 'I'm afraid that was a mortuary photo of George Granston but, as you probably noticed, computer enhanced to show him wearing a beard.'

'Do you mean the disgusting man that night was Margie's husband?' asked Audrey, appalled at the thought.

'Yes. Marcel had already struck up a friendship with him through his marine repair work and had probably realised, quite early on, that Granston, in an effort to stem his own financial problems, had his own little scam going melting down the Hinnerley brothers' church lead. I'm sure he used that knowledge to blackmail George into using the boat he'd had to sell, for the scare job, putting on a false beard and vaguely impersonating poor old Bertie.'

Elsie downed the remains of her vodka. '"Poor old Bertie", indeed, but how was he actually murdered, is what I want to know? 'cos that DI Bailey arrested *Charity* for the murder, not Marcel.'

'I'll tell you now how it was done,' said Jack, 'but I should get yourself another drink first, Elsie, because I think you're going to need it.'

*   *   *

'We know already that Charity had managed to entice Borrett into an affair so she could find out where he kept the gold. But before Lynsey was due to join him late that night on *Merlin Magic*, Charity knew he would have a few hours alone. I'm sure he didn't take much persuading to invite her on board for some illicit love-making until Lynsey arrived, little knowing it was his murder that was really being planned.'

'The old fool really was a sucker for a pretty face,' mourned Elsie into her glass. 'I always said it would be the death of 'im.'

'... which it certainly was,' said Jack, trying not to smile at the irony of her words, 'and I'm reasonably sure how. You see, what Marcel and Charity told us had a kernel of truth. *Faith and Hope* was indeed moored at the *Beauchamp Arms* that night and Charity did go on her bike to the old boatyard, but it wasn't to ghost-watch, but to meet, and murder, Bertie. Before the deed was done though, Marcel cycled to *this* dyke to watch for Lynsey's arrival, because they needed to ensure they really did have her here to take the blame.'

'You mean it was *his* figure I saw, lurking in the background?' asked Lynsey. 'But I was sure it was a female.'

'I think that's what you were intended to think,' said Jack, 'if only to reinforce the "ghostly-girl" story associated with the Cookcraft yard. With hood pulled up and in the fog, it wouldn't have been difficult to pull off such a deception if he was spotted, which he was.'

'But why take that risk?' queried the admiral. 'Why not just get the Hinnerley's to telephone him once they'd dropped Lynsey off?'

'Because I'm sure Granston was forced to be the go-between and not Marcel, who needed to preserve his anonymity. Once he knew Lynsey had arrived, though a bit later than expected due to the fog, he called his sister, who was still on the boat with Borrett, and told her to carry on as planned. Then he headed straight back to *Faith and Hope* so he could take it to pick her up at the head of the village dyke once she'd carried out the murder.'

'My Bertie was a big bloke,' pointed out Elsie, 'and Charity ain't no Charles Atlas, so how did she do it?'

'No doubt by guile and cunning,' answered Jack. 'My guess is she lured Bertie up on deck, clobbered him from behind, and then, knowing he couldn't swim, shoved him overboard. The plan then was for her to cycle to the end of the dyke to meet Marcel in the narrowboat, but by now things weren't running quite to plan.'

'In what way?' asked Lucy Watling, now totally engrossed in the unfolding drama.

'Well, for a start, when Marcel did get back to *Faith and Hope*, it was to find that something had happened to delay that pickup ... a visitor ... someone he hadn't expected to turn up that night of all nights.'

Even Elsie paused in her drinking. 'A visitor?'

'Yes, a ladyfriend, actually. Someone who thought he and Charity really were an item, but was still happy to have a secret affair with this fit and virile man.'

'Yes, well we all know who's the slut around here,' scorned Elsie, giving Lucy a meaningful glare.

'How dare you?' Lucy fired back, before turning and fixing Jack with accusing eyes. 'I suppose it was you who came to this conclusion?'

'No, because I know it wasn't you.'

'Who was it then?'

'It was Elsie.'

'What are you talkin' about?' The widow was half out of her seat and swaying slightly before sinking back. 'Me ... I'm almost old enough to be his bleedin' mother.'

'But still an attractive woman,' appeased Jack. 'Even so, you must have been more than flattered when the handsome Frenchman started making advances.'

Elsie looked down into her drink and nodded. 'He told me him and Charity weren't getting' on so well, and seein' as my Bertie was havin' plenty on the side hisself, I thought why not?'

'Why not, indeed. What you didn't realise, of course, was that Marcel was playing the same game as his sister – simply getting close to someone he thought might know where the gold was hidden.'

'... an' keepin' me away from the farm so his sister could have a good snoop round, no doubt,' realised Elsie. She sighed. 'All I wanted was a bit of romance back in me life. So I got to meetin' up with Marcel on this boat while Charity was up mine cleanin' or when he was off on his boat jobs. I tell yer, I fell for 'im big time and felt a young girl again.'

'I'm not blaming you, Elsie, but tell us what happened the night of the murder.'

'Charity had been up cleanin' for me that mornin',' explained the widow. 'She mentioned her and Marcel were taking their boat to the *Beauchamp* that night, but what with fog forecast, she might be doin' a spot of ghost huntin'. I knew my Bertie was intendin' spendin' the night with his lady lawyer, so I decided to grab the chance and spend time with loverboy.'

'And you call me a slut,' sneered Lucy. 'Well, it takes one to know one, love.'

'Okay,' said Jack, anxious to avoid a catfight, 'so, Elsie, you went to find *Faith and Hope* at the *Beauchamp Arms.*'

'That's right, but when I did, I found the boat empty. Ah well, I think, an' decided to go aboard and wait 'til someone came back.'

'Which Marcel did?'

'Yeah, but he didn't seem that chuffed to see me ... said he was worried Charity might come back and catch us. Eventually, his phone rings and he goes off to answer it. When he comes back he says it's Charity on her way back and kicks me out.'

'But not before you'd delayed his original plan of picking her up,' Jack pointed out, 'but I'm sure that call wasn't from Charity anyway, but from George Granston to say Lynsey had escaped.'

The admiral gave a chuckle. 'That must have messed up their plans.'

'On the contrary,' said Jack. 'You see, I'm reasoning the plan was for Lynsey to be allowed to escape anyway and for Granston to fall overboard, after which she'd then probably contact the police or make her way to Providence Farm. Either way, she'd be the suspect when they found Bertie drowned in the dyke. But now things had worked even better than they hoped, because Lynsey had also hit the man she thought was Borrett with an oil lamp, started a small fire and left her bags onboard. Those factors gave Marcel new possibilities and so, having got Elsie out of the way, he told Charity to cycle back to *Faith and Hope* at the pub and take the boat on to Reedham herself, using the chart plotter to help navigate in the fog. Instead of meeting his sister as planned, he then cycled back here to the old fishing boat and joined Granston under the pretext of helping him return the boat to St Olaves, after his dunking in the dyke.'

'Ah ha, but instead, they first took the old boat to the yard dyke,' realised the admiral, triumphantly, as the penny dropped.

'Yes, although probably, only to the head of the dyke, from where Marcel hotfooted it down the footpath with Lynsey's bags, which he dumped in

Merlin Magic's cabin before setting the boat alight. That way, Lynsey's story would connect even more with the crime-scene and any forensic evidence against his sister would be effectively destroyed. It also explains something else that had intitially puzzled me, which was why the fire on *Merlin Magic* started later than Lynsey reckoned she escaped. Now we know.' Jack turned back to the widow. 'But, tell me this, Elsie – why were you down at the staithe in the early hours when everything was discovered?'

'Ah, well, I knew that hypocrite of a husband was about to divorce me and so, for certain reasons, it was urgent that I got in first ... and quick.'

'... because Bertie was all set to cut you out of his will?'

'Exactly, the rotten beggar. In my mind, if I could get somethin' on him as grounds for a divorce before that happened, I'd still be in line for a nice big settlement.'

'And so, just like you said in your first statement, you went there in the early hours to catch him at it.'

'... because I thought he was spendin' the night with you, love,' confessed Elsie with a nod to Lynsey, 'and that I'd give 'im the shock of 'is life.'

'But, instead, it was you had the shock when you found the boat on fire and him floating in the dyke.'

'Too true. Then I 'ears sirens and the fire brigade arrived. I ducked behind the buildings an' kept out of sight until dear Claude here turned up, just after, to see what all the flames was about, and looked after me.' She gave the admiral's hand a warm squeeze. 'So, there's the story, love, but how did you work out it was me seeing Marcel?'

'Not without a few missfires,' admitted Jack. 'We knew you had a man friend, but we got it wrong a couple of times before I realised who it might be.'

'I can't think how.'

'It was simple in the end, Elsie. When I joined you on this boat the other day at Burgh Castle and you had a bottle of wine, I noticed you knew exactly where to find the corkscrew and glasses. Also, Marcel knew you enjoyed a "little tipple". Small things, but it told me you were familiar with the layout of this boat and that you must have had drinks on it before.'

Elsie raised her glass in mock toast. 'You clever old thing.'

'Here, here to that,' piped up Admiral Ashfordby, 'but what about the Hinnerley and George Granston murders. Why them?'

'Because the Hinnerleys stole the fittings off Merlin Magic after the murder,' explained Jack. 'Perhaps George Granston had let it slip that they were gold. Whatever, the brothers made the mistake of getting the wrong side of an ex- legionnaire, added to which, Marcel knew that Bailey wanted to interview them on the subject. Knowing the trouble the lads would bring if they let the cat out of the bag, Marcel decided they had to be taken out. Margie had told Granston about the shotgun in the cupboard at St Mark's and he must have passed that information on to Marcel who then arranged for the Hinnerleys to meet him there ... and the rest, as they say, is history.'

'But I kept that gun locked in the vestry. How the deuce did he have the keys to get in?'

'George must have copied the set his wife borrowed from the vicar,' replied Jack. 'Being involved in lead theft with the Hinnerleys, he probably thought they could well have a use in the future. Instead, he got murdered by Marcel who took the keys off his body before heaving him into the Yare.'

'So Granston was murdered before the Hinnerleys?'

'Oh yes, he knew far too much to be left alive. My reckoning is that he was murdered en route to St Olaves and dumped in the Yare somewhere after Reedham.'

Audrey gulped. 'You make it all sound so simple, Jack.'

'If I do, I'm doing them an injustice. It was quite a complicated plot.'

'... but one which almost succeeded,' added the admiral, shaking his head. 'Gold. It's been the undoing of many a good man ... and bad ones too. I wonder what happened to the rest of the haul?'

'Ah yes, good question,' answered Jack with a smug smile. 'I told you Bertie had a couple of reasons for buying George Granston's old fishing boat, which he kept moored on Haddiscoe Island, far from prying village eyes and, I suspect, where most of his trysts with other woman and, finally Charity, were conducted. But, having a secret nest for his flings away from Elsie was only of secondary consideration. The main one was that Borrett needed a boat with deep bilges where he could stash his gold until he found a way to dispose of it. Buying Granston's boat might possibly have been how the two men first met, and when he then discovered George owned a foundry and was in financial straights, he knew he'd found the complete solution to his dilemma.'

'So, *Tugger* was being used to move the bars, a few at a time, from the old boat to Granston's foundry to be melted down and cast into fittings,' deduced Audrey.

'Exactly. That was the real reason Bertie kept taking the yard workboat downriver. On the way here today, the police pulled up the floorboards of the fishing boat and, sure enough, there was a load of bullion in the bilges in place of the original lead ballast. Charity and Marcel had said they wanted to shift this narrowboat down to the Waveney, to get away from the yard. The real reason, I'm sure, was to transfer the rest of the gold at the earliest opportunity. In fact, I think they might have done so before now if it hadn't been for one snag.'

'What was that?' asked Elsie.

Jack smiled. 'You ... again. I think they hoped to get quite a few bars onboard the other day when they said they were going for fuel. As it was, you managed to get yourself invited for the trip and pretty-well stymied their plans.'

'That's me for yer,' said the widow with downturned mouth. 'Always messin' up someone's life ... includin' me own.'

'Not at all, dear lady,' comforted the admiral with a pat on her hand. 'You just haven't mixed with the right people, that's all.'

'Oh, thanks, Claude.' Elsie gave a little squeeze back.

Was she mistaken, wondered Audrey, or was there just a little twinkle in the old admiral's eyes? She turned instead to her husband. 'Well done, Jack. I imagine someone's going to be very grateful to get back all that gold.'

'Less a million pound's worth already smuggled across, Aud.'

'The money for which, it seems your Cecil's managed to get his own sticky fingers on,' said Elsie, reluctantly letting go the admiral's hand and fixing Lucy with a hard stare.

'Don't look at me like that. That money's all in Chile. I didn't get any of it,' protested the thwarted wife.

'And it won't bring Cecil any luck either,' said Jack, keen to pour oil once more on potentially troubled waters. 'In my experience, lust for gold only ever brings unhappiness.'

'But it *can* restore life's other values,' broke in Lynsey. 'I've got my freedom again, which has to be more precious than any metal.'

'Well said.' Jack smacked his lips. 'You know what, I could murder a cup of tea. Anyone care to put the kettle on?'

* * *

Epilogue

On the open upper deck of the paddle-wheeler, Lynsey Butterick clapped enthusiastically along with the rest of the passengers as, one deck down, the five-piece jazz band finished a lively medley. 'That was brilliant.'

'Yes, what music *should* sound like,' agreed Jack. The band was obviously stopping for a five-minute break. 'A good time for more drinks. Same again?' He disappeared below.

It was three days since all the revelations on the narrowboat, and an evening jazz trip on the paddle-wheeler *Vintage Broadsman* out of Wroxham had seemed the perfect antidote for all that had gone before. In the twilit stillness, the big open-topped double-decker was just idling around Salhouse Broad where several cruisers lay moored for the night, most of their occupants down in snug, lit cabins relaxing after a day in the fresh air. Others, hearing the sound of music fast approaching, were up on deck to wave as the passenger boat slid by. Lynsey leaned across the varnished guardrail and waved back.

Audrey joined her. 'We're going to miss you, Lynsey.'

'Yes, things are going to be pretty mundane again,' chimed in Jack, arriving back with a tray of drinks and picking up the conversation. He handed Audrey a gin and tonic and Lynsey her white wine. Off to starboard, children, rowing their dinghy in the wherry dyke, gave an enthusiastic wave-off as Broadsman slipped out of the broad. 'And you're going to miss all this.'

She took a sip of her wine. 'Actually, I'm not.'

Audrey looked up, a little shocked. 'But I thought you loved the Broads?'

'Yes, of course I do,' corrected Lynsey with a smile, 'and I mean the reason I'm not going to miss it, is because I'm not leaving.'

'That's wonderful news,' said Jack, with undisguised delight. 'We were afraid you might still decide to head back to London, and your old career, after all you've been through here.'

'No way, Jack. When you've tasted the cherry, it's hard to go back to plain cake.'

'But Lynsey, how will you make a living?' asked the ever-practical Audrey. 'What are you going to do for a job?'

'Ah, that's my good news, which I purposely kept to myself until tonight.' Her blue eyes twinkled. 'I've been offered a position ... well, a partnership actually.'

'Wonderful. Who with?'

'Elsie.'

'What, Elsie Borrett?' Audrey was truly taken aback. 'Doing what?'

'Managing her estate. I rang her the other day while you were both out and told her there was no way I was going to claim my undeserved inheritance, when it was she who'd had to put up with Bertie all those years. But she came back with a perfect solution. We could share the estate and I could manage both Providence Farm and the boatyard.'

'Which I'm sure you'll do brilliantly,' agreed Audrey, clapping her hands in delight, before adding as an afterthought, 'but won't you find living with Elsie just a little bit ... well, trying?'

'Yes, we both thought that, which is why I'm going to be living in the Watling's old cottage.'

'Sounds pretty perfect,' said Jack, smiling. 'I can see there'll be plenty for you to do there ... except ... how about the solar project? Will that be raising its ugly head again?'

Lynsey shook hers. 'No. I agreed with Elsie that shelving that idea might be a good way to rebuild bridges with the village.'

'Very wise and you'll be good for each other,' enthused Audrey. 'Elsie's a lovely lady, but I'm not sure if she's got a business brain. She'll need you keeping a firm hand on the helm.'

'Added to which, I don't think she's going to have much time for the office anyway,' said Lynsey with a chuckle. 'I get the impression she's planning to spend more time with Admiral Ashfordby.'

'The admiral! Well, the old ... seadog.' Jack held up his glass of ale. 'Here's to the happiness they both deserve.'

'Yes, here's to them,' responded Audrey, 'though I'm not sure they have that much in common.'

'Yes they do – loneliness.' Lynsey's smile dropped just slightly. 'Something I'm probably going to have to get used to for a while.'

'Not for very long, I'd wager,' assured Jack, 'but a bit of time on your own will probably help you find yourself again.'

They were back on the main river with *Broadsman*'s paddle-wheels churning as she picked up speed towards Horning. From below came the cheerful beat of the band striking up once more with old-time jazz, and prompting some passengers to break into dance. The activity was probably beneficial in another way because, here on the upper deck, the evening air was becoming just a little chilly. A few less-hardy souls were already filing below to the warmth of the main saloon, but Lynsey seemed reluctant to go inside. Instead, they wandered for'ard into the lee of the funnel and wheelhouse where it was also easier to talk. 'Yes,' she said, taking up Jack's point, 'time alone's definitely preferable to putting up with Miles' company.'

'Have you heard any more from him?' asked Audrey.

Lynsey shook her head. 'No, not a thing ... which is just perfect as far as I'm concerned.'

'You must be having a pretty jaundiced view of all men, what with that dreadful Bertie Borrett enticing you up here for goodness knows what, but definitely not just legal advice.' Audrey sipped her drink and frowned. 'That's one thing I still don't understand – why a man his age should develop such an obsession for a young woman he'd never met.'

'Yes, it is a bit of a mystery,' agreed Lynsey.

'Not really,' said Jack.

Both women looked at him slightly askance, but it was Lynsey who spoke. 'Just what do you mean by that?'

Jack looked at Lynsey. 'I mean I know why Bertie Borrett lured you here.'

'You've kept this to yourself, Jack.' She seemed more puzzled than offended. 'Why didn't you tell me before?'

'Because I was waiting for the right time to explain.' Jack looked around. Most of the other passengers were at the far end of the deck either dancing or just chatting amongst themselves. 'Perhaps this is as good a one as any, but I'm not sure you'll want to hear it.'

'If it's the truth, I will.'

'Okay.' Jack steeled himself. 'Bertie Borrett certainly wasn't the most moral of men and his record with women was, to say the least, questionable.'

'I'd put it stronger than that,' said Audrey. 'The man was downright wicked.'

'In some ways, yes, Aud, but not totally. I think, knowing it would only be a matter of time before his past caught up with him, Bertie was experiencing a sense of mortality which set him thinking of the things he'd done wrong in life and how he could put them right.'

'Tempting me up here with money for immoral purposes doesn't seem a very good way to put anything right, Jack,' argued Lynsey. 'I still don't understand.'

'You will when I explain his intentions weren't immoral. In fact, they were downright honourable.'

'Go on.' Lynsey seemed unconvinced.

'When he was younger, Bertie Borrett was doubtless a serial chaser of girls and I know for a fact that he abandoned one of them, knowing she was pregnant with his child.'

'Typical of the man,' tutted Audrey. 'I bet there were a number of baby Borretts never knowing who their father was.'

'Only the one, as far as I know, Aud ... a daughter who he certainly had no contact with ... that is until age and uncertainty started to creep in to his life. Then, and with no children by Elsie, he must've started thinking about the child he knew he'd fathered, but never seen. And so he made enquiries and found she'd done very well for herself and become a barrister.'

'Jack ... are you saying ...?' Lynsey hesitated, knowing where this was going, '... that Bertie Borrett is ...?'

'Yes ... your father.'

'Good grief.' She put her hand to her mouth. 'Are you sure?'

'Absolutely. Those same DNA profile checks that proved the Calstocks were siblings, also showed Bertie and you to be father and daughter.' Jack paused a few seconds to let it all sink in. 'Doubtless, he started realising how badly he'd behaved to your mother, leaving her to bring you up as a single mum, and especially so when he learned that, sadly, she'd passed away. That was when he probably decided to make amends by ensuring you were financially looked after. I'm convinced he intended to explain it all to you personally that first night on the boat, but he had to get you up here first ...'

'... and so he got his PA to hire me for the solar farm fight ...'

'... and paid you generous sums up front to cement the arrangement.' Jack sat back with a sigh. 'He really was an old rogue, but obviously with a streak of decency in him striving to get out.'

'And this is why he'd changed his will and made Lynsey sole beneficiary,' said Audrey.

'Yep. I think he'd had a premonition that things would soon be turning bad, and so he made appropriate provision for the daughter he'd never known, but was now infinitely proud of.'

'Poor Bertie ... I mean father,' said Lynsey with genuine feeling. 'And so Elsie is, in reality, my stepmother.'

'... which makes it all the more appropriate that you're going to be running the estate together.'

'Yes, I suppose so,' agreed Lynsey. 'I hope that father will be happy with that ... wherever he is.' She brushed back a tear. 'And, in the end, I didn't even get to meet him.'

'No, but you'll live on in his life by looking after all he left behind ... for you.'

They were past Dydler's Mill now, the tree-lined banks already giving way to open marshes over which a full moon was casting its magical beams. Above them, the coloured lighting clusters, strung between *Broadsman*'s mast and funnel, threw just enough light to reveal another tear trickling down Lynsey's cheek. 'More than ever now, I'm so glad I'm staying here.'

'So are we.'

'But there are others whose lives won't have such a happy ending as mine,' she said wistfully, while snuffling away the tears. 'Poor Lucy Watling has been kicked out of her cottage and gone to who-knows-where, and now I even feel sorry for the dreadful Rotherby-Jones. The man's a total pratt, but I don't like the thought of anyone suffering a broken heart.'

'I shouldn't waste time worrying about them,' advised Jack. 'They didn't spare your feelings.' He scanned ahead. 'Horning should be coming up soon.'

Lynsey finished her wine, stood up and took their glasses. 'My round, in celebration. It's not many days you get a new job and a new, be it late, father – in more ways than one,' she added, smiling.

From the marshes on their starboard side, a heron lifted off, silhouetted in the moonlight, while ahead, the lights of bungalows were just appearing down the reach.

* * *

Regardless of whether or not Lynsey was feeling sorry for Rotherby-Jones, the man himself was doing a pretty good job of it on his own. Sitting alone in the cubby-hole of his chambers' office, wig and gown hanging from their hook on the door, he looked down at the dry-as-dust case files still to study for hearings yet to come. He hoped they would end better than today's when he'd made a complete mess of the prosecution and seen an open-and-shut case dissolve into chaos and acquittal.

It was all Lynsey's fault, he told himself, for not having the foresight to recognise a good husbandly catch when she saw one. Now, once again, he sat nursing both an aching heart and extremely bruised ego. The chambers had closed hours before but, with nowhere else to go, he'd stayed on late, telling them he had work to catch up on. In reality, it was the bottle that was getting all his attention and he was just reaching for another top-up when his phone rang.

'Yes!' he barked. They'd put all calls through to his office, so this was probably just some ass of a client calling to complain about their bill.

'Is that Mr Rotherby-Jones?' The voice sounded moderately young and feminine.

'Who wants to know?'

'Perhaps you don't remember me, Mr Rotherby-Jones, but you met me in Norfolk just a few days ago.'

'Really.' Rotherby-Jones wanted nothing less than to be reminded of that unfortunate episode.

'Yes. I'm Lucy ... do you remember? ... Lucy Watling.'

'Er ... perhaps.' He had vague recollections of some reasonably attractive young woman on that infernal narrowboat. 'What can I do for you ... Ms Watling?'

'It's *Mrs* Watling, actually, but that's what I'd like to talk to you about. You see, I'd like to divorce my husband.'

'Well, you'll need to talk to a solicitor about that Mrs Watling. Barristers don't take instructions directly from clients.'

'I know, I'm perfectly aware of that, because my husband *is* a solicitor, but he's cleared off to Chile with a million pounds and I'd like to get some of it.' The tone became rather more vulnerable. 'I don't have any money of my own, but I'd be happy to share anything that could be recovered.'

'Did you say "a million", Mrs Watling?'

'Yes, at least that ... and please call me Lucy,' she replied lowering her voice to a silky whisper, 'and yours is Miles, isn't it? I remember it, because I was so impressed by the way you handled yourself in that horrible situation back there.'

'Oh ...' Rotherby-Jones paused a second to straighten his bands, '... did you think so?'

'Very much so. I always say you can tell a real man by the way he handles himself.'

'You're quite correct, of course but, getting back to this missing million ... Lucy ... I'm not quite sure how we could proceed with its recovery.'

'I think the best way would be for us to get together and discuss it, don't you? It wouldn't have to be in normal working hours. Perhaps we could just meet up for a friendly chat.'

'Yes ... absolutely ... let's make a date ... I mean, an appointment.' Miles reached with shaking hands for his diary. 'Just tell me where and when.'

'Let's say next weekend, shall we? I'll leave you to come up with somewhere nice where we won't be disturbed.'

'Absolutely. Let me get onto that and I'll call you back. Give me your number.'

Lucy duly obliged. 'This is so good of you, Miles. You'll find I'll be terribly grateful.'

'Can't wait.' He put the phone down.

How soon could your fortunes turn around? Miles left his desk, put on his coat and, smiling once more, strode out of chambers. That trip to Norfolk was going to be worthwhile after all.

THE END

Printed in Dunstable, United Kingdom

64551382R00121